# HORRORS UNKNOWN

Also by Sam Moskowitz

**HORRORS IN HIDING**
with Norton

**HORRORS UNSEEN**

# HORRORS UNKNOWN

Edited,
with an Introduction
and Notes by

## Sam Moscowitz

A BERKLEY MEDALLION BOOK
published by
BERKLEY PUBLISHING CORPORATION

To
HANS STEFAN SANTESSON
WHO HAS EXPERIENCED THE THRILL
OF EXPLORING THE FASCINATING BYWAYS
OF FANTASTIC LITERATURE

Berkley Publishing Corporation
200 Madison Avenue
New York, N.Y. 10016

Library of Congress Catalog Card Number 70-155734

SBN 425-03063-6

*BERKLEY MEDALLION BOOKS are published by
Berkley Publishing Corporation
200 Madison Avenue
New York, N.Y. 10016*

BERKLEY MEDALLION BOOK ® TM 757,375

Printed in the United States of America

Berkley Medallion Edition, FEBRUARY, 1976

# CONTENTS

# INTRODUCTION

The title of this book—*Horrors Unknown*—has a double meaning. It is, first, a collection of fine stories whose plots or approach to horror is so different, so unusual, so off-beat, as to present the reader with an element of novelty in the reading of the macabre which will almost seem to broaden the scope of the genre. Secondly, it offers an unparalleled assembly of previously unanthologized, and in many cases literally undiscovered, masterpieces of fantastic terror by authors so famous it seems almost incredible that so many works could have been overlooked.

The stories in this volume are of the type that the successful anthologist rations out at the rate of one, or at the most two, to a book. They are the occasional nuggets of rhetorical gold that the researcher pans out as the result of years of reading and collecting. They are rare and fugitive, and in addition to their individual merit they are virtually collector's items—qualities they possess in common and the rationale of the double-entendre in the title *Horrors Unknown.*

The editor is a historian in the field of fantastic literature. Each year, several thousand books and magazines are added to a collection that expands from room to room. These volumes and periodicals are the tools and the target of research. Scholarship in modern times too frequently consists of accepting existing references as definitive or hardcover printings as the sum total of an author's work. There is also the implied assumption that if something has never been reprinted it is not worth reprinting or if academic approval has not been forthcoming, the item cannot be of superior quality. Needless to say, the editor holds a different view. All stories in this volume were tracked down from their original sources of publication. At the time of collection, only one had ever appeared in an anthology before, either in or out of the fantasy field, and that one ninety years ago! After thirty-seven years of reading and collecting in the field, the editor did not feel he had to lean on someone else's opinion to determine whether the stories were worth preserving.

Actually, it represented a sort of a challenge and a lark. With only the editor of Walker's science fiction and fantasy series, Hans Stefan Santesson, an unregenerate fantasist and bibliophile if there ever was one, aware of my intention, I selected the stories for the following reasons.

"The Challenge from Beyond" brings to the fore an analogy with baseball and football fans, who take great delight in watching all-star games, exhibitions in which the most popular and outstanding competitors from an entire league are assembled to play together. While it is the dream team, it does not necessarily follow that they will play the greatest game of the year. A team, to be truly effective, must learn to function as a group, and a team of the greatest stars is no exception, but just the thrill of assembling them and watching them perform is an end in itself.

Through a series of special circumstances, a group of all-time great writers of fantasy came together to collaborate on a single story. The trick with these particular authors can never be repeated. Of the five involved, three are dead. The authors who wrote it round-robin style were C.L. Moore, A. Merritt, H.P. Lovecraft, Robert E. Howard, and Frank Belknap Long, Jr. Long dead are A. Merritt, once-in-a-lifetime author of such masterpieces as *The Moon Pool, The Ship of Ishtar,* and *Dwellers in a Mirage;* H.P. Lovecraft, who has already become a legend with his fame expanding each year; and Robert E. Howard, whose fabulous barbarian Conan has become a literary landmark. Still alive are C.L. Moore, creator of Northwest Smith and Jirel of Joiry, and Frank

Belknap Long, Jr., a close friend and literary bedfellow of H.P. Lovecraft.

Between the years 1940 and 1960, Edison Marshall was considered one of our finest writers of historical romances. Tyrone Power and Kirk Douglas were among the stars featured in moving picture adaptations of his works, and every paperback store features his books. Long before he had gained such recognition, he was a fine fantasy writer. "The Flying Lion" is an unacclaimed masterpiece of horror, and may also prove a revelation to the followers of Edgar Rice Burroughs, who probably have overlooked it in their collecting of Tarzan-related stories.

Frank Norris, who died tragically young of a burst appendix, was on his way to becoming one of America's great literary figures with his trend-setting novels of naturalism, *The Octopus* and *The Pit*. He is never thought of as one of the important writers of horror and the supernatural. "Grettir at Thorhallstead," never as much as mentioned in scholarly books on occult literature, should prove a bombshell to the academics as well as the *cognoscenti*.

The publication of "Shambleau" in the November, 1933, *Weird Tales,* with its steely-eyed interplanetary mystic adventurer Northwest Smith, created an overnight reputation for C.L. Moore. The promise displayed in that first story was amply vindicated, but despite her literary successes the character of Northwest Smith has remained paramount in the thoughts of her followers, though she has written no new story in the series for over thirty years. However, one work was never professionally published, and appeared in a mimeographed magazine in 1938 with a circulation of sixty copies. That story was "Werewoman." Unlike the others, it is a supernatural fantasy and not a science fantasy, and its printing here is its first truly professional appearance.

Fitz-James O'Brien was probably the finest American short story writer of the strange and unknown in the period between Edgar Allan Poe and Ambrose Bierce, his landmarks "The Diamond Lens" and "What Was It?" being favorably evaluated in any definitive discussion of American literature.

For the first time in ninety years, one of his most striking, surrealistic novelettes, "From Hand To Mouth," is brought back into print, an event not only for his followers but for students of the short story.

There have been a number of occult detectives in British and American literature since the turn of the century, but by odds the most popular was Jules de Grandin, creation of Seabury Quinn in the pages of *Weird Tales*. "Body and Soul" epitomizes the best elements in the series and has never been reprinted since its first appearance forty-two years ago.

The pen name of Francis Stevens hid the identity of Gertrude Bennett, acknowledged by such masters as H.P. Lovecraft and A. Merritt as one of the finest writers the fantasy field ever produced. Her entire production of a handful of novels and short stories, all of them fantastic either in theme or presentation, was believed accounted for until the discovery of "Unseen—Unfeared," never previously listed in a bibliography, let alone reprinted.

Ray Bradbury is today acknowledged as one of the finest of all modern writers of horror. His first story, "Pendulum," written in collaboration with Henry Hasse, has never been included in hard covers. As an intriguing comparison, the first version of the story written entirely on his own and published in his amateur magazine *Futuria Fantasia* is also reprinted so that the differences between it and the final collaboration can be evaluated. This dual presentation is of historical importance to those interested in studying the development of Ray Bradbury as an author.

For something like thirty-one years, A. Merritt worked in various editorial capacities on the *American Weekly*, which at one time claimed the largest circulation of any publication in the world. It has long been conjectured as to whether or not he wrote an identifiable piece of fiction for them during that period. A search has brought to light a short story, "The Pool of the Stone God," credited to one W. Fenimore, which, from internal evidence would seem very likely to be Merritt's work. It is presented here for the readers to evaluate.

The foregoing comprise the contents of an anthology we

believe to be unique of its kind. Each story is prefaced by comprehensive background notes which embody a great deal of special research, much of it revealed for the first time in the pages of this book. What the editor has tried to do is take the readers along with him on a voyage of discovery of lost and almost forgotten masterpieces, so they could experience the thrill of the search as well as the reward in the reading.

# THE CHALLENGE FROM BEYOND

*by* C. L. MOORE, A. MERRITT, H. P. LOVECRAFT, ROBERT E. HOWARD, *and* FRANK BELKNAP LONG, JR.

This utterly remarkable round-robin science fantasy is a one-of-a-kind that owes its creation to an unusual set of circumstances which probably could not be duplicated with a contemporary group of authors of equal stature. It first appeared in the September, 1935, issue of *Fantasy Magazine,* one of the earliest and perhaps still the greatest science fiction and fantasy fan magazine ever published.

The publication wanted something truly outstanding for its third anniversary issue, so its editor, Julius Schwartz, struck upon the idea of two round-robin stories, one of science fiction and the other of fantasy, to be written by the greatest living writers that would cooperate. The magazine had a precedent for securing such cooperation. Beginning with its July, 1933, issue (then titled *Science Fiction Digest*), they published as a serial supplement to the magazine a novel titled *Cosmos,* written by sixteen authors and issued in eighteen segments. As each author completed a chapter, the next took up from where the other had broken off. The individual chapters had to be complete in themselves, yet carry the novel forward. The authors contributed their efforts gratis to make this novel concept a reality.

''The Challenge from Beyond'' was secured the same way, with the difference that each contribution was much shorter in scope than those of *Cosmos,* and rather than being complete in itself would leave a ticklish situation for the next author to extricate himself from. There was a science fiction story also titled ''The Challenge from Beyond,'' which was written cooperatively by Stanley G. Weinbaum, Donald

Wandrei, Edward E. Smith, Harl Vincent, and Murray Leinster; it appeared side-by-side in the September, 1935, *Fantasy Magazine* with the fantasy portion reprinted here.

All the authors included at the time were "hot" then, and most of them have climbed into the category of producers of classics for the genre since that time.

C.L. Moore was acknowledged to be a great discovery upon the publication of her first story, "Shambleu," in the November, 1933, *Weird Tales*, with its sensual presentation of a Medusa-like girl in a Martian setting, and its introduction of Northwest Smith. Her reputation was enhanced by a new series introducing the heroine Jirel of Joiry shortly afterward, and solidified further with the presentation of a number of poetic space fantasies in *Astounding Stories*.

A. Merritt had long been a fixed star in the field, with permanent classics including *The Moon Pool, The Metal Monster, The Ship of Ishtar, Dwellers in a Mirage* and serialized only the year previous in *Argosy, Creep, Shadow!* No one, least of all himself, was aware at the time that his last major work had been completed and with his assumption of full editorship of *American Weekly* in 1937, the opportunities for creative authorship would end.

H.P. Lovecraft, revered by the readers of *Weird Tales* for such unique masterpieces as "The Rats in the Walls," "The Dunwich Horror," and "The Whisperer in Darkness," living in genteel poverty, would be dead of Bright's disease within eighteen months of publication of the story, with recognition never dreamed of, even by his active imagination, yet to come.

An even shorter skein on the thread of life was the destiny of Robert E. Howard, who on June 11, 1936, would end it all at the age of thirty, while still climbing towards the peak of his career. His character of Conan would become an influence treating the entire field of sword and sorcery which exists today, and the vigor and color of his writing method were to be copied by an entire school of fantasy writers.

Frank Belknap Long, Jr., a confidant of H.P. Lovecraft, enjoyed his greatest reputation because he had set many of his stories into a framework, mythology and cosmos similar to that of the Cthulhu series—such stories as "The Space Eaters," "The Hounds of Tindalos," and "The Horror from the Hills"—but had moved into other areas of science fiction and fantasy with a rich, rhythmic writing style which distinguished him from his contemporaries.

The longest portion of the story, about 2,500 words, was written by H.P. Lovecraft, and was presented as a complete story in the May, 1960 issue of *Fantastic Science Fiction Stories*. Probably the finest writing in the story is Frank Belknap Long's poetically done conclusion.

The collaboration was reprinted complete in the H.P. Lovecraft collection *Beyond the Wall of Sleep,* published by Arkham House, 1943, a volume of such rarity and high cost today that it is off-bounds to most readers. Both the science fiction and the fantasy versions of "The Challenge from Beyond" were reprinted as separate mimeographed pamphlets by William Evans and distributed through the Fantasy Amateur Press Association in February, 1954. Since that association has only sixty-five members, copies are even more rare than *Beyond the Wall of Sleep*.

The original printing of the stories in *Fantasy Magazine* was only two hundred copies, of which about twenty or so were run off on coated stock for presentation to the authors and the editors, and the rest appeared on pulp paper.

The appearance of "The Challenge from Beyond" here marks its first availability outside of a limited edition and the first time it has ever been included in an anthology of the fantastic.

# THE CHALLENGE FROM BEYOND

by

**C. L. Moore,**
**A. Merritt,**
**H. P. Lovecraft,**
**Robert E. Howard,**
**and Frank Belknap Long, Jr.**

## I     C. L. MOORE

George Campbell opened sleep-fogged eyes upon darkness and lay gazing out of the tent flap upon the pale August night for some minutes before he roused enough even to wonder what had wakened him. There was in the keen, clear air of these Canadian woods a soporific as potent as any drug. Campbell lay quiet for a moment, sinking slowly back into the delicious borderlands of sleep, conscious of an exquisite weariness, an unaccustomed sense of muscles well used, and relaxed now into perfect ease. These were vacation's most delightful moments, after all—rest. after toil, in the clear, sweet forest night.

Luxuriously, as his mind sank backward into oblivion, he assured himself once more that three long months of freedom lay before him—freedom from cities and monotony, freedom from pedagogy and the University and students with no rudiments of interest in the geology he earned his daily bread by dinning into their obdurate ears. Freedom from—

Abruptly the delightful somnolence crashed about him. Somewhere outside the sound of tin shrieking across tin slashed into his peace. George Campbell sat up jerkily and reached for his flashlight. Then he laughed and put it down again, straining his eyes through the midnight gloom outside where among the tumbling cans of his supplies a dark anonymous little night beast was prowling. He stretched out a long arm and groped about among the rocks at the tent door for a missile. His fingers closed on a large stone, and he drew back his hand to throw.

But he never threw it. It was such a queer thing he had come upon in the dark. Square, crystal-smooth, obviously artificial, with dull rounded corners. The strangeness of its rock surfaces to his fingers was so remarkable that he reached again for his flashlight and turned its rays upon the thing he held.

All sleepiness left him as he saw what it was he had picked up in his idle groping. It was clear as rock crystal, this queer, smooth cube. Quartz, unquestionably, but not in its usual hexagonal crystallized form. Somehow—he could not guess the method—it had been wrought into a perfect cube, about four inches in measurement over each worn face. For it was incredibly worn. The hard, hard crystal was rounded now until its corners were almost gone and the thing was beginning to assume the outlines of a sphere. Ages and ages of wearing, years almost beyond counting, must have passed over this strange clear thing.

But the most curious thing of all was that shape he could make out dimly in the heart of the crystal. For imbedded in its center lay a little disc of a pale and nameless substance with characters incised deep upon its quartz-enclosed surface. Wedge-shaped characters, faintly reminiscent of cuneiform writing.

George Campbell wrinkled his brows and bent closer above the little enigma in his hands, puzzling helplessly. How could such a thing as this have imbedded in pure rock crystal? Remotely a memory floated through his mind of ancient legends that called quartz crystals ice which had frozen too hard to melt again. Ice—and wedge-shaped cuneiforms—yes, didn't that sort of writing originate among the Sumarians who came down from the north in history's remotest beginnings to settle in the primitive Mesopotamian valley? Then hard sense regained control and he laughed. Quartz, of course, was formed in the earliest of earth's geological periods, when there was nothing anywhere but heat and heaving rock. Ice had not come for tens of millions of years after this thing must have been formed.

And yet—that writing. Man made, surely, although its characters were unfamiliar save in their faint hinting at cuneiform shapes. Or could there, in a Paleozoic world, have been things with a written language who might have graven these cryptic wedges upon the quartz-enveloped disc he held? Or—might a thing like this have fallen meteor-like out of space into the unformed rock of a still molten world? Could it—

Then he caught himself up sharply and felt his ears going hot at the luridness of his own imagination. The silence and the solitude and the queer thing in his hands were conspiring to play tricks with his common sense. He shrugged and laid the crystal down at the edge of his pallet, switching off the light. Perhaps morning and a clear head would bring him an answer to the questions that seemed so insoluble now.

But sleep did not come easily. For one thing, it seemed to him as he flashed off the light, that the little cube had shone for a moment as if with sustained light before it faded into the surrounding dark. Or perhaps he was wrong. Perhaps it had been only his dazzled eyes that seemed to see the light forsake it reluctantly, glowing in the enigmatic deeps of the thing with queer persistence.

He lay there unquietly for a long while, turning the unanswered questions over and over in his mind. There was something about this crystal cube out of the unmeasured past, perhaps from the dawn of all history, that constituted a challenge that would not let him sleep.

## II    A. MERRITT

He lay there it seemed to him for hours. It had been the lingering light, the luminescence that seemed so reluctant to die, which held his mind. It was as though something in the heart of the cube had awakened, stirred drowsily, become suddenly alert . . . and intent upon him.

Sheer fantasy, this. He stirred impatiently and flashed his light upon his watch. Close to one o'clock; three hours more before the dawn. The beam fell and was focused upon the warm crystal cube. He held it there closely, for minutes. He snapped it out, then watched.

There was no doubt about it now. As his eyes accustomed themselves to the darkness, he saw that the strange crystal was glimmering with tiny fugitive lights deep within it like threads of sapphire lightnings. They were at its center and they seemed to him to come from the pale disc with its disturbing markings. And the disc itself was becoming larger . . . the markings shifting shapes . . . the cube itself was growing . . . was it illusion brought about by the tiny lightnings . . .

He heard a sound. It was the very ghost of a sound, like the ghosts of harp strings being plucked with ghostly fingers. He bent closer. It came from the cube . . .

There was squeaking in the underbrush, a flurry of bodies and an agonized wailing like a child in death throes and swiftly stilled. Some small tragedy of the wilderness, killer and prey. He stepped over to where it had been enacted, but could see nothing. He again snapped off the flash and looked toward his tent. Upon the ground was a pale blue glimmering. It was the cube. He stooped to pick it up; then obeying some obscure warning, drew back his hand.

And again, he saw, its glow was dying. The tiny sapphire lightnings flashing fitfully, withdrawing to the disc from which they had come. There was no sound from it.

He sat, watching the luminescence glow and fade, glow and fade, but steadily becoming dimmer. It came to him that two elements were necessary to produce the phenomenon. The electric ray itself, and his own fixed attention. His mind must travel along the ray, fix itself upon the cube's heart, if its beat were to wax, until . . . what?

He felt a chill of spirit, as though from contact with some alien thing. It was alien, he knew it; not of this earth. Not of earth's life. He conquered his shrinking, picked up the cube, and took it into the tent. It was neither warm nor cold; except for its weight he would not have known he held it. He put it upon the table, keeping the torch turned from it; then stepped to the flap of the tent and closed it.

He went back to the table, drew up the camp chair, and turned the flash directly upon the cube, focusing it so far as he could upon its heart. He sent all his will, all his concentration, along it; focusing will and sight upon the disc as he had the light.

As though at command, the sapphire lightnings burned forth. They burst from the disc into the body of the crystal cube, then beat back, bathing the disc and the markings. Again these began to change, shifting, moving, advancing, and retreating in the blue gleaming. They were no longer cuneiform. They were things . . . objects.

He heard the murmuring music, the plucked harp strings. Louder grew the sound and louder, and now all the body of the cube vibrated to their rhythm. The crystal walls were melting, growing misty as though formed of the mist of diamonds. And the disc itself was growing . . . the shapes shifting, dividing, and multiplying as though some door had been opened and into it companies of phantasms were pouring. While brighter, more bright grew the pulsing light.

He felt swift panic, tried to withdraw sight and will, dropped the flash. The cube had no need now of the ray . . . and he could not withdraw . . . could not withdraw? Why, he himself was being sucked into that disc which was now a globe within which unnameable shapes danced to a music that bathed the globe with steady radiance.

There was no tent. There was only a vast curtain of sparkling mist behind which shone the globe . . .

He felt himself drawn through that mist, sucked through it as if by a mighty wind, straight for the globe.

## III          H.P. LOVECRAFT

As the mist-blurred light of the sapphire suns grew more and more intense, the outlines of the globe ahead wavered and dissolved to a churning chaos. Its pallor and its motion and its music all blended themselves with the engulfing mist—bleaching it to a pale steel-color and setting it undulantly in motion. And the sapphire suns, too, melted imperceptibly into the greying infinity of shapeless pulsation.

Meanwhile the sense of forward, outward motion grew intolerably, incredibly, cosmically swift. Every standard of speed known to earth seemed dwarfed, and Campbell knew that any such flight in physical reality would mean instant death to a human being. Even as it was—in this strange, hellish hypnosis or nightmare—the quasi-visual impression of meteor-like hurtling almost numbed his mind. Though there were no real points of reference in the grey, pulsing, void, he felt that he was approaching and passing the speed of light itself. Finally his consciousness did go under—and merciful blackness swallowed everything.

It was very suddenly, and amidst the most impenetrable darkness, that thoughts and ideas again came to George Campbell. Of how many moments—or years—or eternities—had elapsed since his flight through the grey void, he could form no estimate. He knew only that he seemed to be at rest and without pain. Indeed, the absence of all physical sensation was the salient quality of his condition. It made even the blackness seem less solidly black—suggesting as it did that he was rather a disembodied intelligence in a state beyond physical senses, than a corporeal being with senses deprived of their accustomed objects of perception. He could think sharply and quickly—almost preternaturally so—yet could form no idea whatsoever of his situation.

Half by instinct, he realized that he was not in his own tent. True, he might have awaked there from a nightmare to a world equally black; yet he knew this was not so. There was no camp cot beneath him—he had no hands to feel the blankets and canvas surface and flashlight that ought to be around him—there was no sensation of cold in the air—no flap through which he could glimpse the pale night outside . . . something was wrong, dreadfully wrong . . .

He cast his mind backward and thought of the fluorescent cube which had hypnotized him—of that, and all which had followed. He had known that his mind was going, yet had been unable to draw back. At the last moment there had been a shocking, panic fear—a subconscious fear beyond even that caused by the sensation of demoniac flight. It had come from some vague flash of remote recollection—just what, he could not at once tell. Some cell-group in the back of his head had seemed to find a cloudily familiar quality in the cube— and that familiarity was fraught with dim terror. Now he tried to remember what the familiarity and the terror were.

Little by little it came to him. Once—long ago, in connection with his geological life-work—he had read of something like that cube. It had to do with those debatable and disquieting clay fragments called the Eltdown Shards, dug up from precarboniferous strata in southern England thirty years before. Their shape and markings were so queer that a few scholars hinted at artificiality, and made wild conjectures about them and their origin. They came, clearly, from a time when no human beings could exist on the globe—but their contours and figurings were damnably puzzling. That was how they got their name.

It was not, however, in the writings of any sober scientist that Campbell had seen that reference to a crystal, disc-holding globe. The source was far less reputable, and infinitely more vivid. About 1912 a deeply learned Sussex clergyman of occultist leanings—the Reverend Arthur Brooke Winters-Hall—had professed to identify the markings on the Eltdown Shards with some of the so-called ''pre-human heiroglyphs'' persistently cherished and esoterically handed down in certain mystical circles, and had published at his own expense what purported to be a ''translation'' of the primal and baffling ''inscriptions''—a ''translation'' still quoted frequently and seriously by occult writers. In this ''translation''—a surprisingly long brochure in view of the limited number of ''shards'' existing—had occurred the narrative, supposedly of pre-human authorship, containing the now frightening reference.

As the story went, there dwelt on a world—and eventually on countless other worlds—of outer space a mighty order of wormlike beings whose attainments and whose control of nature surpassed anything within the range of terrestrial imagination. They had mastered the art of interstellar travel early in their career, and had peopled every habitable planet in their own galaxy—killing off the races they found.

Beyond the limits of their own galaxy—which was not ours—they could not navigate in person; but in their quest for knowledge of all space and time they discovered a means of spanning certain trans-galactic gulfs with their minds. They devised peculiar objects—strangely energized cubes of a curious crystal containing hypnotic talismans and enclosed in space resisting spherical envelopes of an unknown substance—which could be forcibly expelled beyond the limits of their universe, and which would respond to the attraction of cool solid matter only.

These, of which a few would necessarily land on various inhabited worlds in outside universes, formed the ether-bridges needed for mental communication. Atmospheric friction burned away the protecting envelope, leaving the cube exposed and subject to discovery by the intelligent minds of the world where it fell. By its very nature, the cube would attract and rivet attention. This, when coupled with the action of light, was sufficient to set its special properties working.

The mind that noticed the cube would be drawn into it by the power of the disc and would be sent on a thread of obscure energy to the place whence the disc had come—the remote world of the worm-like space-explorers across stupendous galactic abysses. Received in one of the machines to which each cube was attuned, the captured mind would remain suspended without body or senses until examined by one of the dominant race. Then it would, by an obscure process of interchange, be pumped of all its contents. The investigator's mind would now occupy the strange machine while the captive mind occupied the interrogator's worm-like body.

Then, in another interchange, the interrogator's mind would leap across boundless space to the captive's vacant and unconscious body on the trans-galactic world—animating the alien tenement as best it might, and exploring the alien world in the guise of one of its denizens.

When done with exploration, the adventurer would use the cube and its disc in accomplishing his return—and sometimes the captured mind would be restored safely to its own remote world. Not always, however, were the dominant race so kind. Sometimes, when a potentially important race capable of space travel was found, the worm-like folk would employ the cube to capture and annihilate minds by the thousand, and would extirpate the race for diplomatic reasons—using the exploring minds as agents of destruction.

In other cases, sections of the worm-folk would permanently occupy a trans-galactic planet—destroying the captured minds and wiping out the remaining inhabitants preparatory to settling down in unfamiliar bodies. Never, however, could the parent civilization be quite duplicated in such a case; since the new planet would not contain all the materials necessary for the worm race's arts. The cubes, for example, could be made only on the home planet.

Only a few of the numberless cubes sent forth ever found a landing and response on an inhabited world—since there was no such thing as *aiming* them at goals beyond sight or knowledge. Only three, ran the story, had ever landed on peopled worlds in our own particular universe. Of these, one had struck a planet near the galactic rim two thousand billion years ago, whilst another had lodged three billion years ago on a world near the center of gravity. The third—and the only one ever known to have invaded the solar system—had reached our own earth 150,000,000 years ago.

It was with this latter that Dr. Winters-Hall's "translation" chiefly dealt. When the cube struck the earth, he wrote, the ruling terrestrial species was a huge, cone-shaped race surpassing all others before or since in mentality and achievements. This race was so advanced that it had actually sent minds abroad in both space *and* time to explore the cosmos, hence recognized something of what had happened when the cube fell from the sky and certain individuals had suffered mental change after gazing at it.

Realizing that the changed individuals represented invading minds, the race's leaders had them destroyed—even at the cost of leaving the displaced minds exiled in alien space. They had had experience with even stranger transitions. When, through a mental exploration of space and time, they formed a rough idea of what the cube was, they carefully hid the thing from light and sight, and guarded it as a menace. They did not wish to destroy a thing so rich in later experimental possibilities. Now and then some rash, unscrupulous adventurer would furtively gain access to it and sample its perilous powers despite the consequences—but all such cases were discovered, and safely and drastically dealt with.

Of this evil meddling the only bad result was that the worm-like outside race learned from the new exiles what had happened to their explorers on earth, and conceived a violent hatred of the planet and all its life-forms. They would have depopulated it if they could, and indeed sent additional cubes into space in the wild hope of striking it by accident in unguarded places—but that accident never came to pass.

The cone-shaped terrestrial beings kept the one existing cube in a special shrine as a relique and basis for experiments, till after aeons it was lost amidst the chaos of war and the destruction of the great polar city where it was guarded. When, fifty million years ago, the beings sent their minds ahead into the infinite future to avoid a nameless peril of inner earth, the whereabouts of the sinister cube from space were unknown.

This much, according to the learned occultist, the Eltdown Shards had said. What now made the account so obscurely frightful to Campbell was the minute accuracy with which the alien cube had been described. Every detail tallied—dimensions, consistency, hieroglyphed central disc, hypnotic effects. As he thought the matter over and over amidst the darkness of his strange situation, he began to wonder whether his whole experience with the crystal cube—indeed, its very existence—were not a nightmare brought on by some freakish subconscious memory of this old bit of extravagant, charlatanic reading. If so, though, the nightmare must still be in force, since his present apparently bodiless state had nothing of normality in it.

Of the time consumed by this puzzled memory and reflection, Campbell could form no estimate. Everything about his state was so unreal that ordinary dimensions and measurements became meaningless. It seemed an eternity, but perhaps it was not really long before the sudden interruption came. What happened was as strange and inexplicable as the blankness it succeeded. There was a sensation—of the mind rather than of the body—and all at once Campbell felt his thoughts swept or sucked beyond his control in tumultuous and chaotic fashion.

Memories arose irresponsibly and irrelevantly. All that he knew—all his personal background, traditions, experiences, scholarship, dreams, ideas, and inspirations—welled up abruptly and simultaneously, with a dizzying speed and abundance which soon made him unable to keep track of any separate concept. The parade of all his mental contents became an avalanche, a cascade, a vortex. It was as horrible and vertiginous as his hypnotic flight through space when the crystal cube pulled him. Finally it sapped his consciousness and brought on a fresh oblivion.

Another measureless blank—and then a slow trickle of sensation. This time it was physical, not mental. Sapphire light, and a low rumble of distant sound. There were tactile impressions—he could realize that he was lying at full length on something, though there was a baffling strangeness about the feel of his posture. He could not reconcile the pressure of the supporting surface with his own outlines—or with the outlines of the human form at all. He tried to move his arms, but found no definite response to the attempt. Instead, there were little ineffectual nervous twitches all over the area which seemed to mark his body.

He tried to open his eyes more widely, but found himself unable to control their mechanism. The sapphire light came in a diffused, nebulous manner, and could nowhere be voluntarily focused into definiteness. Gradually, though, the visual images began to trickle in curiously and indecisively. The limits and qualities of vision were not those which he was used to, but he could roughly correlate the sensation with what he had known as sight. As this sensation gained some degree of stability, Campbell realized that he must still be in throes of nightmare.

He seemed to be in a room of considerable extent—of medium height, but with a large proportionate area. On every side—and he could apparently see all four sides at once—were high, narrowish slits which seemed to serve as combined doors and windows. There were singular low tables or pedestals, but no furniture of normal nature and proportions. Through the slits streamed floods of sapphire light, and beyond them could be mistily seen the sides and roofs of fantastic buildings like clustered cubes. On the walls—in the vertical panels between the slits—were strange markings of an oddly disquieting character. It was some time before Campbell understood why they disturbed him so—then he saw that they were, in repeated instances, precisely like some of the hieroglyphs on the crystal cube's disc.

The actual nightmare element, though, was something more than this. It began with the living thing which presently entered through one of the slits, advancing deliberately toward him and bearing a metal box of bizarre proportions and glassy, mirror-like surfaces. For this thing was nothing human—nothing of earth—nothing even of man's myths and dreams. It was a gigantic, pale-grey worm or centipede, as large around as a man and twice as long, with a disc-like, apparently eyeless, cilia fringed head bearing a purple central orifice. It glided on its rear pairs of legs, with its fore part raised vertically—the legs, or at least two pairs of them, there serving as arms. Along its spinal ridge was a curious purple comb, and a fan-shaped tail of some grey membrane ended its grotesque bulk. There was a ring of flexible red spikes around its neck, and from the twistings of these came clicking, twanging sounds in measured, deliberate rhythms.

Here, indeed was outré nightmare at its height—capricious fantasy as its apex. But even this vision of delirium was not what caused George Campbell to lapse a third time into unconsciousness. It took one more thing—one final, unbearable touch—to do that. As the nameless worm advanced with its glistening box, the reclining man caught in the mirror-like surface a glimpse of what should have been his own body. Yet—horribly verifying his disordered and unfamiliar sensations—it was not his own body at all that he saw reflected in the burnished metal. It was, instead, the loathsome, pale-grey bulk of one of the giant centipedes.

## IV    ROBERT E. HOWARD

From that final lap of senselessness, he emerged with a full understanding of his situation. His mind was prisoned in the body of a frightful native of an alien planet, while, somewhere on the other side of the universe, his own body was housing the monster's personality.

He fought down an unreasoning horror. Judged from a cosmic standpoint, why should his metamorphosis horrify him? Life and consciousness were the only realities in the universe. *Form* was unimportant. His present body was hideous only according to terrestrial standards. Fear and revulsion were drowned in the excitement of titanic adventure.

What was his former body but a cloak, eventually to be cast off at death anyway? He had no sentimental illusions about the life from which he had been exiled. What had it ever given him save toil, poverty, continual frustration, and repression? If this life before him offered no more, at least it offered no less. Intuition told him it offered more—much more.

With the honesty possible only when life is stripped of its naked fundamentals, he realized that he remembered with pleasure only the physical delights of his former life. But he had long ago exhausted all the physical possibilities of pleasure contained in that earthly body. Earth held no new thrills. But in the possession of this new, alien body he felt promises of strange, exotic joys.

A lawless exultation rose in him. He was a man without a world, free of all conventions or inhibitions of earth, or of this strange planet, free of every artificial restraint in the universe. He was a god! With grim amusement he thought of his body moving in earth's business and society, with all the while an alien monster staring out of the windows that were George Campbell's eyes on people who would flee if they knew.

Let him walk the earth slaying and destroying as he would. Earth and its races no longer had any meaning to George Campbell. There he had been one of a billion nonenities, fixed in place by a mountainous accumulation of conventions, laws, and manners, doomed to live and die in his sordid niche. But in one blind bound he had soared above the commonplace. This was not death, but rebirth—the birth of a full-grown mentality, with a newfound freedom that made little of physical captivity on Yekub.

He started. Yekub! It was the name of this planet, but how had he known? Then he knew, as he knew the name of him whose body he occupied—Tothe. Memory, deep-grooved in Tothe's brain, was stirring in him—shadows of the knowledge Tothe had. Carved deep in the physical tissues of the brain, they spoke dimly as implanted instincts to George Campbell; and his human consciousness seized them and translated them to show him the way not only to safety and freedom, but to the power his soul, stripped to its primitive impulses, craved. Not as a slave would he dwell on Yekub, but as a king! Just as of old barbarians had sat on the throne of lordly empires.

For the first time he turned his attention to his surroundings. He still lay on the couch-like thing in the midst of that fantastic room, and the centipede-man stood before him, holding the polished metal object, and clashing its neck-spikes. Thus it spoke to him, Campbell knew, and what it said he dimly understood, through the implanted thought processes of Tothe, just as he knew the creature was Yukth, supreme lord of science.

But Campbell gave no heed, for he had made his desperate plan, a plan so alien to the ways of Yekub that it was beyond Yukth's comprehension and caught him wholly unprepared. Yukth, like Campbell, saw the sharp-pointed metal shard on a nearby table, but to Yukth it was only a scientific implement. He did not even know it could be used as a weapon.

Campbell's earthly mind supplied the knowledge and the action that followed, driving Tothe's body into movements no man of Yekub had ever made before.

Campbell snatched the pointed shard and struck, ripping savagely upward. Yukth reared and toppled, his entrails spilling on the floor. In an instant Campbell was streaking for a door. His speed was amazing, exhilarating, first fulfilment of the promise of novel physical sensations.

As he ran, guided wholly by the instinctive knowledge implanted in Tothe's physical reflexes, it was as if he were borne by a separate consciousness in his legs. Tothe's body was bearing him along a route it had traversed ten thousand times when animated by Tothe's mind.

Down a winding corridor he raced, up a twisting stair, through a carved door, and the same instincts that had brought him there told him he had found what he sought. He was in a circular room with a doomed roof from which shone a livid blue light. A strange structure rose in the middle of the rainbow-hued floor, tier on tier, each of a separate, vivid color. The ultimate tier was a purple cone, from the apex of which a blue smoky mist drifted upward to a sphere that poised in midair—a sphere that shone like translucent ivory.

This, the deep-grooved memories of Tothe told Campbell, was the god of Yekub, though why the people of Yekub feared and worshipped it had been forgotten a million years. A worm-priest stood between him and the altar which no hand of flesh had ever touched. That it could be touched was a blasphemy that had never occurred to a man of Yekub. The worm-priest stood in frozen horror until Campbell's shard ripped the life out of him.

On his centipede-legs Campbell clambered the tiered altar, heedless of its sudden quiverings, heedless of the change that was taking place in the floating sphere, heedless of the smoke that now billowed out in blue clouds. He was drunk with the feel of power. He feared the superstitions of Yekub no more than he feared those of earth. With that globe in his hands he would be king of Yekub. The worm-men would dare deny him nothing when he held their god as hostage. He reached a hand for the ball—no longer ivory hued, but red as blood . . .

## V     FRANK BELKNAP LONG, JR.

Out of the tent into the pale August night walked the body of George Campbell. It moved with a slow, wavering gait between the bodies of enormous trees, over a forest path strewed with sweet-scented pine needles. The air was crisp and cold. The sky was an inverted bowl of frosted silver flecked with stardust, and far to the north the aurora borealis splashed streamers of fire.

The head of the walking man lolled hideously from side to side. From the corners of his lax mouth drooled thick threads of amber froth, which fluttered in the night breeze. He walked upright at first, as a man would walk, but gradually as the tent receded his posture altered. His torso began almost imperceptibly to slant, and his limbs to shorten.

In a far-off world of outer space the centipede-creature that was George Campbell clasped to its bosom a god whose lineaments were red as blood, and ran with insect-like quiverings across a rainbow-hued hall and out through massive portals into the bright glow of alien suns.

Weaving between the trees of earth in an attitude that suggested the awkward lopings of a werebeast, the body of George Campbell was fulfilling a mindless destiny. Long, claw-tipped fingers dragged leaves from a carpet of odorous pine needles as it moved toward a wide expanse of gleaming water.

In the far-off, extra-galactic world of the worm-people, George Campbell moved between cyclopean blocks of black masonry down long, fern-planted avenues, holding aloft the round red god.

There was a harsh animal cry in the underbrush near the gleaming lake on earth where the mind of a worm-creature dwelt in a body swayed by instinct. Human teeth sank into soft animal fur, tore at black animal flesh. A little silver fox sank its fangs in frantic retaliation into a furry human wrist, and thrashed about in terror as its blood spurted. Slowly the body of George Campbell arose, its mouth splashed with fresh blood. With upper limbs swaying oddly it moved toward the waters of the lake.

As the veriform creature that was George Campbell crawled between the black blocks of stone thousands of worm-shapes prostrated themselves in the scintillating dust before it. A god-like power seemed to emanate from its weaving body as it moved with a slow, undulant motion toward a throne of spiritual empire transcending all the sovereignties of earth.

A trapper stumbling wearily through the dense woods of earth near the tent where the worm-creature dwelt in the body of George Campbell came to the gleaming waters of the lake and discerned something dark floating there. He had been lost in the woods all night, and weariness enveloped him like a leaden cloak in the pale morning light.

But the shape was a challenge that he could not ignore. Moving to the edge of the water he knelt in the soft mud and reached out toward the floating bulk. Slowly he pulled it to the shore.

Far off in outer space the worm-creature holding the glowing red god ascended a throne that gleamed like the constellation Cassiopeia under an alien vault of hyper-suns. The great deity that he held aloft energized his worm-tenement, burning away in the white fire of a supermundane spirituality all animal dross.

On earth the trapper gazed with unutterable horror into the blackened and hairy face of the drowned man. It was a bestial face, repulsively anthropoid in contour, and from its twisted, distorted mouth black ichor poured.

"He who sought your body in the abysses of time will occupy an unresponsive tenement," said the red god. "No spawn of Yekub can control the body of a human."

"On all earth, living creatures rend one another, and feast with unutterable cruelty on their kith and kin. No worm-mind can control a bestial man-body when it yearns to raven. Only man-minds instinctively conditioned through the course of ten thousand generations can keep the human instincts in thrall. Your body will destroy itself on earth, seeking the blood of its animal kin, seeking the cool water where it can wallow at its ease. Seeking eventually destruction, for the death-instinct is more powerful in it than the instincts of life and it will destroy itself in seeking to return to the slime from which it sprang.''

Thus spoke the round red god of Yekub in a far-off segment of the space-time continuum to George Campbell as the latter, with all human desire purged away, sat on a throne and ruled an empire of worms more wisely, kindly, and benevolently than any man of earth had ever ruled an empire of men.

# THE FLYING LION

*by* EDISON MARSHALL

Those who viewed the motion pictures *The Viking* with Kirk Douglas and, earlier, *Son of Fury,* starring Tyrone Power, were being treated to the work of Edison Marshall. During the forties and fifties, critics frequently cited him as the nation's leading historical novelist, of which his best-known work is probably *Yankee Pasha.*

As early as 1920, Edison Marshall's short stories were included among the fifteen best of the year in the annual O'Henry volume. In 1921 another short story, "The Heart of Little Shikara," a tale of a brave Indian boy who saves an injured white man from a tiger, also won an O'Henry prize as one of the finest short stories of the year and was the title yarn of a successful collection of his works that followed.

Edison Marshall, in addition to being master of a rich, captivating writing style, was a great traveler and his story backgrounds held real authenticity. His ability at characterization was outstanding, and his skill at making animals emerge as personalities in their own right may be favorably compared to that of Rudyard Kipling and Edgar Rice Burroughs.

He was born in Rensselaer, Indiana, August 28, 1894, and died in Augusta, Georgia, October 30, 1967. Son of a newspaperman, he began writing at the University of Oregon in 1915, and seems to have been unable to accumulate enough funds to complete his fourth year of education there.

The first story he sold was titled "When the Fire Dies," and appeared in *The Argosy* for May, 1915 under his full name of Edison Tesla Marshall, with the title changed to "The Sacred Fire." His first work of science fiction, "Who is Charles Avison?," which is regarded as a minor classic in its theme of a twin earth which revolves always out of sight on the other side of the earth with parallel people and events, appeared to be written under a nom de plume because of the two very famous scientists he was named after. This may very well have been a contributing factor in the dropping of his middle name in future stories. The original title for "Who is Charles Avison?" was "Here and There."

In the field of fantasy he has done four major novels. The best known, "Og, The Dawn Man," tells of a pilot injured when his plane crashes in the Canadian wilds, whose mind, through ancestral memory, relinquishes control to a caveman ancestor. Originally published in four installments in the March 24 to April 14, 1928 issues of *The Popular Magazine*, it was published in hardcover by Kinsey in 1934 as "Ogden's Strange Story" and eventually reprinted in *Famous Fantastic Mysteries* for December, 1949. Almost as popular was "Dian of the Lost Land," which appeared in hardcover from Kinsey in 1935 and was reprinted in *Famous Fantastic Mysteries* for April, 1939 and deals with a lost race of Cro-Magnons in an Antarctic valley ruled over by Dian, blonde daughter of a previous explorer.

"The Flying Lion" is one of Edison Marshall's least known works, listed in no bibliography of the fantastic, despite the fact that it was the first in a truly outstanding series which began in the August, 1919 issue of *The Blue Book Magazine*. Searchers after the fantastic and horrifying may have been fooled by the overall title of the series, which was "From a Frontiersman's Diary," but this masterpiece does not deserve to remain in obscurity and unreprinted. It has a dual appeal both to the lovers of the true horror story and for those who dote on the Tarzan-like tales which Edgar Rice Burroughs made so popular and of which school it is a variant. In fact, the entire series of which it is the first, is of the Kipling and Burroughs tradition.

The second story in the series, "The Blood of Kings," in the September, 1919 issue is built around a frontiersman who tames a baby mountain-lion; "The Son of the Wild Things" in October, 1919, is a superlatively human and imaginative story of an Eskimo boy raised with the musk-oxen; "The

Serpent City,'' November, 1919 is a frightening masterpiece of a man who discovers a ''city'' of snakes and masters their customs and ''speech''; and ''Jungle Justice'' in December, 1919 tells of an Indian who raises a bear cub and the feeling that develops between them.

It is safe to say that ''The Flying Lion'' will whet the appetites of its readers to secure some of the other stories in this fine group.

# THE FLYING LION

by

**Edison Marshall**

When my old friend gave me the letter of introduction, he
made a number of promises that I think would be grounds for
a lawsuit. "You'll find complete rest for nerves and muscles," said he. "You'll find mountain air and the smell of
balsam and wild huckleberries served with cream and the best
trout-fishing in the world." He was right in some particulars.
I found lakes and streams where the trout leaped for the fly
before it ever struck the water. I ate mountain food, and the
smell of balsam was an unceasing delight when the wind blew
from the forests. The mountain air stole into every capillary,
and made a man feel as if he could stride from peak to peak.
But instead of complete rest for nerves and muscles—I have a
limp that will remain in my body till I die, and a story no
sensible man on earth will believe.

It doesn't make any difference, one way or another,
whether or not anyone believes it. I believe it. The old
mountaineer who was my host believes it. You may say I was
delirious; and of course I had been. But what the moon
showed me on the cliff-top was just as distinct, just as real, as
the sun in the sky or my hand that I hold before my face.

Rest for nerves and muscles! I can laugh at the phrase now.
But it wasn't so easy to laugh on that strange, moonlight night
in April.

The long shadows of the mountains had dropped down on Dead Indian Ranch when the stage left me at the gate. I will never cease wondering at those mountain shadows. They fall all at once, like a curtain, and they seem to be a strange blue in color. They make the hills look purple instead of green, and the sky a queer lavender for which there is no name. It is the signal for the gaunt wolves to leave their coverts, and for the deer to steal out like shadows themselves, and feed along the narrow deer-trails.

The house was typical for a mountain ranch—square, comfortable, with big fireplaces and a white sweep of un-adorned walls. Jelt, my host, was a typical mountain ranch-man, sinewy, silent, rather grim and severe.

He welcomed me to supper. After supper we sat before a logfire. And we went together to the window, and saw the moon hanging over the dark woods.

"We are the last outpost," said Jelt. "Beyond here is only—Beyond. Miles and miles and miles of ridges, one just like the other, and it isn't well to be lost up there."

Then I pointed to what looked like a dark slit between the mountains. "What is that?" I asked.

He turned to me, with a sparkle of interest in his eyes. "Funny you noticed that right off. It's a place worth seeing, if any place is. We call it the Dark Cañon."

We walked back to the fire, and he told me about it. It was nothing more or less than a box cañon, found often in the mountains. A box cañon is a glen between hills bound about with cliffs, and usually with a narrow opening. It was given over to freakish tendencies in the way of creeks that started up and disappeared, and caves that had no end, and brush-thickets through which no man could push his way. On three sides, he said, it had sheer cliffs, impassable to human feet. Its mouth was a steep and difficult descent, rugged and treacherous; and even the tried mountaineers that have a sixth sense to lead them at the brink of precipices in darkest night, would never attempt it after twilight. "The deer don't go in there often," said Jelt. "It doesn't give them space to run from the cats. But there are plenty of them, and plenty of wolves."

"I suppose you mean mountain-lions?"

"Yes—cougars we call them. They grow ungodly large down there, too, and come up on the ridges to hunt."

I know old Jelt. I know his annoying reticence, and I have not the slightest doubt but that he would never have taken the trouble to tell me about the Flying Lion if it had not been for a little incident just before we went to bed. The fire was almost burned out, by then. Jelt and I and his big, rawboned son were smoking a last pipe together. Then we heard it.

It was the kind of noise that a man would not relish hearing alone at night. I don't know why, either—except that it sounded like nothing under heaven. There is simply nothing with which a man can compare it, and I don't think a word has ever been coined to name it. For it wasn't exactly a scream. It wasn't a howl, like a wolf makes. And the thing sounded just below our window.

It was a long, wild cry that rose and rose to an unbelievable height, and wailed away. It came so suddenly, like a blade thrown out of the darkness, and it was so terribly loud in the perfect stillness that it startled us more than a mere vibration of sound-waves could ever startle three healthy men. It came to a sharp crescendo, then streamed away in a long, shuddering wail; and it wouldn't fit it exactly to say that it was a sound of someone in terror. It had some of the qualities of a death-scream of a woman, and yet I knew just as soon as I knew anything, that it was not the death-scream of a woman.

"And what in heaven's name was that?" I asked. I smiled at them, although I knew that it was no smiling matter.

But they did not return my smile, or answer me. They paid no attention to me whatever. All they did was sigh, one with the other. I find it hard to describe the way in which these long sighs affected me. I felt that it would have been a great deal better for them to exclaim in fear, and ask startled questions of each other, than just to stand and sigh. Such sounds were in a moment an expression of utter futility and helplessness. And as I watched them, they soberly turned and unhooked their rifles from the wall. I followed them to the door.

As we opened it, Jelt's hound pushed through and startled us. It was naturally a magnificent animal, the kind of creature a man likes to imagine is courageous in all circumstances. But it was not magnificent now. It was whimpering and sweating in a way a dog should never do.

The two men walked in front of me, along the hillside on which the house was built, and they seemed to be marching as if in a rank of soldiers. They walked steadily, swiftly; and they spoke no words at all. When they came to a point where the lower valleys were revealed to them, they paused, and I saw them looking here and there, down over the glens.

In just a moment, almost before I could reach them, they had started back to the house. And they sighed again, both of them. I could hear them in the stillness.

"I s'pose it was one of the calves in the South Lot that'll be gone this time," said the younger man.

"I suppose so." And we trooped together into the house.

They hung up their rifles, and they sat down again before the fire. Jelt quietly refilled his pipe.

"I suppose you're wondering what it's all about," he said at last.

"Wondering a great deal. Would you mind telling me?"

"There isn't much that I can tell you. You know as much about it as we do now, only we've heard it eight times, and you've heard it just once. If you hadn't heard it too, I'd say that everyone in this house was stark staring mad. What did it sound like to you?"

"I've been trying to think, and I don't know. Nothing like I ever heard before."

The mountaineer smoked calmly a long moment before he spoke again. "Did you ever hear a mountain-lion?" he asked at last.

"No. Was that what it was? A mountain-lion?"

He waited endless seconds before he answered. "Young man," he said at last, "in my time I've heard a hundred mountain-lions. I've killed a good score of them, I've heard bobcats, and I've heard wolves. That thing that screamed out there in the South Lot tonight is not a mountain-lion.

"The sound was something like the scream of a mountain-lion—like the cougar's cry when he knocks down a deer. It's high and wild and kind of creepy. And yet it isn't one, and I can't tell you why I know it isn't. It has a quality no man ever heard in a mountain-lion before. I've heard it eight times, and the first few times we went out and hunted up and down the mountains. But we didn't hear anything or see anything. We still go out and have a look, but it never does any good. The thing is always gone, and with it a calf. Our hound runs out and barks when a cougar or a wolf comes too near; but he comes into the house and whimpers and sweats when this thing makes its kill. I've got it figured out that it lives in the Dark Cañon somewhere, But heavens! A troop of goblins could live in the Dark Cañon, and no one would ever see them. But there's one other strange thing. In fact, it's the strangest thing of all.''

He turned his head and spoke so low I could hardly hear. ''The thing doesn't leave any tracks,'' he said.

He said it perfectly simply. I couldn't think of an intelligent remark to make in answer. So we sat still, and listened to the wind in the tree-tops.

''I've gone out dozens of times, and searched all over the trails for the track of a beast of prey big enough to carry off a calf and not drag its legs. That would mean a cougar, or something bigger. A wolf can kill a calf, but it has to eat it where it falls or drag it to its lair. A bear—the little bears we have here can't even kill them. But this thing not only fails to make a track, but it doesn't even drag its meat. I feel like a fool to sit here and tell you something you won't believe—but it is unfortunately the truth. And a calf weighing one hundred and fifty pounds isn't an easy thing to carry without dragging.

''Well, that's all there is to it. Figure it out any way you like. Son and I have a little name for the thing—we call it the Flying Lion. You see why—we don't see how it can carry away one of my calves and leave no trace unless it flies. I admit that's a silly lot of stuff to tell a man and expect him to believe, and I don't expect you to. Only don't call me a liar, for I'm telling you exactly what I know. It doesn't make much difference. Like as not we won't hear the thing again for another year. I think it just kills my calves when it misses its wild kill down in the Cañon.''

We were still again. ''Paw!'' his son said at last. ''Better tell him about that bear with the crooked foot whose track we saw that day. I've always kind of figured that had something to do with it.''

''Son, I keep telling you that was nothing.'' He turned to me. ''The boy found what looked like a track of a young bear a time or two, and he's always thought it had cards in the deal some way. But it hasn't. A bear that size couldn't kill a lamb; besides, the little black bears eat berries, not meat. There are bears all around. We see their tracks all the time.'' He laughed once, grimly. ''And no bear on earth would scream like that thing did!''

And soon after this, we went to bed.

There was a kind of grim fascination about the Dark Cañon. Often I stood on the rocky ledge at its mouth, and looked down into its fastnesses; but the weeks grew to months before ever I went into it. In the first place, I was not yet enough accustomed to the mountain-trails to trust myself on the precipitate path.

The sunlight seemed never to enter it. Of course, around noon, a few lame beams used to steal down between the dark pines; but as a whole the Dark Cañon was always in shadow. It had been well named.

But there came a day when I felt skilled enough to try the trail. It was worse than I thought. Part of the time I had to go on hands and knees; and part, I had to cling to the stunted shrubbery to hold fast at all. My breath was coming hard, and my nerves were ragged and jumpy by the time I reached the floor of the ravine.

I had a queer feeling of being out of the world. It was very still down here. The stream that trickled through it made a little noise, and the trees kept up their solemn chant, and I had a dim realization that bees were plying in the thickets, but all these noises combined together and made only silence. I can't describe my feeling. It was one of those elusive sensations that is some way connected with the realm of dreams. It was as if I had been projected out of my boundaries of time, to a period infinitely remote and strange.

I remembered, more clearly than ever since the night it reached us through the cry of the Flying Lion; and all at once I knew that here was its source and home. No other place in the world would be fitting. It was as much a part of this savage Cañon as laughter is part of a children's nursery, or prayer part of a church. But I did hope that it would not sound out now. It would not be the sort of thing to quiet a man's already jumping nerves. I was absolutely unarmed.

Adding to the sense of isolation and loneliness, I remembered all at once that I had neglected to notify my hosts in the ranch-house of my expedition; and they would have no idea to which of the thousand hills I had gone.

Moss grew on the glen floor, and strong, rank ferns made lush carpets along the creek-banks. The trees were tremendous and solemn and dark and still.

I went farther down into the glen, and all the time the walls of the Cañon grew more steep. The creek disappeared, as if a spirit had wished it away. I could hear my own footfall in the moss, and that was all.

It was about four o'clock in the afternoon when I arrived on the valley floor; and all at once I realized that I must turn at once if I were going to mount the ridge before night came. I had seen enough of the Dark Cañon for one day.

It was then that the shadow fell, as always like a purple drapery. It was not darkness yet. That falling curtain was only the harbinger of the darkness that would come in less than an hour. The sky grew curiously green, and the mountains changed color.

But the queerest thing of all was that the falling shadow seemed to be the signal for the wakening of the forest life. The Cañon had seemed dead and still on my descent. Yet I had not gone a dozen steps in return until a crash and tumult in the thicket beside my trail told me of a startled forest-creature. I don't know what it was. I know that I heard it spring; and then I heard the *pit-pat* of its feet upon a trail.

They stopped, and I stopped. I would have greatly preferred to have them continue.

I hurried on, and a covey of mountain quail sprang up from the shrubbery. The explosion of their starting wings was preternaturally loud. But I did not pause again. I hurried on to the foot of the steep ascent.

All the way the start and stir of the wild creatures sounded in the dead forest. Once I thought I caught a glimpse of a tawny body in the shrubbery; but I could not be sure. And once the limbs of a dark pine above my head crashed and rustled strangely; but the shadows were too deep for me to see. Something kept patting the trail behind me.

To this day I cannot be quite certain as to what happened on the steep trail when I had mounted sixty feet. I had reached for the root of a shrub to aid me, and the thing broke in my grasp. I have a dim memory of reeling, staggering, trying to check my fall; and after that was only darkness.

It was night in the Dark Cañon when I wakened. There was a great, white moon somewhere above; but I could not see it, and I only knew it was hanging there from the silver mystery that was on the top of the pines. None of its beams streamed down through the great trees to me; only a dim pallor to which my eyes had not yet grown accustomed. The stars signaled down, a whole sky of them.

I was lying at the very foot of the steep trail. I had fallen fully sixty feet. Of course the descent had not been straight down; yet to a casual glance it was a sheer precipice. And I think that the first impression that I had, on wakening, was the realization that I could not move.

There is no sensation in the world quite so terrible as that of helplessness and futility. Men who are caught in burning buildings have it, and men who are starving in desert wastes. I had it now.

It wasn't just weakness. A man can overcome weakness by some fortitude within himself. It was not just unconsciousness or pain. I knew that a burning, stabbing pain was all over me, and that I was hovering at the very brink of unconsciousness into which I would presently fall; but I knew too that I had sustained severe and actual injuries. I focused all my thought to determine the extent of them. It was work, such work as I do not care to do again. "My leg is broken—I know that," I told myself. "There is a cave-in somewhere in my ribs. And my head is bleeding."

All these things were true. They were not just delusions. And I could not even crawl along the ground.

I did not have many seconds to think of my own broken bones, because all at once I knew that there were other, more poignant things to think about. They were things that stirred, here and there, in the thickets about me.

At first all I heard was the quick *pit-pat* of soft feet upon a trail. They were running feet, and they stopped short. Then I heard a long body snap the twigs and rustle the branches of the buck-brush just to my right. They were not altogether silent things. It seemed to me that they leaped about, and were curiously excited. Forest creatures as a rule try to be silent. The things in the thickets about me were making no such try. A wolf or a lion is never noisy; but when they wish they can drift like mist through the forest. I heard them step quite freely; and sometimes I heard them sniff and grunt. And the *pit-pat* of their feet was nearer.

I fell vaguely to wondering why they were so excited. And then I spoke and told myself.

"It is the smell of blood," I said.

It was perfectly evident that my return to consciousness had startled them a moment. They were only waiting for me to go to sleep again. They knew it would not be long. But they weren't patient, as are vultures on a desert. I was not even certain that they would wait until unconsciousness came again.

Then the faint light that there was, suddenly caught and reflected in a pair of eyes in the thicket just beside me. It was not just a flash, such as may easily be the gleam of something much less terrible. They were unmistakably eyes; for they stared and stared, unwinking. They were green and very bright. And then I began to see them anywhere I looked.

They were the eyes of the great, gaunt timber-wolves. And the timber-wolf, foresters know, is the most terrible creature in the Cascades. He is not quite so strong as a full-grown cougar. He has not the magnificence and fury in a long charge that marks a wounded brown bear. But he is less educated. He is less schooled in his relations with man—or else, with his dog-like sagacity, he better understands man's weaknesses. He travels in packs, and this fact makes his strength the greater. And finally, he seems to have no forest law against eating human flesh—the law that is obeyed by most of the larger forest-creatures. It is the wolf's law that whatever is meat, and whatever can be safely attacked without too great loss to the pack, is food.

They had ranged about on all sides of me, and I heard the twigs crack beneath their feet as they drew ever nearer. Their eyes gleamed, ever brighter, and ever they seemed more restless and excited. And then I turned my head to find one just behind me.

I raised my one good arm; and his teeth clicked as he snapped at it. Two of the other wolves ran in as I turned, but I drove them back with a shout. They only retreated a little way. And in some dim, remote corner of my mind it seemed to me I heard an answer to my cry. It was so far away, so dim, that I only perceived it at the outer limits of hearing. If it was anything, it was a long half-scream, half-howl that rose and shuddered away.

The wolves stood near enough for me to see the dim outlines of the forms, and for a moment they all seemed to be standing rigid. They all seemed to be listening. Then they came on again.

"A useless fight!" I told myself. "A lost fight already!"

And I prayed that unconsciousness might come before I felt their fangs.

The wolves were quite close now. I struck at them to the right and left. I caught the gleam of their fangs sometimes; and only my frenzied shouts kept them off at all. But it was sickeningly evident how long mere shouts would frighten them. The smell of blood was an intoxication in the air—and even now they were crouching to spring upon me.

Then above the suppressed noise of the leaping wolves and the echo of my own shouts and the sad moan of the wind, I heard another sound. It was the rapid patter of feet upon the trail—running very swiftly down the Cañon. It burst upon us all at once.

Most four-footed creatures race at a gallop, and their feet sound *pit-pat—pit-pat* on a trail. Two impacts so close together that it seems as one sound, then a pause of a fraction of a second, and then two more impacts. But this creature that was advancing so rapidly from the farther reaches of the glen came *pat—pat—pat—pat;* with every impact at an exact interval. Why, in the face of the death that even now was upon me, I perceived this fact, I do not know. The human brain acts queerly in a crisis. Men that have fallen from great heights are known to have observed physical phenomena while in their lightning descent that had escaped their gaze before. I know that even as I struck at the wolves and shouted, I marked the cadence of those approaching feet.

For once, I seemed to hear the sound before the wolves heard it. And all at once they stopped short, like forms suddenly stricken to stone. Slowly they turned their heads. They seemed to have forgotten me. The hair was erect upon their necks, and they were growling in an uneasy fashion in their throats. They turned, advancing to meet the newcomer.

It was a moment's interlude; and exhausted beyond words to tell, I sank back prone. The shadows of unconsciousness began to gather and deepen. And only in some outer realm of my thought was I aware that great forces were ranged against each other in the thicket beyond; and I was the subject of the conflict.

The growls rose to furious, angry barks; and in between I heard queer, chattering, snarling noises that I was too tired and dazed to try to name or trace. Animals always fought over their food . . . Some greater beast had come from the far stretches of the Dark Cañon to fight these wolves for their

meat. It did not matter which won. The teeth of one would be
no less sharp, no less remorseless than those of the other. And
then I began to drift away into unconsciousness.

Once I was wakened out of it by the death-cry of a wolf—a
strangling scream ending in a sob that was almost human.
The strange dark fight went on. Another wolf howled in
agony, and it seemed to me from time to time that I heard the
*pit-pat—pit-pat* of feet that hastened in flight up the trail.

I heard the spring of bodies, and the snap of teeth that
missed their hold, and now and then the terrible tearing of
flesh. I heard all these things as in a dream, as things not
particularly mattering one way or the other. And then the feet
of the vanquished party pattered on the trail.

" *'Pat—pat—pat'* wins, and *'pit-pat'* is beaten," I
thought as the darkness grew around me. And all at once there
was silence in the Dark Cañon, except for the ever-fading
patter of fleeing feet. I tried to probe the shadows, to see what
kind of thing had come and had fought for my helpless body.
But I could not see. The curtain of unconsciousness dropped
between.

What occurred between this moment and the moment
when I opened my eyes again, I can never be quite sure. I can
only tell of the impressions that I had through the mists of
delusion and delirium; and they don't make particularly good
sense. I only know this—that some living creature took me up
as tenderly as a baby and carried me over that awful trail to the
mouth of the Dark Cañon up above.

A mountain-lion can be tender, in a terrible way. It is
tender as is a cat with a mouse, striking just hard enough to
agonize and not to kill. It can seize its prey between its teeth,
and with an excruciating tenderness carry it away to torture.
But this was not the kind of tenderness with which I was
carried. I did not feel the slightest sense of pain. And I felt as
secure, as safe, as when long ago my mother bore me in her
arms.

I am a fair-sized man, physically—weighing one hundred
and sixty pounds. The trail was straight up and down. It was a

bare foothold in bright day, to be aided with empty hands and the strength of an unloaded back. And yet the creature on whose back I hung bounded up the trail with me easily.

If I had not heard it breathing, it wouldn't have seemed a thing of flesh at all—so securely I rode, so free from jar. My senses were blurred by pain and the shadow of unconsciousness; and besides the trail was lost in darkness; so I could not see even the outline of the thing that carried me.

We reached the top of the cliff, and through my half-closed eyes I could see the full moon. We darted through shadow, out of the shrubbery, and at the boundary of what Jelt called his South Lot. We seemed to move like the wind—and the only sound was the swift *pat—pat—pat* of its feet on the trail. It was a distance of six hundred yards from the top of the cliff, and it seemed to me we covered it between sixty beats of my heart.

And then, in the grass of the South Lot, the creature laid me down. Never was motion more gentle, more tender; and so near was its body to me that at first I could not open my eyes and see it. And then the thing threw back its head and called.

It stood on its hind feet, and I saw it plain. The bright moon was on it. I could see every line, every feature. I could see the nails on its paws. I was not unconscious. Every detail of the scene, the huge moon above, the Dark Cañon spreading in mystery below the house with its lighted windows, the tall pines were all remarkably plain. I was not delirious. As often after the channel of unconsciousness has been crossed, my senses seemed abnormally acute and sharp. Every mist that pain and fear had brought had passed away, and only a great awe remained.

It was not a large form. It did not stand quite erect, and its arms dropped down in front of it like the arms of an ape; but I judged it must be about six feet from extremity to extremity. It was slender as a panther. It was terribly wrinkled, and seemingly older than the hills themselves. It opened its mouth like a beast and I saw its white teeth; and the thing was hideous beyond the power of words to describe. Something gray and tenuous hung wild about its shoulders. I could see now the thing that held me on its back. It was a hand, brown and long-nailed and strong as a thing of steel. It wore a strip of fur about its body, in remembrance of an instinct almost forgotten. And the cry that it uttered was the long, wild, rising and falling scream of the Flying Lion.

It stood with head thrown back a long moment before it darted back toward the Cañon. It was too plain to mistake. I would love to say that it was something else than what it was; I would have loved to believe that my eyes were lying to me, as I lay at its feet. I can do neither.

It was the Flying Lion at last; and true, it was a beast in posture and voice. But it had not been born a beast. As surely as old Jelt was at that moment emerging from his house with his rifle, the Flying Lion had been born a woman.

This is the story. I carry a limp from the fall. And anyone has the liberty of believing I have given a wrong interpretation to the events—or forgetting them.

There are three considerations, however, that should be remembered.

One of them is that a legend has been passed down, and the name of the ranch seems to bear it out, that in a long-forgotten spring a girl-papoose wandered away from the side of a dead squaw, and was carried off to a cougar's cave.

The second is that a human being, even growing up among the lions, living the way the lions lived, climbing the same trees and eating the same meat, attaining a lion's strength—a strength so formidable that not even a pack of wolves remained to fight after one of their number had been slain—might not descend so far but that a spark of humanity, an instinct of tenderness and protection and motherhood toward its own kind, might linger in its savage heart.

The third point is that the naked foot of a human being, with long-nailed toes that had never been confined in shoes and long from climbing trees, makes a track not greatly different from that of the most amiable of the forest people, the small black bear.

# GRETTIR AT THORHALL-STEAD
## *by* FRANK NORRIS

Frank Norris is acknowledged to be one of the great transitional figures in American literary history. Even earlier and more effectively than Theodore Dreiser, he paved the way for naturalism in serious American novels and helped sound the literary equivalent of "taps" on the vogue for excessive sentimentalism.

The work that brought him his greatest reputation was *The Octopus,* published in 1901, a powerful novel of the struggle of the ranchers against the railroads in the West. The novel was criticized for the ambivalence of the author in failing to present a simplistic situation of good against evil, but instead showing that the forces at work were far more complex than commonly believed. Despite the hailing of *The Octopus* as a triumph of realism, there was a strain of mysticism in which the wheat crop of the West is invested with an awareness of itself as an entity and through virtual self-determination wills itself to grow and to be ultimately consumed for food.

A strain of fantasy touching upon real horror had run through Norris' work previously. There was an almost baroque distortion in the literary techniques utilized in *McTeague* (1899), an early success telling of a dentist warped by heredity and environment, who degenerates into an alcoholic, becomes the murderer of his wife, and in flight from justice retreats physically as well as psychologically to the region of his youth.

The grim masterpiece to come from his pen was *Vandover and the Brute,* begun in 1894 and when finished lost in the San Francisco fire, and never recovered and published until 1914. "The most revolting story of lycanthrophy," was the description given the novel by Dorothy Scarborough in her book *The Supernatural in Modern English Fiction* (1917). *Vandover and the Brute* tells of the gradual disintegration of the personality of a fine, sensitive young man who consistently takes the course of least resistance, to finally end up naked and insane, crawling on all fours and barking the word "Wolf!"

Knowing the early genesis of this novel and its subject matter, it is easier to understand why the man who continued the trend toward naturalism in America started by Stephen Crane, and helped perpetuate it by the discovery of Theodore Dreiser's *Sister Carrie* in a slush pile of manuscripts while working as a first reader for Doubleday, could have produced a number of short works of the supernatural. Among them, "Grettir at Thorhall-Stead" is a particularly remarkable tale of possession and the animation of the dead by another will. It first appeared in *Everybody's Magazine* for April, 1903 with eight illustrations plus page ornamentations by the artist J.J. Gould. The story is set in ancient Iceland, a background so bleak and dour that it is strange it has not been used more frequently for tales of horror and the supernatural. Told with some of the flavor of the Norsemen, the story upon this reprinting will be recognized as a neglected masterpiece of the art of the macabre.

In the same issue, *Everybody's* ran Mary E. Wilkins-Freeman's supernatural classic, *The Southwest Chamber*. The magazine would run the entire contents of what was to become one of the most coveted books in the genre, *The Wind in the Rose-Bush* (Doubleday Page & Co., 1903), and the volume would be illustrated by the work of artist Peter Newell which adorned the stories in their original publication.

It is not generally recognized, but in the ten years preceding and following 1900, the United States produced a small but outstanding body of horror fiction which included, in addition to the works of Frank Norris previously discussed, and Mary E. Wilkins-Freeman, such masters as Robert W. Chambers, W.C. Morrow, Henry James, Ralph Adams

Cram, Ambrose Bierce, Edith Wharton, Jack London, J. Marion Crawford, Edward Lucas White, and Gertrude Atherton. It raises the question as to whether or not the American contribution to horror fiction in this era has not been greatly underrated.

# GRETTIR AT THORHALL-STEAD

by

**Frank Norris**

## I    GLAMR

Thorhall the bonder had been to the great Thingvalla, or annual fair of Iceland, to engage a shepherd, and was now returning. It had been a good two-days' journey home, for his shaggy little pony, though sure-footed, was slow. For the better part of three hours on the evening of the second day he had been picking his way cautiously among the great boulders of black basalt that encumbered the path. At length, on the summit of a low hill, he brought the little animal to a standstill and paused a moment, looking off to the northward, a smile of satisfaction spreading over his broad, sober face. For he had just passed the white stone that marked the boundary of his own land. Below him opened the little valley named the Vale of Shadows, and in its midst, overshadowed by a single Norway pine, black, wind-distorted, was the stone farmhouse, the byre, Thorhall's home.

Only an Icelander could have found pleasure in that prospect. It was dreary beyond expression. Save only for the deformed pine, tortured and warped by its unending battle with the wintry gales, no other tree relieved the monotony of the landscape. To the west, mountains barred the horizon—

volcanic mountains, gashed, cragged, basaltic, and still blackened with primeval fires. Bare of vegetation they were—somber, solitary, empty of life. To the eastward, low, rolling sand dunes, sprinkled thinly with gorse, bore down to the sea. They shut off a view of the shore, but farther on the horizon showed itself, a bitter, inhospitable waste of gray water, blotted by fogs and murk and sudden squalls. Though the shore was invisible, it nonetheless asserted itself. With the rushing of the wind was mingled the prolonged, everlasting thunder of the surf, while the taint of salt, of decaying kelp, of fish, of seaweed, of all the pungent aromas of the sea, pervaded the air on every hand.

Black gulls, sharply defined against the gray sky, slanted in long tacking flights hither and thither over sea and land. The raucous bark of the seal hunting mackerel off the shore made itself occasionally heard. Otherwise there was no sign of life. Veils of fine rain, half fog, drove across the scene between ocean and mountain. The wind blew incessantly from off the sea with a steady and uninterrupted murmur.

Thorhall rode on, inclining his head against the gusts and driving wind. Soon he had come to the farmhouse. The servants led the pony to the stables and in the doorway Thorhall found his wife waiting for him. They embraced one another and—for they were pious folk—thanked God for the bonder's safe journey and speedy return. Before the roaring fire of drift that evening Thorhall told his wife of all that had passed at the Thingvalla, of the wrestling, and of the stallion fights.

"And did you find a shepherd to your liking?" asked his wife.

"Yes, a great fellow with white teeth and black hair. Rather surly, I believe, but strong as a troll. He promised to be with me by the beginning of the winter night. His name is Glamr."

But the summer passed, the sun dipped below the horizon not to reappear for six months, the winter night drew on, snow buried all the landscape, hurricanes sharp as boarspears descended upon the Vale of Shadows; in their beds the dwellers in the byre heard the grind and growl of the great bergs careering onward through the ocean, and many a night the howl of hunger-driven wolves startled Thorhall from his sleep; yet Glamr did not come.

Then at length and of a sudden he appeared; and Thorhall on a certain evening, called hastily by a frightened servant, beheld the great figure of him in the midst of the kitchen floor, his eyebrows frosted yet scowling, his white teeth snapping with cold, while in a great hoarse voice, like the grumble of a bear, he called for meat and drink.

From thenceforward Glmar became a member of Thorhall's household. Yet seldom was he found in the byre. By day he was away with the sheep; by night he slept in the stables. The servants were afraid of him, though he rarely addressed them a word. He was not only feared, but disliked. This aversion was partly explained by Glamr's own peculiar disposition—gloomy, solitary, uncanny, and partly by a fact that came to light within the first month of his coming to the Vale of Shadows.

He was an unbeliever. Never did his broad bulk darken the lich-gate of the kirk; the knolling of matin and vesper-bell put him in a season of even deeper gloom than usual. It was noticed that he could not bear to look upon a cross; the priest he abhorred as a pestilence. On holy days he kept far from home, absenting himself upon one pretext or another, withdrawing up into the chasms and gorges of the hills.

So passed the first months of the winter.

Christmas day came, and Christmas night. It was bitter, bitter cold. Snow had fallen since second cockcrow the day before, and as night closed in such a gale as had not been known for years gathered from off the Northern Ocean and whirled shrieking over the Vale of Shadows. All day long Glamr was in the hills with the sheep, and even above the roaring of the wind his bell-toned voice had occasionally been heard as he called and shouted to his charges. At the candlelighting time he had not returned. The bonder and his family busked themselves to attend the Christmas mass.

Some two hours later they were returning. The wind was going down, but even yet shreds of torn seaweed and scud of foam, swept up by the breath of the gale, drove landward across the valley. The clouds overhead were breaking up, and between their galloping courses one saw the sky, the stars glittering like hoar frost.

The bonder's party drew near the farmhouse, and the servants, going before with lanthorns and pine torches, undid the fastenings of the gate. The wind lapsed suddenly, and in the stillness between two gusts the plunge of the surf made itself heard.

Then all at once Thorhall and his wife stopped and her hand clutched quickly at his wrist.

"Hark! What was that?"

What, indeed? Was it an echo of the storm sounding hollow and faint from some thunder-split crag far off there in those hills toward which all eyes were suddenly turned; was it the cry of a wolf, the clamor of a falcon, or was it the horrid scream of human agony and fury, vibrating to a hoarse and bell-like note that sounded familiar in their ears?

"Glamr! Where is Glamr?" shouted Thorhall, as he entered the byre. But those few servants who had been left in charge of the house reported he had not yet returned.

Night passed and no Glamr; and in the morning the search-party set out toward the hills. Half way up the slope, the sheep—a few of them—were found, scattered, half buried in drifts; then a dog, dead and frozen hard as wood. From it led a track up into the higher mountains, a strange track indeed, not human certainly, yet whether of wolf or bear no one could determine. Some had started to follow when a lad who had looked behind the shoulder of a great rock raised a cry.

There was the body of Glamr. The shepherd was stretched upon his back, dead, rigid. The open eyes were glazed, the face livid; the tongue protruding from the mouth had been bitten through in the last agony. All about the snow was trampled down, and the bare bushes crushed and flattened out. Even the massive boulder near which the body had been found was moved a little from its place. A fearful struggle had been wrought out here, yet upon the body of Glamr was no trace of a wound, no mark of claw or hand. Only among his footprints was mingled that strange track that had been noticed before, and as before it led straight up toward the high part of the mountains.

The young men raised the body of the shepherd and the party moved off toward the kirk and the graveyard. Even though Glamr had shunned the mass, the priest might be prevailed upon to bury him in consecrated ground. But soon the young men had to pause to rest. The body was unexpectedly heavy. Once again, after stopping to breathe, they raised the bier upon their shoulders. Soon another helper was summoned, then another; even Thorhall aided. Ten strong men though they were, they staggered and trembled under that earthly weight. Even in that icy air the perspiration streamed from them. Heavier and still heavier grew the burden; it bore them to the earth. Their knees bowed out from under them, their backs bent. They were obliged to give over.

Later in the day they returned with oxen and a sledge. They repaired to the spot where the body had been left; then stared at each other with paling faces. In the snow at their feet there was the impression made by the great frame of the shepherd. But that was all; the body was gone, nor was there any footprint in the snow other than they themselves had made.

A cairn was erected over the spot, and for many a long day the strange death of the shepherd of the Vale of Shadows was the talk of the countryside. But about a month or so after the death of Glamr a strange sense of uneasiness seemed to invade the household of the byre. By degrees it took possession of first one and then another of the servants and family. No one spoke about this. It was not a thing that could be reduced to words, and for the matter of that, each one believed that he or she was the only one affected. This one thought himself sick; that one believed herself merely nervous. But nevertheless a certain perplexity, a certain disturbance of spirit was in the air.

One evening Thorhall and his wife met accidentally in the passage between the main body of the house and the dairy. They paused and looked at each other for no reason that they could imagine. Thus they stood for several seconds.

"Well," said Thorhall at length, "what is it?"

"Ay," responded his wife. "Ay, what *is* it?"

"Nothing," he replied; and she, echoing his words, also answered "Nothing."

Then they laughed nervously, yet still looking fixedly into each other's eyes for all that.

"I believe," said Thorhall the next day, "that I am to be sick. I cannot tell—I feel no pain—no fever—and yet—"

"And I, too," declared his wife. "I am—no, not sick—but distressed. I—I am troubled. I cannot tell what it is. I sometimes think I am *afraid.*"

A week later, on a certain evening just after curfew, the whole family was aroused by a wild shriek as of someone in mortal terror. Thorhall and his wife rushed into the dairy whence the cry came and found one of the maids in a fit upon the floor.

When she recovered she cried out that she had seen at one of the windows the face of Glamr.

## II    GRETTIR

The cold, bright Icelandic summer shone over Thorhall's byre and the Vale of Shadows. There was no cloud in the sky. The void and lonely ocean was indigo blue. But still the prospect was barren, inhospitable. Only a few pallid flowers, hardy bluebells and buttercups, appeared here and there on the sand dunes in the hollows beneath the gorse and bracken. In the lower hills, on the far side of the valley, a tenuous skim of verdure appeared. At times a ptarmigan fluttered in and out of the crevices of these hills searching for blueberries; at times on the surfaces of the waste of dunes a sandpiper uttered its shrill and feeble piping. Always, as ever, the wind blew from off the ocean; always, as ever, the solitary pine by the farmhouse writhed and tossed its gaunt arms; always the gorse and bracken billowed and weltered under it. The sand drifted like snow, encroaching forever upon the cultivated patches around the house. Always the surf—surge on surge

—boomed and thundered on the shore, casting up broken kelp and jetsam of wreck. Always, always forever and forever, the monotony remained. The bleakness, the wild, solitary stretches of sea and sky and land turned to the eye their staring emptiness. At long intervals the figure of a servant, a herdsman or at times Thorhall himself moved—a speck of black on the illimitable gray of nature—across the landscape. Ponies, shagged, half wild, their eyes hidden under tangled forelocks, sometimes wandered down upon the shore—their thick hair roughing in the wind—to snuff at the salty seaweeds. The males sometimes fought here on the shore, their hoofs thudding on the resounding beach, their screams mingling with the incessant roar of the breakers.

Once even, at Eastertide, during a gale, an empty galley drove ashore, a *snekr* with dragon prow, the broken oars dangling from the thole-pins; and in the waist of her a Viking chieftain, dead, the salt rime rusting on his helmet.

With the advent of summer the mysterious trouble at the farmhouse in the Vale of Shadows disappeared. But the fall equinox drew on, the nights became longer; soon the daylight lasted but a few hours and the sun set before it could be said to have actually risen.

As the winter darkness descended upon the farmhouse the trouble recommenced. During the night the tread of footsteps could be heard making the rounds of the byre. The fumbling of unseen fingers could be distinguished at the locks. The low eaves of the house were seized in the grip of strong hands and wrenched and pulled till the rafters creaked. Outhouses were plucked apart and destroyed, fences uprooted. After nightfall no one dared venture abroad.

Thorhall had engaged a new shepherd, one Thorgaut, a young man, who professed himself fearless of the haunted sheep-walks and farmyard. He was as popular as Glamr had been disliked. He made love to the housemaids, helped in the butter-making, and rode the children on his back. As to the Vampire, he snapped his fingers and asked only to meet him in the open.

The snow came in August, and was followed by sleet and icy rains and blotting sea-fogs. As the time went on the nightly manifestations increased. Windows were broken in; iron bars shaken and wrenched; sheep and even horses killed.

At length one night a terrible commotion broke out in the stables—the shrill squealing of the horses and the tramping and bellowing of cows, mingled with deep tones of a dreadful voice. Thorhall and his people rushed out. They found that the stable door had been riven and splintered, and they entered the stable itself across the wreckage. The cattle were goring each other, and across the stone partition between the stalls was the body of Thorgaut, the shepherd, his head upon one side, his feet on the other, and his spine snapped in twain.

It chanced that about this time Grettir, well known and well beloved throughout all Iceland, came into that part of the country and one eventide drew rein at Thorhall's farmhouse. This was before Grettir had been hunted from the island by the implacable Thorbjorn, called The Hook, and driven to an asylum and practical captivity upon the rock of Drangey.

He was at this time in the prime of his youth and of a noble appearance. His shoulders were broad, his arms long, his eye a bright blue, and his flaxen hair braided like a Viking's. For cloak he wore a bearskin, while as for weapons he carried nothing but a short sword.

Thorhall, as may be easily understood, welcomed the famous outlaw, but warned him of Glamr.

Grettir, however, was not be dissuaded from remaining overnight at the byre.

"Vampire or troll, troll or vampire, here bide I till daybreak," he declared.

Yet despite the bonder's fears the night passed quietly. No sound broke the stillness but the murmur of the distant surf, no footfall sounded around the house, no fingers came groping at the doors.

"I have never slept easier," announced Grettir in the morning.

"Good; and Heaven be praised," declared the bonder fervently.

They walked together toward the stables, Thorhall in-

structing Grettir as to the road he should follow that day. A
they drew near, Grettir whistled for his horse, but no answering whicker responded.

"How is this?" he muttered, frowning.

Thorhall and the outlaw hurried into the building, and
Grettir, who was in the advance, stopped stock-still in the
midst of the floor and swore a great oath.

His horse lay prone in the straw of his stall, his eyeballs
protruding, the foam stiff upon his lips. He was dead. Grettir
approached and examined him. Between shoulder and
withers, the back—as if it had been a wheat-straw—was
broken.

"Never mind," cried the bonder eagerly, "I have another
animal for you, a piebald stallion of Norway stock, just the
beast for your weight. Here is your saddle. On with it. Up you
go and a speedy journey to you."

"Never!" exclaimed Grettir, his blue eyes flashing.
"Here will I stay till I meet Glamr face to face. No man did
me an injury that he did not rue it. I sleep at the byre another
night."

Dark as a wolf's mouth, silent as his footfalls, the night
closed down. There was no moon as yet, but the heavens
were bright. Steadily as the blast of some great huntsman's
horn, the wind held from the northeast. The sand skimming
over the dunes and low hills near the coast was caught up and
carried landward and drifted in at crevice and door-chink of
the farmhouse. A young seal—lost, no doubt, from the herd
that had all day been feeding in the offing—barked and
barked incessantly from a rock in the breakers. In the pine
tree by the house a huge night-bird, owl or hawk, stirred
occasionally with a prolonged note. By and by the weather
grew colder, the ground began to freeze and crack. Inside in
the main hall of the house, covered by his bearskin cloak,
Grettir lay wakeful and watching. He reclined in such a
manner—his head pillowed on his arm—that he could see the
door. At the other end of the hall the fire of drift was dying
down upon the flags. On the other side of the partition, in the
next room, lay the bonder, alternately dozing and waking.

The time passed heavily, slowly. From far off toward the

shore could be heard the lost seal raising from time to time his hoarse, sobbing bark.

Then at length a dog howled, and an instant after the bonder spoke aloud. He had risen from his bed and stood in the door of his room.

"Hark! Did you not hear something?"

"I hear the barking of the seal," said Grettir, "the baying of the hound, the cry of the night-bird, and the break of the surges; nothing else."

"No. This was a footstep. There. Listen!"

A heavy footfall sounded crunching in the snow from without and close by. It passed around and in front of the house; and the wooden shutter of a window of the hall was plucked at and shaken. Then an outhouse was attacked—a shed where in summertime the calves were fed. Grettir could hear the snap and rasp of splintering boards.

"It has a strong arm," he muttered.

Once more the tread encircled the house. In a very short time it sounded again in the front of the byre.

"It has a long stride," said Grettir.

The tread ceased. For a long moment there was silence, while the scurrying sand rattled delicately against the house like minute hailstones. Suddenly a corner eave was seized. Something tugged at it, wrenching, and the thatch gave with the long swish of rent linen.

"It has a tall figure," said Grettir.

For nearly a quarter of an hour these different sounds continued, now distinct, now confused, now distant, now near at hand. Suddenly from overhead there came a jar and a crash, and Grettir felt the dust from the rafters descend upon his face; the Vampire was on the roof. But soon he leaped down and now the footsteps came straight to the door of the hall. The door itself was gripped with colossal strength. In the crescent-shaped openings of the upper panels a hand appeared, black against the faint outside light, groping, picking. It seized upon the edge of the board in the lower bend of the crescent and pulled. The board gave way, ripped to the very door-sill; then an arm followed the hand, reaching for one of the two iron bars with which the door was fenced.

Evidently it could not find these, for the effort was soon abandoned and another panel was split and torn away. The cross-panel followed, the nails shrieking as they were drawn from out the wood. Then at last the door, shattered to its very hinges, gave way, leaving only the bars set in the stone sockets of the jamb, and against the square of gray light of the entrance stood, silhouetted, the figure of a monster. Stood but for a moment, for almost at once the bars were pulled out.

The Vampire was within the house, the light from the smoldering logs illuminating the face.

Glamr's face was livid. The pupils of the eyes were white, the hair matted and thick. The whole figure was monstrously enlarged, bulked like a *jotun,* and the vast hands, white as those of the drowned, swung heavily at his sides.

Once in the hall, he stood for a long moment looking from side to side, then moved slowly forward, reaching his great arms overhead, feeling and fumbling with the roofbeams with his fingers, and guiding himself thus from beam to beam.

Grettir, watching, alert, never moved, but lay in his place, his eyes fixed upon the monster.

But at length Glamr made out the form stretched upon the couch and came up and laid hold of a flap of the bearskin under Grettir's shoulders and tugged at it. But Grettir, bracing his feet against the foothand of the couch, held back with all his strength. Glamr seized the flap in both hands and set his might to pull, till the tough hide fetched away, and he staggered back, the corner of skin still in his grip. He looked at it stupidly, wondering, bewildered.

Then suddenly the bonder, listening from within his bolted door, heard the muffled crashing shock of the onset. The rafters cracked, the byre shook, the shutters rocked in their grooves, and Grettir, eyes alight, hair flying like a torch, thews rigid as iron, leaped to the attack.

Down upon the hero's arms came the numbing, crushing grip of the dead man's might. One instant of that inhuman embrace and Grettir knew that now peril of his life was toward. Never in all his days of battle and strength had such colossal might risen to match his own. Back bore the wrestlers, back, back toward the sides of the hall. Benches ironed to the wall were overturned, wrenched like paper from their fastenings. The great table crashed and splintered beneath their weight. The floor split with their tramping, and the fire was scattered upon the hearth. Now forward, now back, from side to side and from end to end of the wrecked hall drove the fight. Great of build though the fighters were, huge of bone, big of muscle, they yet leaped and writhed with the agility, the rapidity of young lambs.

But fear was not in Grettir. Never in his life had he been afraid. Only anger shook him, and fine, above-board fury, and the iron will to beat his enemy.

All at once Grettir, his arms gripped about the Vampire's middle, his head beneath the armpit, realized that the creature was dragging him toward the door. He fought back from this till the effort sent the blood surging in his ears, for he knew well that ill as the fight had fared within the house it must go worse without. But it was all one that he braced his feet against the broken benches, the wreck of the table, the every unevenness of the floor. The Vampire had gripped him close and dragged and clutched and heaved at his body, so that the white nails drove into his flesh, and the embrace of those arms of steel shut in the ribs till the breath gushed from the nostrils in long gasps of agony.

And now they swayed and grappled in the doorway. Grettir's back was bent like a bow and Grettir's arms at fullest stretch strained to their sockets, till it seemed as though the very tendons must tear from off the bones. And ever the foul thing above him drew him farther and yet farther from out the entrance-way of the house.

"God save you, Grettir!" cried the bonder, "God save you, brave man and true. Never was such fight as this in all Iceland. Are you spent, Grettir?"

Muffled under the arms of his foe, the voice of Grettir shouted: "Stand from us. I am much spent, but I fear not."

Then with the words, feeling the half-sunk stone of the threshold beneath his feet, he bowed his knees, and with his shoulder against the Vampire's breast drove, not, as hitherto, back, but forward, and that with all the power of limb and loin.

The Vampire reeled from the attack. His shoulder crashed against the outer doorcase, and with that gigantic shock the roof burst asunder. Down crushed and roared the frozen thatch, and then in that hideous ruin of splintering rafters, grinding stones, and wreck of panel and beam the Vampire fell backward and prone to the ground, while Grettir toppled down upon him till his face was against the dead man's face, his eye to the dead eye, his forehead against his front, and the gray bristle of his beard between his teeth.

The moon was bright outside, and all at once, lighted by her rays, Grettir for the first time saw the Vampire's face.

Then the soul of him shrank and sank, and the fear that all his days he had not known leaped to life in his heart. Terror of that glare of the dead man's gaze caught him by the throat, till his grip relaxed, and his strength dwindled away and he crouched there motionless but for his trembling, looking, looking into those blind, white, dead eyes.

And then the Vampire began to speak:

"Eagerly hast thou striven to match thyself with me, and ill hast thou done this night. Now thou art weak with the fear and the rigor of this fight, yet never henceforth shalt thou be stronger than at this moment. Till now thou hast won much fame by great deeds, yet henceforth ill-luck shall follow thee and woe and man-slayings and untoward fortune. Outlawed shalt thou be, and thy lot shall be cast in lands far from thine home. Alone shalt thou dwell and in that loneliness, this weird I lay upon thee: Ever to see these eyes with thine eyes, till the terror of the Dark shall come upon thee and the fear of night, and the twain shall drag thee to thy death and thy undoing."

As the voice ceased, Grettir's wits and strength returned, and suddenly seizing the hair of the creature in one hand and his short sword in the other, he hewed off the head.

But within the heart of him he knew that the Vampire had said true words, and as he stood looking down upon the great body of his enemy and saw the glazed and fish-like eyes beneath the lids, he could for one instant look ahead to the days of his life yet to be, to the ill-fortune that should dog him from henceforth, and knew that at the gathering of each night's dusk the eyes of Glamr would look into his.

Thorhall came out when the fight was done, praising God for the issue, and he and Grettir together burned the body and, wrapping the ashes in a skin, buried them in a corner of the sheep-walks.

In the morning Thorhall gave Grettir the piebald horse and new clothes and set him a mile on his road. They rode through the Vale of Shadows and kissed each other farewell on the shore where the road led away toward Waterdale.

The clouds had gathered again during the dawn and the rain was falling, driven landward by the incessant wind. The seals again barked and hunted in the offing, and the rough-haired ponies once more wandered about on the beach snuffing at the kelp and seaweed.

Long time Thornhall stood on the ridge watching the figure of Grettir grow small and indistinct in the waste of north country and under the blur of the rain. Then at last he turned back to the byre.

But Grettir after these things rode on to Biarg, to his mother's house, and sat at home through the winter.

# WEREWOMAN

### *by* C. L. MOORE

On October 4, 1956, the late Henry Kuttner wrote me from Santa Monica, California: "I tried to reach you in New York, but didn't get through, and since Catherine and I were staying only about three weeks, things were so hectic that we had to leave before I could reach you by telephone . . . What I wanted to ask you about was whether or not you had a record of publication for a story by C.L. Moore about Northwest Smith called ''Werewoman.'' It was unfinished, written in the late thirties, I think, and Catherine doesn't remember its being published anywhere. But we keep running across references to it, and there's a possibility it may have been given to some fan mag which Catherine has forgotten about. Since you're about the only one who'd really have complete records for this sort of thing, I'm wondering if you happen to recall any publication data on this yarn. If you do and could let us know, we'd be very grateful.''

C.L. Moore is probably the most talented woman writer of science fiction to appear on the scene since Mary Wollstonecraft Shelley wrote *Frankenstein* and it was published in London on March 11, 1818. Moore's first love was science fiction and she unsuccessfully tried to sell stories to *Amazing Stories* and *Wonder Stories;* when they rejected them because of an atmosphere of near fantasy and grim horror of the themes, she tried *Weird Tales* magazine with ''Shambleau.'' Lead character of ''Shambleau'' was Northwest Smith, ''a man nearing forty, with steely no-color eyes, a streak of murder in his makeup, and a psychological hardness that . . . resisted the most soul-destroying horrors . . .'' Northwest Smith rescues a strange brown girl from a Martian mob and takes her to his lodgings. When she unloosens her turban, instead of hair a cascade of worm-like tendrils falls like a cloak almost to her feet." She is, in truth, a Martian Medusa. That was but the first of many nightmarish and fascinating adventures of Northwest Smith on Mars, Venus, the asteroids, and other dimensions. His legendary exploits have been collected in *Shambleau and Others* (Gnome Press, 1953) and *Northwest of Earth* (Gnome Press, 1954). That is, most of them were, but there are several that for one reason or another were not included. Among those was "Werewoman," of which C.L. Moore did not even own a copy.

"Werewoman" appeared in only one place, the second, 1938 issue of mimeographed amateur magazine published by H.P. Lovecraft's good friend R.H. Barlow and titled *Leaves*. The first issue of *Leaves* was dated Summer, 1937 and was edited, stenciled, and mimeographed by R.H. Barlow when he resided in Leavenworth, Kansas. It was an outstanding collector's item, containing original material by Clark Ashton Smith, H.P. Lovecraft, Donald Wandrei, and Frank Belknap Long, and reprints of stories by A. Merritt and August W. Derleth.

The second issue was stenciled by R.H. Barlow between July, 1937 and December, 1938 in Kansas City, Mexico City, and Lakeport, California and sixty copies were ostensibly run off for sale at 50 cents each. It contained new material by H.P. Lovecraft, Donald Wandrei, and Fritz Leiber, Jr., but its real coup was the first and only publication of "Werewoman" by C.L. Moore, a Northwest Smith story completely atypical of any other in the series. It is a supernatural fantasy, superbly written, and deserves a better fate than the obscurity it has been consigned to.

At my suggestion, Henry Kuttner wrote to Clyde Beck, still living in Lakeport, California, who published the second issue of *Leaves,* with the following result, concerning which he wrote me on January 19, 1957: "We did get in touch with Clyde Beck, who had one copy of the issue. We certainly didn't expect him to present it to Catherine, but that's what he did, a hell of a nice gesture . . . I am sorry we don't have a second copy. If we had, we'd be happy to pass it along to you. As it is, if you should ever want to borrow this issue of

*Leaves,* or if photostats would do any good, just let us know.''

I eventually secured the second issue from other sources, for after Henry Kuttner's death, C.L. Moore stated that she was unable to locate her copy. For those many thousands already familiar with C.L. Moore and Northwest Smith, settle back to enjoy a novelette of fantastic horror which has languished in a literary limbo for thirty-one years. For those who have never experienced this phase of C.L. Moore's writing, you are in for a reader's voyage of discovery.

# WEREWOMAN

by

## C.L. MOORE

With the noise of battle fading behind him down the wind,
Northwest Smith staggered into the west and the twilight,
stumbling as he went. Blood spattered brightly behind him on
the rocks, leaving a clear trail to track him by, but he knew he
would not be followed far. He was headed into the salt
wastelands to the westward, and they would not follow him
there.

He urged his reluctant feet faster, for he knew that he must
be out of sight in the grey waste before the first of the
scavengers came to loot the dead. They would follow—that
trail of blood and staggering footsteps would draw them like
wolves on his track, hot in the hope of further spoils—but
they would not come far. He grinned a little wryly at the
thought, for he was going into no safety here, though he left
certain death behind. He was stumbling, slow step by step,
into almost as certain a death, of fever and thirst and hunger in
the wastelands, if no worse death caught him first. They told
tales of this grey salt desert . . .

He had never before come even this far into the cold waste
during all the weeks of their encampment. He was too old an
adventurer not to know that when people shun a place completely and talk of it in whispers and tell little half-finished,
fearful stories of it over campfires, that place is better left

59

alone. Some might have been spurred by that very reticence into investigation, but Northwest Smith had seen too many strange things in his checkered career to doubt the basis of fact behind folk-tales or care to rush in heedlessly where others had learned by experience not to tread.

The sound of battle had dwindled to a faint murmur on the evening breeze. He lifted his head painfully and stared into the gathering dark ahead with narrowed eyes the no-color of pale steel. The wind touched his keen, scarred face with a breath of utter loneliness and desolation. No man-smell of smoke or byre or farmstead tainted it, blowing clear across miles beyond miles of wastelands. Smith's nostrils quivered to that scent of unhumanity. He saw the greyness stretching before him, flat and featureless, melting into the dark. There was a sparse grass growing, and low shrub and a few stunted trees, and brackish water in deep, still pools dotted the place at far intervals. He found himself listening . . .

Once in very long-ago ages, so campfire whispers had told him, a forgotten city stood here. Who dwelt in it, or what, no man knew. It was a great city spreading over miles of land, rich and powerful enough to wake enmity, for a mighty foe had come at last out of the lowlands and in a series of tremendous battles razed it to the ground. What grievance they had against the dwellers in the city no one will ever know now, but it must have been dreadful, for when the last tower was laid to earth and the last stone toppled from its foundation they had sown the land with salt, so that for generations no living thing grew in all the miles of desolation. And not content with this, they had laid a curse upon the very earth wherein the city had its roots, so that even today men shun the place without understanding why.

It was very long past, that battle, and history forgot the very name of the city, and victor and vanquished alike sank together into the limbo of the forgotten. In time the salt-sown lands gained a measure of life again and the sparse vegetation that now clothed it struggled up through the barren soil. But men still shunned the place.

They said, in whispers, that there were dwellers yet in the saltlands. Wolves came out by night sometimes and carried off children straying late; sometimes a new-made grave was found open and empty in the morning, and people breathed of ghouls . . . late travellers had heard voices wailing from the wastes by night, and those daring hunters who ventured in search of the wild game that ran through the underbrush spoke fearfully of naked werewomen that howled in the distances. No one knew what became of the adventurous souls who travelled too far alone into the desolation of the place. It was accursed for human feet to travel, and those who dwelt there, said the legends, must be less than human.

Smith discounted much of this when he turned from the bloody shambles of that battle into the wastelands beyond. Legends grow, he knew. But a basis for the tales he did not doubt, and he glanced ruefully down at the empty holsters hanging low on his legs. He was completely unarmed, perhaps for the first time in more years than he liked to remember; for his path had run for the most part well outside the law, and such men do not go unarmed anywhere—even to bed.

Well, no help for it now. He shrugged a little, and then grimaced and caught his breath painfully, for that slash in the shoulder was deep, and blood still dripped to the ground, though not so freely as before. The wound was closing. He had lost much blood—the whole side of his leather garment was stiff with it, and the bright stain spattering behind him told of still greater losses. The pain of his shoulder stabbed at him yet, but it was being swallowed up now in a vast, heaving greyness . . .

He drove his feet on stubbornly over the uneven ground, though the whole dimming landscape was wavering before him like a sea—swelling monstrously—receding into the vague distances . . . The ground floated up to meet him with surprising gentleness.

He opened his eyes presently to a grey twilight, and after awhile staggered up and went on. No more blood flowed, but the shoulder was stiff and throbbing, and the wasteland heaved still like a rolling sea about him. The singing in his ears grew loud, and he was not sure whether the faint echoes of sound he heard came over grey distances or rang in his own

head—long, faint howls, like wolves wailing their hunger to
the stars. When he fell the second time he did not know it, and
was surprised to open his eyes upon full dark with stars
looking down on him and the grass tickling his cheek.

He went on. There was no great need of it now—he was
well beyond pursuit, but the dim urge to keep moving dinned
in his weary brain. He was sure now that the long howls were
coming to him over the waste stretches; coming nearer. By
instinct his hand dropped to clutch futilely at the empty
holster.

There were queer little voices going by overhead in the
wind. Thin, shrill. With immense effort he slanted a glance
upward and thought he could see, with the clarity of exhaus-
tion, the long, clean lines of the wind streaming across the
sky. He saw no more than that, but the small voices shrilled
thinly in his ears.

Presently he was aware of motion beside him—life of
some nebulous sort moving parallel to his course, invisible in
the starlight. He was aware of it through the thrill of evil that
prickled at the roots of his hair, pulsing from the dimness at
his side—though he could see nothing. But with that clarity
of inner vision he felt the vast and shadowy shape lurching
formlessly through the grass at his side. He did not turn his
head again, but the hackles of his neck bristled. The howls
were nearing, too. He set his teeth and drove on, unevenly.

He fell for the third time by a clump of stunted trees, and
lay for a while breathing heavily while long, slow waves of
oblivion washed over him and receded like waves over sand.
In the intervals of lucidity he knew that those howls were
coming closer over the greyness of saltlands.

He went on. The illusion of that formless walker-in-the-
dark still haunted him through the grass, but he was scarcely
heeding it now. The howls had changed to short, sharp yaps,
crisp in the starlight, and he knew that the wolves had struck
his trail. Again, instinctively, his hand flashed downward
toward his gun, and a spasm of pain crossed his face. Death
he did not mind—he had kept pace with it too many years to
fear that familiar visage—but death under fangs, unarmed

. . He staggered on a little faster, and the breath whistled through his clenched teeth.

Dark forms were circling his, slipping shadowily through the grass. They were wary, these beasts of the outlands. They did not draw near enough for him to see them save as shadows gliding among the shadows, patient and watching. He cursed them futilely with his failing breath, for he knew now that he dared not fall again. The grey waves washed upward, and he shouted something hoarse in his throat and called upon a last reservoir of strength to bear him up. The dark forms started at his voice.

So he went on, wading through oblivion that rose waist-high, shoulder-high, chin-high—and receded again before the indomitable onward drive that dared not let him rest. Something was wrong with his eyes now—the pale-steel eyes that had never failed him before—for among the dark forms he was thinking he saw white ones, slipping and gliding wraithlike in the shadow . . .

For an endless while he stumbled on under the chilly stars while the earth heaved gently beneath his feet and the greyness was a sea that rose and fell in blind waves, and white figures weaved about his through the hollow dark.

Quite suddenly he knew that the end of his strength had come. He knew it surely, and in the last moment of lucidity left to him he saw a low tree outlined against the stars and staggered to it—setting his broad back against the trunk, fronting the dark watchers with lowered head and pale eyes that glared defiance. For that one moment he faced them resolutely—then the tree-trunk was sliding upward past him—the ground was rising—he gripped the sparse grass with both hands, and swore as he fell.

When he opened his eyes again he stared into a face straight out of hell. A woman's face, twisted into a diabolical smile, stooped over him—glare-eyed in the dark. White fangs slavered as she bent to his throat.

Smith choked back a strangled sound that was half oath, half prayer, and struggled to his feet. She started back with a soundless leap that set her wild hair flying, and stood staring

him in the face with wide slant eyes that glared greenly from
the pallor of her face. Through dark hair, her body was white
as a sickle moon, half-veiled in the long, wild hair.

She glared with hungry fangs a-drip. Beyond her he sensed
other forms, dark and white, circling restlessly through the
shadows—and he began to understand dimly, and knew that
there was no hope in life for him, but he spread his long legs
wide and gave back glare for glare, pale-eyed and savage.

The pack circled him, dim blurs in the dark, the green glare
of eyes shining alike from white shapes and black. And to his
dizzied eyes it seemed that the forms were not stable; shifting
from dark to light and back again with only the green-glowing
eyes holding the same glare through all the changing. They
were closing in now, the soft snarls rising and sharp yaps
impatiently breaking through the guttural undernotes, and he
saw the gleam of teeth, white under the stars.

He had no weapon, and the wasteland reeled about him and
the earth heaved underfoot, but he squared his shoulders
savagely and fronted them in hopeless defiance, waiting for
the wave of darkness and hunger to come breaking over him
in an overwhelming tide. He met the green desire of the
woman's wild eyes as she stooped forward, gathering herself
for the lunge, and suddenly something about the fierceness of
her struck a savage chord within him, and—facing death as
he was—he barked a short, wild laugh at her, and yelled into
the rising wind. "Come on, werewoman! Call your pack!"

She stared for the briefest instant, half-poised for leaping
—while something like a spark seemed to flash between
them, savageness calling to savageness across the barriers of
everything alive—and suddenly she flung up her arms, the
black hair whirling, and tossed back her head and bayed to the
stars; a wild, long ululating yell and tossed it from voice to
voice across the saltlands until the very stars shivered at the
wild, exultant baying.

And as the long yell trembled into silence something
inexplicable happened to Smith. Something quivered in answer within him, agonizingly, the grey oblivion he had been
fighting so long swallowed him up at a gulp—and then he
leaped within himself in a sudden, ecstatic rush; and while

one part of him slumped to its knees and then to its face in the grass, the living vital being that was Smith sprang free into the cold air that stung like sharp wine.

The wolf-pack rushed clamorously about him, the wild, high yells shivered delightfully along every nerve of his suddenly awakened body. And it was as if a muffling darkness had lifted new eyes, and his nostrils caught fresh, exciting odors on the streaming wind, and in his ears a thousand tiny sounds took on sudden new clarity and meaning.

The pack that had surged so clamorously about him was a swirl of dark bodies for an instant—then in a blur and a flash they were dark no longer—rose on hind legs and cast off the darkness as they rose—and slim, white, naked werewomen swirled around him in a tangle of flashing limbs and streaming hair.

He stood half-dazed at the transition, for even the wide salt moor was no longer dark and empty, but pale grey under the stars and peopled with nebulous, unstable beings that wavered away from the white wolf-pack which ringed him, and above the clamour of wild voices that thin, shrill chattering went streaming down the wind overhead.

Out of the circling pack a white figure broke suddenly, and he felt cold arms about his neck and a cold, thin body pressing his. Then the white whirl parted violently and another figure thrust through—the fierce-eyed woman who had called him across the barriers of flesh into this half-land of her own. Her green-glaring eyes stabbed at the sister-wolf whose arms twined Smith's neck, and the growl that broke from her lips was a wolf's guttural. The woman fell away from Smith's embrace, crouching at bay, as the other, with a toss of wild hair, bared her fangs and launched herself straight at the throat of the interloper. They went down in a tangle of white and tossing dark, and the pack fell still so that the only sound was the heavy breathing of the fighters and the low, choked snarls that rippled from their throats. Then over the struggle of white and black burst a sudden torrent of scarlet. Smith's nostrils flared to the odor that had a new, fascinating sweetness now—and the werewoman rose, bloody-mouthed, from

the body of her rival. The green-glowing eyes met his, and a
savage exultation flowing from them met as savage a delight
wakening in his, and her keen, moon-white face broke into a
smile of hellish joy.

She flung up her head again and bayed a long, triumphant
cry to the stars, and the pack about her took up the yell, and
Smith found his own face turned to the sky and his own throat
shouting a fierce challenge to the dark.

Then they were running—jostling one another in savage
play, flying over the coarse grass on feet that scarcely
brushed the ground. It was like the rush of the wind, that
effortless racing, as the earth flowed backward under their
spurning feet and the wind streamed in their nostrils with a
thousand tingling odors. The white werewoman raced at his
side, her long hair flying behind her like a banner, her
shoulder brushing his.

They ran through strange places. The trees and the grass
had taken on new shapes and meanings, and in a vague,
half-realized way he was aware of curious forms looming
round him—buildings, towers, walls, high turrets shining in
the starlight, yet so nebulous that they did not impede their
flight. He could see these shadows of a city very clearly
sometimes—sometimes he ran down marble streets, and it
seemed to him that his feet rang in golden sandals on the
pavement and rich garments whipped behind him in the wind
of his speed, and a sword clanked at his side. He thought the
woman beside him fled in bright-colored sandals too, and her
long skirts rippled away from her flying limbs and the streaming hair was twined with jewels—yet he knew he ran naked
beside a moon-bare wolf-woman over coarse grass that rustled to his tread.

And sometimes, too, it seemed to him that he fled on four
legs, not two—fleetly as the wind, thrusting a pointed muzzle
into the breeze and lolling a red tongue over dripping
fangs . . .

Dim shapes fled from their sweeping onward rush—great,
blurred, formless things; dark beings with eyes; thin wraiths
wavering backward from their path. The great moor teemed
with these half-seen monstrosities; fierce-eyed, some of

them, breathing out menace, and evil, angry shapes that gave way reluctantly before the werepack's sweep. But they gave way. There were terrible things in that wasteland, but the most terrible of all were the werewomen, and all the dreadful, unreal beings made way at the bay of those savage voices. All this he knew intuitively. Only the thin chattering that streamed down the wind did not hush when the werevoices howled.

There were many odors on the wind that night, sharp and sweet and acrid, wild odors of wild, desolate lands and the dwellers therein. And then, quite suddenly on a vagrant breeze, lashing their nostrils like a whip—the harsh, rich, blood-tingling scent of man. Smith flung up his head to the cold stars and bayed long and shudderingly, and the wild wolf-yell rang from throat to throat through the pack until the whole band of them was shaking the very air to that savage chorus. They loped down the wind-stream, nostrils flaring to that full, rich, scent.

Smith ran at the forefront, shoulder to shoulder with the wild white creature who had fought for him. The man-smell was sweet in his nostrils, and hunger wrenched at him as the smell grew stronger and faint atavistic stirrings of anticipation rose in his memory . . . Then they saw them.

A little band of hunters was crossing the moorland, crashing through the underbrush, guns on their shoulders. Blindly they walked, stumbling over hummocks that were clear to Smith's new eyes. And all about them the vague denizens of the place were gathering unseen. Great, nebulous, cloudy shapes dogged their footsteps through the grass, lurching along formlessly. Dark things with eyes flitted by, turning a hungry glare unseen upon the hunters. White shapes wavered from their path and closed in behind. The men did not see them. They must have sensed the presence of inimical beings, for now and then one would glance over his shoulder nervously, or hitch a gun forward as if he had almost seen— then lower it sheepishly and go on.

The very sight of them fired that strange hunger in Smith's new being, and again he flung back his head and yelled fiercely the long wolf-cry toward the frosty stars. At the sound of it a ripple of alarm went through the unclean, nebulous crowd that dogged the hunters' footsteps. Eyes turned toward the approaching pack, glaring angrily from bodies as unreal as smoke. But as they drew nearer the press began to melt away, the misty shapes wavering off reluctantly into the pallor of the night before the sweep of the wolves.

They skimmed over the grass, flying feet spurning the ground, and with a rush and a shout they swooped down around the hunters yelling their hunger. The men had huddled into a little knot, backs together and guns bristling outward as the werepack eddied round them. Three or four men fired at random into the circling pack, the flash and sound of it sending a wavering shudder through the pale things that had drawn back to a safe distance, watching. But the wolf-women paid no heed.

Then the leader—a tall man in a white fur cap—shouted suddenly in a voice of panic terror. "No use to fire! No use—don't you see? These aren't real wolves . . ."

Smith had a fleeting realization that to human eyes they must, then, seem wolf-formed, though all about him in the pale night he saw clearly only white, naked women with flying hair circling the hunters and baying hungrily with wolf-voices as they ran.

The dark hunger was ravaging him as he paced the narrowing circle with short, nervous steps—the human bodies so near, smelling so richly of blood and flesh. Vaguely memories of that blood running sweetly eddied through his mind, and the feel of teeth meeting solidly to flesh; and beyond that a deeper hunger, inexplicably, for something he could not name. Only he felt he would never have peace again until he had sunk his teeth into the throat of that man in the white fur cap; felt blood gushing over his face . . .

"Look!" shouted the man, pointing as his eyes met Smith's ravenous glare. "See—the big one with white eyes, running with the she-wolf . . ." He fumbled for something inside his coat. "The Devil himself—all the rest are green-eyed, but—white eyes—see!"

Something in the sound of his voice lashed that hunger in

Smith to the breaking point. It was unbearable. A snarl
choked up in his throat and he gathered himself to spring. The
man must have seen the flare of it in the pale eyes meeting his,
for he shouted, "God in Heaven! . . ." and clawed desperately at his collar. And just as Smith's feet left the ground in a
great, steel-muscled spring straight for that tempting throat,
the man ripped out what he had been groping for and the
starlight caught the glint of it exposed—a silver cross dangling from a broken chain.

Something blinding exploded in Smith's innermost brain.
Something compounded of thunder and lightning smote him
in midair. An agonized howl ripped itself from his throat as
he fell back, blinded and deafened and dazed, while his brain
rocked to its foundations and long shivers of dazzling force
shuddered through the air about him.

Dimly, from a great distance, he heard the agonized howls
of the werewomen, the shouts of men, the trample of shod
feet on the ground. Behind his closed eyes he could still see
that cross upheld, a blinding symbol from which streamers of
forked lightning blazed away and the air crackled all around.

When the tumult had faded in his ears and the blaze died
away and the shocked air shuddered into stillness again, he
felt the touch of cold, gentle hands upon him and opened his
eyes to the green glare of other eyes bending over him. He
pushed her away and struggled to his feet, swaying a little as
he stared round the plain. All the white werewomen were
gone, save the one at his side. The huntsmen were gone. Even
the misty denizens of the place were gone. Empty in the grey
dimness the wasteland stretched away. Even the thin piping
overhead had fallen into shocked silence. All about them the
plain lay still, shuddering a little and gathering its forces
again after the ordeal.

The werewoman had trotted off a little way and was
beckoning to him impatiently over her shoulder. He followed, instinctively anxious to leave the spot of the disaster.
Presently they were running again, shoulder to shoulder
across the grass, the plain spinning away under their flying
feet. The scene of that conflict fell behind them, and strength
was flowing again through Smith's light-footed body, and

overhead, faintly, the thin, shrill chattering began anew.

With renewed strength the old hunger flooded again through him, compellingly. He tossed up his head to test the wind, and a little whimper of eagerness rippled from his throat. An answering whine from the running woman replied to it. She tossed back her hair and sniffed the wind, hunger flaming in her eyes. So they ran through the pale night, hunter and huntress, while dim shapes wavered from their path and the earth reeled backward under their spurning feet.

It was pleasant to run so, in perfect unison, striding effortlessly with the speed of the wind, arrogantly in the knowledge of their strength, as the dreadful dwellers of the aeon-cursed moor fled from their approach and the very air shuddered when they bayed.

Again the illusion of misty towers and walls wavered in the dimness before Smith's eyes. He seemed to run down marble-paved streets, and felt again the clank of a belted sword and the ripple of rich garments, and saw the skirts of the woman beside him moulded to her limbs as she fled along with streaming, jewel-twined hair. He thought that the buildings rising so nebulously all around were growing higher as they advanced. He caught vague glimpses of arches and columns and great domed temples, and began, somehow uneasily, to sense presences in the streets, unseen but thronging.

Then simultaneously his feet seemed to strike a yielding resistance, as if he had plunged at a stride knee-deep into heavy water, and the woman beside him threw up her arms wildly in a swirl of hair and tossed back her head and screamed hideously, humanly, despairingly—the first human sound he had heard from her lips—and stumbled to her knees on the grass that was somehow a marble pavement.

Smith bent to catch her as she fell, plunging his arms into unseen resistance as he did so. He felt it suck at her as he wrenched the limp body out of those amazing, invisible wavelets that were lapping higher and higher up his legs with incredible swiftness. He swung her up clear of them, feeling the uncontrollable terror that rippled out from her body course in unbroken wavelets through his own, so he shook with nameless panic, not understanding why. The thick tide had risen mufflingly about his thighs when he turned back the way he had come and began to fight his way out of the clinging horror he could not see, the woman a weight of terror in his arms.

It seemed to be a sort of thickness in the air, indescribable, flowing about him in deepening waves that lapped up and up as if some half-solidified jelly were swiftly and relentlessly engulfing him. Yet he could see nothing but the grass underfoot, the dim, dreamlike marble pavement, the night about, the cold stars overhead. He struggled forward through the invisible thickness. It was worse than trying to run through water, with the retarded motion of nightmares. It sucked at him, draggingly, as he struggled forward through the deeps of it, stumbling, not daring to fall, the woman a dead weight in his arms.

And very slowly he won free. Very slowly he forced his way out of the clinging horror. The little lapping waves of it ceased to mount. He felt the thickness receding downward, past his knees, down about his ankles, until only his feet sucked and stumbled in invisibility, the nameless mass shuddering and quaking. And at long last he broke again, and as his feet touched the clear ground, he leaped forward wildly, like an arrow from a bow, into the delightful freedom of the open air. It felt like pure flying after that dreadful struggle through the unseen. Muscles exulting at the release, he fled over the grass liked a winged thing while the dim building reeled away behind him and the woman stirred a little in his arms, an inconsidered weight in the joy of freedom.

Presently she whimpered a little, and he paused by a stunted tree to set her down again. She glanced round wildly. He saw from the look on her bone-white face that the danger was not yet past, and glanced round himself, seeing nothing but the dim moor with wraith-like figures wavering here and there and the stars shining down coldly. Overhead the thin shrilling went by changelessly in the wind. All this was familiar. Yet the werewoman stood poised for instant flight, seeming unsure in just what direction danger lay, and her eyes glared panic into the dimness. He knew then that dreadful though the werepack was, a more terrible thing haunted

the wasteland—invisibly, frightfully indeed to wake in the
wolf-woman's eyes that staring horror. Then something
touched his foot.

He leaped like the wild thing he was, for he knew that
feel—even in so short a time he knew that feel. It was flowing
round his foot sucking at his ankle even as he poised for
flight. He seized the woman's wrist and twisted round,
wrenching his foot from the invisible grip, leaping forward
arrow-swift into the pale darkness. He heard her catch her
breath in a sobbing gasp, eloquent of terror, as she fell into
stride beside him.

So they fled, invisibility ravening at their heels. He knew,
somehow, that it followed. The thick, clutching waves of it
were lapping faster and faster just short of his flying feet, and
he strained to the utmost, skimming over the grass like
something winged and terror-stricken, the sobbing breath of
the woman keeping time to his stride. What he fled he could
not even guess. It had no form in any image he could conjure
up. Yet he felt dimly that it was nothing alien, but rather
something too horribly akin to him . . . and the deadly danger
he did not understand spurred on his flying feet.

The plain whirled by blurrily in their speed. Dim things
with eyes fluttered away in panic as they neared, clearing a
terror-stricken way for the dreadful werepeople who fled in
such blind horror something more dreadful yet.

For eternities they ran. Misty towers and walls fell away
behind them. In his terror-dimmed mind it seemed to him in
flashes that he was the other runner clad in rich garments and
belted with the sword, running beside that other fleeing
woman from another horror whose nature he did not know.
He scarcely felt the ground underfoot. He ran blindly, knowing only that he must run and run until he dropped, that
something far more dreadful than any death he could die was
lapping hungrily at his heels, threatening him with an
unnameable, incomprehensible horror—that he must run and
run and run . . .

And so, very slowly, the panic cleared. Very gradually
sanity returned to him. He ran still, not daring to stop, for he

knew the invisible hunger lapped yet not far behind—knew it surely without understanding how—but his mind had cleared enough for him to think, and his thoughts told curious things, half-realized things that formed images in his brain unbidden, drawn from some far source beyond his understanding. He knew, for instance, that the thing at their heels was unescapable. He knew that it would never cease its relentless pursuit, silent, invisible, remorseless, until the thick waves of it had swallowed up its quarry, and what followed that—what unimaginable horror—he somehow knew, but could not form even into thought-pictures. It was something too far outside any experience for the mind to grasp it.

The horror he felt instinctively was entirely within himself. He could see nothing pursuing him, feel nothing, hear nothing. No tremor of menace reached toward him from the following nothingness. But within him horror swelled and swelled balloon-like, a curious horror akin to something that was part of him, so it was as if he fled in terror of himself, and with no more hope of ever escaping than if indeed he fled his own shadow.

The panic had passed. He no longer ran blindly, but he knew now that he must run and run forever, hopelessly . . . but his mind refused to picture the end. He thought the woman's panic had abated, too. Her breathing was evener, not the frantic gasping of that first frenzy, and he no longer felt the shaking waves of pure terror beating out from her against the ephemeral substance that was himself.

And now, as the grey landscape slid past changelessly and the thin shapes still wavered from their path and the piping went by overhead, he became conscious as he ran of a changing in the revulsion that spurred him on. There were little moments when the horror behind drew him curiously, tightening its hold on that part of his being so strangely akin to it. As a man might stare over a precipice-edge and feel the mounting urge to fling himself over, even in the face of his horror of falling, so Smith felt the strong pull of the thing that followed, if thing it might be called. Without abatement in his horror the curious desire grew to turn and face it, let it come

lapping over him, steep himself in the thick invisibility—
even though his whole being shuddered violently from the
very thought.

Without realizing it, his pace slackened. But the woman
knew, and gripped his hand fiercely, a frantic appeal rippling
through him from the contact. At her touch, the pull abated
for a while and he ran on in an access of revulsion, very
conscious of the invisibility lapping at their heels.

While the access was at its height he felt the grip of her
hand loosen a little and knew that the strange tugging at
something within was reaching out for her. His hand tight-
ened over hers and he felt the little shake she gave to free
herself of that blind pull.

So they fled, the strength in each bearing the other up.
Behind them relentlessly the Something followed. Twice a
forward lapping wave of it brushed Smith's heel. And
stronger and stronger grew the blind urge within him to turn,
to plunge into the heavy flow of what followed, to steep
himself in invisibility until—until— He could form no picture of that ultimate, but each time he reached the point of
picturing it a shudder went over him and blankness clouded
his mind.

And ever within him that thing akin to the Follower
strengthened and grew, a blind urge from his innermost
being. It grew so strong that only the grip of the werewoman's hand held him from turning, and the plain faded from
about him like a grey dream and he ran through a curving
void—a void that he somehow knew was bending back upon
itself so that he must eventually, if he ran on, come round
behind his pursuer and overtake it, wade head-on into the
thick deeps of invisibility . . . yet he dared not slacken his
running, for then it would catch him from behind. So he spun
in the treadmill, terror ahead, terror behind, with no choice
but to run and no hope for all his running.

When he saw the plain at all it was in dim flashes, unac-
countably blurred and not always at the correct angles. It
tilted without reason. Once he saw a dark pool of water
slanting before him like a door, and once a whole section of
landscape hung mirage-like above his head. Sometimes he

panted up steep inclines, sometimes he skimmed fleetly down steeper slopes—yet he knew the plain in reality lay flat and featureless from edge to edge.

And now, though he had long ago left those misty towers and walls far behind, he began to be aware that his flight had somehow twisted and they loomed once more, shadowily, overhead. With a sickening sense of futility he fled again down the dream-vague marble pavements between rows of cloudy palaces.

Through all these dizzy metamorphoses the pursuer flowed relentlessly behind, lapping at his heels when he slowed. He began to realize, very dimly, that it might have overtaken him with ease, but that he was being spurred on thus for some vast, cloudy purpose—perhaps so that he might complete the circle he was so vaguely aware of and plunge of his own effort headlong into the very thing from which he fled. But he was not fleeing now, he was being driven.

The dim shapes of buildings reeled past. The woman running at his side had become something cloudy and vague too, a panting presence flying from the same peril—into the same peril—but unreal as a dream. He felt himself unreal too, a phantom fleeing hand-in-hand with another phantom through the streets of a phantom city. And all reality was melting away save the unreal, invisible thing that pursued him, and only it had reality while everything else faded to shapes of nothingness. Like driven ghosts they fled.

And as reality melted about them, the shadowy city took firmer shape. In the reversal everything real became cloudy, grass and trees and pools dimming like some forgotten dream, while the unstable outlines of the towers loomed up more and more clearly in the pale dark, colors flushing them as if reviving blood ran through the stones. Now the city stood firm and actual around them, and vague trees thrust themselves mistily through unbroken masonry, shadows of grass waved over firm marble pavements. Superimposed upon the unreal, the real world seemed vague as a mirage.

It was a curious architecture that rose around them now, so old and so forgotten that the very shapes of it were fantastic to Smith's eyes. Men in silk and steel moved down the streets, wading to their greave-clad knees in shadowy grass they did not seem to see. Women, too brushed by in mail as fine-linked and shining as gowns of silver tissue, belted with swords like the men. Their faces were set in a strained stare, and though they hurried they gave an impression of aimlessness, as if moved by some outer compulsion they did not understand.

And through the hurrying crowd, past the strange-colored towers, over the grass-shadowed streets, werewoman and wolf-man fled like the shadows they had become, pale wraiths blowing through the crowds unseen, the invisible follower lapping at their feet when they faltered. That force within which had urged them to turn and meet the pursuer now commanded them irresistibly to flee—to flee toward that same ending, for they knew now that they ran toward what they fled, roundaboutly; yet dared not stop running for deadly fear of what flowed along behind.

Yet in the end they did turn. The werewoman ran now in blind submission, all the strength dissolved that at first had carried her on. She was like a ghost blowing along on a gale, unresisting, unquestioning, hopeless. But in Smith a stouter spirit dwelt. And something strong and insistent was urging him to turn—an insistence that had no relation to the other urge to wait. It may have been a very human revolt against being driven, it may have been a deeply ingrained dislike of running from anything, or of allowing death to overtake him from behind. It had been bred in him to face danger when he could not escape it, and the old urge that every fighting thing knows—even a cornered rat will turn—drove him at last to face what followed him and die resisting—not in flight. For he felt that the end must be very near now. Some instinct stronger than the force that harried them told that.

And so, ignoring the armored crowd that eddied round them, he gripped the werewoman's wrist hard and slackened his speed, fighting against the urge that would have driven him on, choking down the panic that rose involuntarily as he waited for the thick waves to begin their surging round his feet. Presently he saw the shadow of a tree leaning through the smooth stone of a building, and instinctively he chose that misty thing he knew to be real for a bulwark to set his back against, rather than the unreal wall that looked so solid to his eyes. He braced his shoulders, holding a firm grip on the woman's wrist as she struggled and whimpered and moaned in her wolf-voice, straining to break the hold and run on. About, the mail-clad crowd hurried by heedlessly.

And very soon he felt it—the lapping wavelets touching his toes. He shuddered through all his unreal body at the feel, but he stood steady, gripping the struggling wolf-woman in a resolute hold, feeling the thick waves flowing around his feet, creeping up to his ankles, lapping higher and higher round his legs.

For a while he stood at bay, feeling terror choke up and up in his throat as the waves rose round him, scarcely heeding the woman's struggles to be free. And then a further rebellion began to stir. If die he must, let it be neither in headlong flight nor in dazed and terrified quiescence, but violently, fighting against it, taking some toll, if he could, to pay for the life he was to lose. He gasped a deep breath and plunged forward into the quaking, unseen mass that had risen almost to his waist. Behind him at arm's length the werewoman stumbled unwillingly.

He lurched forward. Very swiftly the unseen rose about him, until arms and shoulders were muffled in thickness, until the heavy invisibility brushed his chin, his closed mouth, sealed his nostrils . . . closed over his head.

Through the clear deeps he forged on, moving like a man in a nightmare of retarded motion. Every step was an immense effort against that flow, dragged through resisting depths of jelly-like nothingness. He had all but forgotten the woman he dragged along behind. He had wholly forgotten the colored city and the shining, armored people hurrying past. Blinded to everything but the deep-rooted instinct to keep moving, he forced his slow way onward against the flow. And indescribably he felt it begin to permeate him, seeping in slowly through the atoms of his ephemeral being. He felt it, and felt a curious change coming over him by degrees, yet could not define it or understand what was happening. Something urged him fiercely to go on, to struggle ahead, not to surrender—and so he fought, his mind whirling and the strange stuff of the thing that engulfed him soaking slowly through his being.

Presently the invisibility took on a faint body, a sort of clear opaqueness, so that the things outside were streaked and blurred a little and the splendid dream city with its steel-robed throngs wavered through the walls of what had swallowed him up. Everything was shaking and blurring and somehow changing. Even his body no longer obeyed him completely, as if it trembled on the verge of transition into something different and unknown. Only the driving instinct to fight on held clear in his dazed mind. He struggled forward.

And now the towered city was fading again, its mailed people losing their outlines and melting into the greyness. But the fading was not a reversal—the shadow-grass and trees grew more shadowy still. It was as if by successive steps he was leaving all matter behind. Reality had faded almost to nothing, even the cloudy unreality of the city was going now, and nothing but a grey blankness remained, a blankness through which he forged stubbornly against the all-engulfing flow that steeped him in nothingness.

Sometimes in flashes he ceased to exist—joined the grey nothing as part of it. The sensation was not that of unconsciousness. Somehow utter nirvana swallowed him up and freed him again, and between the moments of blank he fought on, feeling the transition of his body taking place very slowly, very surely, into something that even now he could not understand.

For grey eternities he struggled ahead through the clogging resistance, through darknesses of nonexistence, through flashes of near-normality, feeling somehow that the path led in wild loops and whorls through spaces without name. His time-sense had stopped. He could hear and see nothing, he could feel nothing but the immense effort of dragging his limbs through the stuff that enfolded him, and the effort was so great that he welcomed those spaces of blankness when he did not exist even as an unconsciousness. Yet stubbornly, unceasingly, the blind instinct drove him on.

There was a while when the flashes of nonexistence

crowded closer and closer, and the metamorphosis of his body was all but complete, and only during brief winks of consciousness did he realize himself as an independent being. Then in some unaccountable way the tension slackened. For a long moment without interludes he knew himself a real being struggling upstream through invisibility and dragging a half-fainting woman by the wrist. The clarity of it startled him. For a while he could not understand—then it dawned upon him that his head and shoulders were free—free! What had happened he could not imagine, but he was free of it.

The hideousness grey nothingness had gone—he looked out over a plain dotted with low trees and low, white, columned villas like no architecture he had ever seen before. A little way ahead a stone slab no higher than himself leaned against a great boulder in a hollow fringed with trees. Upon the slab an indescribable symbol was incised. It was like no symbol of any writing he had ever seen before. It was so different from all the written characters men make that it scarcely seemed akin to writing at all, nor traced by any human hand. Yet there was a curious familiarity about it, that did not even puzzle him. He accepted it without question. He was somehow akin to it.

And between him and the engraved slab the air writhed and undulated. Streamers of invisibility flowed toward him, mounting as they flowed. He struggled forward, exultation surging within him. For—he knew, now. And as he advanced the thick resistance fell away from him, sliding down his shoulders, ebbing lower and lower about his struggling body. He knew that whatever the invisibility was, its origin lay in that symbol on the stone. From that it flowed. Half-visibly, he could see it. And toward that stone he made his way, a dim purpose forming in his brain.

He heard a little gasp and quickened breathing behind him, and turned his head to see the werewoman, moon-white in the undulating, almost-visible flow, staring about with wakened eyes and incomprehension clouding her face. He saw that she did not remember anything of what had happened. Her green-glowing eyes were empty as if they had just opened from deep slumber.

He forged on swiftly now through the waves that lapped futilely around his waist. He had won. Against what he did not yet know, nor from what cloudy terror he had saved himself and her, but he was not afraid now. He knew what he must do, and he struggled on eagerly toward the slab.

He was still waist-deep in the resisting flow when he reached it, and for a dizzy instant he thought he could not stop; that he must wade on into the very substance of that unnameable carving out of which came the engulfing nothingness. But with an effort he wrenched round and waded cross-stream, and after a while of desperate struggle he broke free into the open air.

It was like a cessation of gravity. In the release from that dragging weight he felt he must scarcely be touching the ground, but there was no time now to exult in his freedom. He turned purposefully toward the slab.

The werewoman was just floundering clear of the stream when she saw what he intended, and she flung up her hands with a shriek of protest that startled Smith into a sidewise leap, as if some new terror were coming upon him. Then he saw what it was and gave her an amazed stare as he turned again to the stone, lifting his arms to grapple with it. She reeled forward and seized him in a cold, desperate embrace, dragging backward with all her might. Smith glared at her and shook his shoulders impatiently. He had felt the rock give a little. But when she saw that, she screamed again piercingly, and her arms twined like snakes as she struggled to drag him away.

She was very strong. He paused to unwind the fierce clasp and she fought savagely to prevent it. He needed all his strength to break her grip, and he pushed her from him then with a heavy shove that sent her reeling. The pale eyes followed her, puzzling why, though she had fled in such a frenzy of terror from what flowed out of the stone, she still strove to prevent him from destroying it. For he was quite sure that if the slab were broken and the symbol destroyed that stream would cease to flow. He could not understand her. He shook his shoulders impatiently and turned again to the stone.

This time she was on him with an animal spring, snarling low in her throat and clawing with frantic hands. Her fangs snapped just clear of his throat. Smith wrenched free with a great effort, for she was steel-strong and very desperate, and gripped her by the shoulder, swinging her away. Then he set his teeth and drove a heavy fist into her face, smashing against the fangs. She yelped, short and sharply, and collapsed under his hand, sinking to the grass in a huddle of whiteness and wild black hair.

He turned to the stone again. This time he got a firm grip on it, braced his legs wide, heaved. And he felt it give. He heaved again. And very slowly, very painfully, he uprooted its base from the bed where for ages it must have lain. Rock ground protestingly against rock. One edge rose a little, then settled. And the slab tilted. He heaved again, and very deliberately he felt it slipping from his hands. He stood back, breathing heavily, and watched.

Majestically, the great slab tottered. The stream flowing invisibly from its incised symbol twisted in a streaked path through the air, long whorls of opacity blurring the landscape beyond. Smith thought he felt a stirring in the air, a shiver as of warning. All the white villas dimly seen through the dark wavered a little before his eyes, and something hummed through the air like a thin, high wailing too sharp to be heard save as a pain to the ears. The chattering overhead quickened suddenly. All this in the slow instant while the slab tottered.

Then it fell. Deliberately slow, it leaned outward and down. It struck the ground with a rush and a splintering crash. He saw the long cracks appear miraculously upon its surface as the great fantastic symbol broke into fragments. The opacity that had flowed outward from it writhed like a dragon in pain, flung itself high-arching into the shivering air—and ceased. In that moment of cessation the world collapsed around him. A mighty wind swooped down in a deafening roar, blurring the landscape. He thought he saw the white villas melting like dreams, and he knew the werewoman on the grass must have recovered consciousness, for he heard a wolf-yell of utter agony from behind him. Then the great wind blotted out all other things, and he was whirling through space in a dizzy flight.

In that flight understanding overtook him. In a burst of illumination he knew quite suddenly what had happened and what would happen now—realized without surprise, as if he had always known it, that the denizens of this wasteland had dwelt here under the protection of that mighty curse laid upon the land in the long-past century when the city fell. And he realized that it must have been a very powerful curse, laid down by skill and knowledge that has long since vanished even from the legends of man, for in all the ages since, this accursed moor had been safe haven for all the half-real beings that haunt mankind, akin to the evil that lay like a blanket over the moor.

And he knew that the curse had its origin in the nameless symbol which some sorcerer of forgotten times had inscribed upon the stone, a writing from some language which can have no faintest kinship with man. He knew that the force flowing out from it was a force of utter evil, spreading like a river over the whole salt waste. The stream of it lapped to and fro in changing courses over the land, and when it neared some dweller of the place the evil that burnt for a life-force in that dweller acted as a magnet to the pure evil which was the stream. So, evil answering to evil, the two fused into one, the unfortunate dweller swallowed up into a nirvana of nonexistence in the heart of that slow-flowing stream.

It must have worked strange changes in them. That city whose shapes of shadow still haunted the place assumed reality, taking on substance and becoming more and more actual as the reality of the captive waned and melted into the power of the stream.

He thought, remembering those hurrying throngs with their strained, pale faces, that the spirits of the people who had died in the lost city must be bound tenuously to the spot of their death. He remembered that young, richly garmented warrior he had been one with in fleeting moments, running golden-sandaled through the streets of the forgotten city in a panic of terror from something too long past to be remembered—the jeweled woman in her colored sandals and rippling robes running at his side—and wondered in the space of a second what their story had been so many ages ago. He thought that curse must somehow have included the dwellers in the city, chaining them in earthbound misery for centuries. But of this he was not sure.

Much of all this was not clear to him, and more he realized without understanding, but he knew that the instinct which guided him to turn upstream had not been a false one—that something human and alien in him had been a talisman to lead his staggering feet back toward the source of his destroyer. And he knew that with the breaking up of the symbol that was a curse, the curse ceased to be, and the warm, sweet, life-giving air that humanity breathes swept in a flood across the barrens, blowing away all the shadowy, unclean creatures to whom it had been haven for so long. He knew—he knew . . .

Greyness swooped round him, and all knowledge faded from his mind and the wind roared mightily in his ears. Somewhere in that roaring flight oblivion overtook him.

When he opened his eyes again he could not for an instant imagine where he lay or what had happened. Weight pressed upon his entire body suffocatingly, pain shot through it in jagged flashes. His shoulder ached deeply. And the night was dark, dark about him. Something muffling and heavy had closed over his senses, for no longer could he hear the tiny, sharp sounds of the plain or scent those tingling odors that once blew along the wind. Even the chattering overhead had fallen still. The place did not even smell the same. He thought he could catch from afar the odor of smoke, and somehow the air, as nearly as he could tell with his deadened senses, no longer breathed of desolation and loneliness. The smell of life was in the wind, very faintly. Little pleasant odors of flower-scent and kitchen smoke seemed to tinge it.

"—wolves must have gone," someone was saying above him. "They stopped howling a few minutes ago—notice?— first time since we came into this damned place. Listen."

With a painful effort Smith rolled his head sideways and stared. A little group of men was gathered around him, their eyes lifted just now to the dark horizon. In the new density of the night he could not see them clearly, and he blinked in irritation, striving to regain that old, keen, clarity he had lost. But they looked familiar. One wore a white fur cap on his head. Someone said, indicating something beyond Smith's limited range of vision, "Fellow here must have had quite a tussle. See the dead she-wolf with her throat torn out? And look—all the wolf-tracks everywhere in the dust. Hundreds of them. I wonder . . ."

"Bad luck to talk about them," broke in the fur-capped leader. "Werewolves, I tell you—I've been in this place before, and I know. But I never saw or heard tell of a thing like what we saw tonight—that big white-eyed one running with the she-wolves. God! I'll never forget those eyes."

Smith moved his head and groaned. The men turned quickly.

"Look, he's coming to," said someone, and Smith was vaguely conscious of an arm under his head and some liquid, hot and strong, forced between his lips. He opened his eyes and looked up. The fur-capped man was bending over him. Their eyes met. In the starlight, Smith's were colorless as pale steel.

The man choked something inarticulate and leaped back so suddenly that the flask spilled its contents half over Smith's chest. He crossed himself frankly with a hand that shook.

"Who—who are you?" he demanded unsteadily.

Smith grinned wearily and closed his eyes.

# FROM HAND TO MOUTH
*by* FITZ-JAMES O'BRIEN

"No more electric and versatile genius had ever appeared among American authors," stated Fred Lewis Pattee in *The Development of the American Short Story,* in describing the work and activities of Fitz-James O'Brien, *doyen* of the American Bohemian movement in the years prior to the Civil War. O'Brien's work was popular during his day in journals of poetry, on the stage, in the columns of newspapers, or almost anywhere because he had the feel of the contemporary public pulse and could improvise to order. Of his voluminous contributions, his most remarkable and influential works have been his fantasies, the most famous of which is "The Diamond Lens," and close behind in popularity, "The Wondersmith" and "What Was It?" In science fiction, supernatural, and fantasy, his imagination was exotic as well as original, and all the more effective since the locale was frequently the realistic setting of the New York City of his time.

It seems almost inexplicable that one of his most extraordinary novelettes, a story which may very well prove the single most striking example of surrealistic fiction to precede *Alice in Wonderland,* should have remained unreprinted for over ninety years! That story is "From Hand to Mouth," first published in the weekly *New York Picayune* in eight installments from the issues of March 27, 1858, to May 15, 1858.

The *New York Picayune* was co-published by an artist who was a carousing buddy of O'Brien's, named Frank H. Bellow. The paper had originally been started in 1847 by Dr. Richard B. Hutchings and Joseph Woodward to promote a patent medicine called Hutchings Dyspepsia Bitters, but the humorous fillers intended to attract readers to the advertisements so adequately fulfilled their purpose that the paper was continued as a regular comic weekly. Bellow was its last editor, seeing it through to its demise in 1860.

Securing the O'Brien story was quite a coup for Bellow, because "The Diamond Lens" had only a short time previously created a minor sensation and established a following for its author. Each weekly chapter was written to meet the deadline. At the seventh installment O'Brien didn't come through and after skipping one issue, Frank Bellow wrote the final chapter, ending it with a few hundred words titled "How It All Happened." It is believed that O'Brien had fabricated so wild a situation that he could not think of any way to conclude the story.

For one who knows the history of the period, any of the names and places in "From Hand to Mouth" are inside jokes which O'Brien's friends must have chuckled over at the time. Today, all of the names and the double meanings are forgotten or missed, but that "loss" is overwhelmingly eclipsed by the manner in which the story anticipates many of the elements of the surrealistic movement to emerge after World War I, and in fact is one of the most successful surrealistic fantasies ever written. Despite the "wildness" of situations, the reader is able to follow every situation without confusion and with perfect clarity. It is not an experiment at writing surrealism—it is a success. Had O'Brien been able to properly end the story with the ingenuity he displayed in "What Was It?" or "The Diamond Lens" he might have had a masterpiece of considerable stature.

Its value was recognized at the time and it was collected in *Good Stories* Part IV, Boston, 1868, with a frontispiece which portrayed Fitz-James O'Brien as the lead character in the story as drawn by his friend S. Eythinge, Jr. It was reprinted for the last time in the anthology *Famous Stories*, published by R. Worthington, New York, in 1880 and the frontispiece was again used.

Its republication here is an event, for the work is absolutely original, its like having never been seen before or since. Should there be a future collection of O'Brien's fantasies, it will undoubtedly be included among them.

# FROM HAND
# TO MOUTH

by

## Fitz-James O'Brien

## I     HOW I FELL IN WITH COUNT GOLOPTIONS.

The evening of the 8th of November, in the present year, was
distinguished by the occurrence of two sufficiently remarkable events. On that evening Mr. Ullman produced Meyerbeer's opera of "The Huguenots," for the first time in this
country, and we were unexpectedly visited by a snowstorm.
Winter and the great lyrical dramatist made their debut
together. Winter opened with a slow movement of heavy
snowflakes,—an andante, soft and melancholy, and breathing of polar drowsiness. The echoing streets were muffled,
and the racket and din of thoroughfares sounded like the roar
of a far-off ocean. The large flakes fell sleepily through the
dim blue air, like soft white birds that had been stricken with
cold in the upper skies, and were sinking benumbed to earth.
The trees and lamp-posts, decorated with snowy powder,
gave the city the air of being laid out for a grand supper-party,

with ornamental confectionery and embellishing the long white table. Through the hoar drifts that lay along the streets peeped the black tips of building-stones and mud-piles in front of half-finished houses, until Broadway looked as if it was enveloped in an ermine robe, dotted with the black tails with which cunning furriers ornament that skin.

Despite the snow, I sallied forth with my friend Cobra, the musical critic of the New York *Daily Cockchafter,* to hear Meyerbeer's masterpiece. We entered a mute omnibus with a frozen driver, whose congealed hands could scarcely close upon our faces—which accounted perhaps for a slight error in the change he gave us—and so rolled up silently to Union Square, whence we floundered into the Academy. I listened to that wonderful picture of one of France's anniversaries of massacre, with bloody copies of which that "God-protected country" (*vide* speech from the throne of any public occasion) is continually furnishing the civilized world. The roar of Catholic cannon—the whistle of Huguenot bullets—the stealthy tread of conspiring priests—the mournful wailing of women whose hearts foretell evil before it comes—the sudden outburst of the treacherous, bloodthirsty Romish tiger —the flight and shrieks of men and women about to die— the valiant, despairing fighting of the stern Protestants—the voice of the devilish French king, shouting from his balcony to his assassins the remorseless command, "Tuez! tuez!"— the ominous trickling of the red streams that sprung from cloven Lutheran hearts, and rolled slowly through the kennels:—all this arose before me vital and real, as the music of that somber opera smote the air. Cobra, whose business it was—being a critic—not to attend to the performance, languidly surveyed the house, or availed himself of the intermission between the acts to fortify himself with certain refreshing but stimulating beverages.

The opera being concluded, we proceeded to Pilgarlik's— Pilgarlik keeps a charming private restaurant at the upper end of Broadway—and there, over a few reed-birds and a bottle of Burgundy, Cobra concocted his criticism on "The Huguenots,"—in which he talked learnedly of dominants, sub-dominants, ascending by thirds, and descending by twenty-thirds, and such like, while I, with nothing more weighty on my mind than paying for the supper, smoked my cigar and sipped my concluding cup of black coffee in a state of divine repose.

The snow was deep, when, at about one o'clock, A.M., Cobra and myself parted at the corner of Eight Street and Broadway, each bound for his respective home. Cobra lived on Fourth Avenue—I live, or lived, on Bleecker Street. The snow was deep, and the city quite still, as I half ran, half floundered down the sidewalk, thinking what a nice hot brandy-toddy I would make myself when I got home, and the pleasure I would have in boiling the water over my gas-light on a lately invented apparatus which I had acquired, and in which I took much pride; I also recollected with a thrill of pleasure that I had purchased a fresh supply of lemons that morning, so that nothing was needed for the scientific concoction of a nightcap. I turned down Bleecker Street and reached my door. I was singing a snatch of Pierre Dupont's song of *La Vigne* as I pulled out my night-key and inserted it in that orifice so perplexing to young men who have been to a late supper. One vigorous twist, and I was at home. The half-uttered triumphal chant of the Frenchman, who dilates with metrical malice on the fact that the vine does not flourish in England, died on my lips. The key turned, but the door, usually so yielding to the members of our family, obstinately refused to open. A horrible thought flashed across my mind. They had locked me out! A new servant had perhaps arrived, and cautiously barricaded the entrance; or the landlady—to whom, at the moment, I was under some slight pecuniary responsibility—had taken this cruel means of recalling me to a sense of my position. But it could not be. There was some mistake. There was fluff in my key—yes, that was it—there was fluff in the barrel of my night-key. I instantly proceeded to make a Pandean pipe of that instrument, and blew into the tube until my face resembled that queer picture of the wind in Aesop's fables, as it is represented in the act of endeavoring to make the traveller take off his cloak. A hopelessly shrill sound responded to my efforts. The key was clear as a flute. Was it the wrong key? I felt in every pocket, vaguely expect-

ing a supernumerary one to turn up, but in vain. While thus
occupied, the conviction forced itself on my mind that I had
no money.

Locked out, with a foot of snow on the ground, and nothing
but a three-cent piece and two new cents—so painfully bright
that they presented illusory resemblances to half-eagles—in
my pocket!

I knew well that an appeal to the bell was hopeless. I had
tried it once before for three hours at a stretch, without the
slightest avail. It is my private conviction that every member
of that household, who slept at all within hearing of the bell,
carefully stuffed his or her ears with cotton before retiring for
the night, so as to be out of the reach of temptation to answer
it. Every inmate of that establishment, after a certain hour,
determinedly rehearsed the part of Ulysses when he was
passing the Sirens. They were deaf to the melody of the bell. I
once knew a physician who, to keep up appearances, had a
night-bell affixed to his door. The initiated alone knew that he
regularly took the tongue out before he went to bed. His
conscience was satisfied, and he slept calmly. I might just as
well have been pulling his bell.

Break the windows! Why not? Excellent idea; but, as I
before stated, my pecuniary position scarcely allowed of
such liberties. What was I to do? I could not walk up and
down the city all night. I would freeze to death, and there
would be a horrible paragraph in the morning papers about
the sad death of a destitute author. I ran over rapidly in my
mind every hotel in the city with which I was at all
acquainted, in order to see if there was in any one of them a
night-porter who knew me. Alas! Night-porters knew me
not. Why had I not a watch or a diamond ring? I resolved on
the instant to purchase both as soon as I got ten or twelve
hundred dollars. I began to wonder where the newsboys'
depot was, and recollected there was a warm spot somewhere
over the *Herald* press-room, on which I had seen ragged
urchins huddling as I passed by late of night. I was ruminating
gravely over the awful position in which I was placed, when a
loud but somewhat buttery voice disturbed me by shouting

from the sidewalk: "Ha, ha! Capital joke! Locked out, eh? You'll never get in."

A stranger! perhaps benevolent, thought I. If so, I am indeed saved. To rush down the steps, place my hand upon his shoulder, and gaze into his face with the most winning expression I was capable of assuming, was but the work of several minutes—which, however, included two tumbles on the stoop.

"Can it—can it be," I said, "that you have a night-key?"

"A night-key!" he answered with a jolly laugh, and speaking as if his mouth was full of turtle—"a night-key! What the deuce should I do with a night-key? I never go home until morning."

"Sir," said I, sadly, "do not jest with the misery of a fellow-creature. I conjure you by the sanctity of your fireside to lend me your night-key."

"You've got one in your hand; why don't you use that?"

I had. In the excitement of the moment I had quite over-looked the fact that, if I had fifty night-keys, I would still have found myself on the wrong side of the door.

"The fact is—pardon me—but I forgot that the door was locked on the inside."

"Well, you can't get in, and you can't stay out," said the stranger, chuckling over a large mouthful of turtle. "What are you going to do?"

"Heavens only knows, unless you are in a position to lend me a dollar, which, sir, I assure you, shall be returned in the morning."

"Nonsense. I never lend money. But if you like, you shall come to my hotel and spend the night there, free of charge."

"What hotel?"

"The Hotel de Coup d'OEil, on Broadway."

"I never heard of such an establishment."

"Perhaps. Nevertheless, it is what is called a first-class hotel."

"Well, but who are you, sir?" I inquired; for, in truth, my suspicions began to be slightly excited by this time. My interlocutor was rather a singular-looking person, as well as I could make out his features in the dusk. Middle height, broad shoulders, and a square, pale face, the upper part of which seemed literally covered with a pair of huge blue spectacles, while the lower portion was hidden in a frizzly beard. A small space on either cheek was all that was uncovered, and that shone white and cold as the snow that lay on the streets. "Who are you, sir?"

"I—I am Count Goloptious, Literary Man, *Bon vivant*, Foreign Nobleman, Linguist, Duellist, Dramatist, and Philanthropist."

"Rather contradictory pursuits, sir," I said, rather puzzled by the man's manner, and wishing to say something.

"Of course. Every man is a mass of contradictions in his present social state."

"But I never heard your name mentioned in the literary world," I remarked. "What have you written?"

"What have I not written? Gory essays upon Kansas for the New York *Tribune*. Smashing personal articles for the *Herald*. Carefully constructed noncommittal double-reflex-action with escape-movement leaders for the *Daily Times;* sensation dramas for the Phantom Theatre. Boisterous practical joke comedies for Mr. Behemoth the low comedian; and so on *ad infinitum*."

"Then as a *bon vivant*—?"

"I have been immensely distinguished. When Brillat Savarin was in this country, I invented a dish which nearly killed him. I called it *Surprise des Singes avec petite verole.*"

"Linguist?"

"I speak seventeen languages, sir."

"Duellist?"

"I was elected a Member of Congress for South Carolina."

"Philanthropist?"

"Am I not offering to you, a stranger, the hospitality of the Hotel de Coup d'OEil?"

"Enough, sir," I cried; "I accept your offer. I thank you for your timely assistance."

"Then let us go," answered the Count Goloptious, offering me his arm.

## II    THE HOTEL DE COUP D'OEIL.

The Count led me out of Bleecker Street into Broadway. We trudged a few blocks in silence, but whether towards Union Square or the Battery I could not for the life of me tell. It seemed as if I had lost all my old landmarks. The remarkable corners and signposts of the great thoroughfare seemed to have vanished.

We stopped at length before a large edifice, built of what seemed at first glance to be a species of variegated marble; on examining more closely, I perceived that every stone in the front of the building was a mosaic, in which was represented one of the four chief organs of the body. The stones were arranged in the form of a cross, with these designs depicted on them.

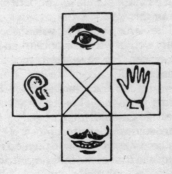

The effect of the entire front of this huge building, staring at you with a myriad painted eyes, listening to you with a myriad painted ears, beckoning to you with a myriad painted hands, and grinning at you with a myriad painted mouths, was inconceivably strange and bewildering.

"This is the hotel," said Count Golopious. "Let us enter."

We passed under a gigantic portal towards two gleaming doors of plate-glass, which voluntarily unclosed as we approached. A magnificent hall lay before us. The pavement was of tessellated marble, on every square of which the

strange emblems which decorated the front of the establishment were repeated. From the center of this vast chamber a
spiral staircase arose, from each coil of which small bridges
of delicate gilt iron work branched off, and led into what
seemed to be the corridors of the building. At one end of the
hall stood a curious Oriental-looking structure, within which,
seated upon a sort of throne, I beheld a portly bearded
personage whose breast was festooned with gold chains, and
whose fingers were covered with rings.

"That is the night clerk," whispered the Count to me,
pointing to this person. "Go and enter your name on the
book."

I approached the Oriental temple, and, finding a hotel
register with leaves of vellum and bound in silver and mother-
of-pearl, open on a shelf close by, took up a pen and wrote
down my name. The clerk did not even condescend to glance
at me, while doing this.

"Would you like some supper?" asked the Count.

"No, no," I answered; "I want only to go to bed." The
truth is, the whole scene so bewildered me, that I began to
fear that I had gone mad.

"Very well. I will call for your candle." So saying the
Count approached a large model of a human ear, which was
fixed in the wall of the Oriental temple, and putting his lips to
it called out, "A bedroom light for 746."

In an instant a continuous murmur seemed to fill the hall
and ascend towards the roof of the building. It appeared to me
that ten thousand voices took up the words, "A bedroom light
for 746," one after the other, until the sentence rolled along
like the fire of a line of infantry. I turned, startled, towards the
direction from which those echoes proceeded, and on casting
my eyes upon the great spiral staircase beheld the cause.


III     EYE, EAR, HAND, AND MOUTH.

The balustrades of the staircase on either side, and the sides of
the different galleries branching off, were all decorated with
two of the mystical emblems I had before seen so often

repeated in this strange hotel. On the one side a line of human mouths ran up the edges of the staircase, while on the other a line of human hands occupied a corresponding position. There was, however, this difference between them and the symbols occupying the front of the establishment. They were all modelled in high relief. The balustrades seemed as if they had been decorated with the pillage of numberless anatomical museums. As I turned suddenly and glanced towards the staircase, I saw the lips of those ten thousand mouths moving, and whispering softly but distinctly the words, "A bedroom light for 746."

I had scarcely recovered from the astonishment with which this sight overwhelmed me, and the rolling whisper had hardly died away in the domed roof of the hall, when my attention was attracted by a speck of light which appeared far away up on the staircase, and seemed to be travelling slowly down the huge spiral. I watched it with a sort of stupid interest, and when it came nearer discovered that it was nothing less than a chamber wax-light in a silver candlestick, which the ten thousand hands that lined the edge of the balustrade opposite to the balustrade of the mouths were carefully passing from one to the other. In a few moments it reached the bottom, where the last hand, a huge muscular-looking fist, held it.

"There is your light," said the Count; "follow it up stairs, and it will lead you to your room. I will, for the present, wish you a good-night, as I have to go and take my before-morning walk."

I confusedly wished my strange friend good night, and walked towards the hand that held my candle. As I approached, the hand passed it to the hand next above, and the candle so began to ascend the stairs. I followed. After toiling up an interminable number of steps, the hands suddenly took the candle off into one of the side galleries, in which at last it stopped before a huge polished door, on the upper panels of which were painted again a huge eye and an equally gigantic ear. I could not help noticing that the eye had a demoniac expression.

I pushed the door open, and, taking the candle from the

attendant hand, was about to enter the room, when my
attention was attracted by that member giving my coat a
gentle twitch. I turned, and there beheld the hand stretched
out with an expression—if ever hand had an expression—
which was inexpressibly pleading. I was puzzled. What
could it want? I would follow the example of my friend Count
Goloptious, and speak to the ear. Approaching my lips to the
ear painted over my door, I put the question, ''What does this
amiable hand want?'' In an instant a fusillade of whispers
came rolling up the line of mouths, answering, ''He wants a
quarter for his trouble.'' My heart sank—I had only five
cents.

''Pshaw!'' said I, trying to bluff the thing off, ''I can't
attend to it now''; and so saying, stepped towards my room.
As I entered and hurriedly closed the door, I beheld every
hand down the long coil of stairs simultaneously double up
and shake at me in menace, while a horrid sardonic laugh ran
down the line of mouths. I never beheld anything more
devilish than that spiral smile of scorn.

On closing the door of my room, I was not a little annoyed
to find that the eye and the ear, which were on the outside,
were on the inside also, so exactly alike that they seemed to
have come through for the purpose of watching me, and
listening to my sleep-talk. I felt wretchedly uncomfortable at
the idea of undressing before that eye. It was fixed on me
wherever I moved in the room. I tried to pin a handkerchief
over it, but the wood of the door was too hard and the pins
would not stick. As the handkerchief fell to the ground, I
beheld the horrid eye wink at me with a devilish expression of
derision. Determined not to be overlooked, I put out the light
and undressed in the dark, when I tumbled into bed in a state
of confusion of mind not easily described. I had scarcely laid
my head on the pillow, when I heard a distinct knock at my
door. Cursing the intrusion, and not without some tremor,
being uncertain what new enchantment might be brewing, I
opened it. There was the hand outstretched, and pleading for
its infernal quarter. The abominable member was evidently
determined to keep me awake all night. There was but one
thing to be done—to bribe him with a promise. I put my lips

to the ear and said: "If the hand does not disturb me, I will put a gold ring on his finger tomorrow."

The ten thousand mouths repeated with tones of approval, "He will put a gold ring on his finger tomorrow," and the ten thousand hands waved their thanks. I shut my door, congratulating myself on my escape, and, flinging myself on the bed, soon fell fast asleep.

## IV    DR. KITCHENER IN A DREAM.

A horrible heat seemed to surround my head. I suffered intolerable agony. Count Goloptious had unscrewed my caput just at the point known to anatomists as the condyles, and deliberately placed it in the center of a ring of burning brands which he had laid on the floor. The Philanthropic Duellist then drew a volume from his pocket, which, even in my excited condition, I could not help recognizing as Doctor Kitchener's cookery-book, and commenced deliberately to read aloud the recipe for roasting a goose alive, which is contained in that immortal work. I now perceived with unutterable indignation that he intended to cook my head after Kitchener's inhuman instructions.

The flames leaped higher and higher around my blistering cheeks. My whiskers—whiskers on which countless barbers had exhausted the resources of their art—shrivelled into ashy nothings. My eyeballs protruded, my lips cracked; my tongue, hard and wooden, beat against the roof of my mouth. I uttered a half-inarticulate cry for water. The Count laughed a devilish laugh, and consulted his book.

"True," he said, "the worthy doctor says, that when the goose thirsteth let her be fed with water, so that the flesh shall be tender when cooked. Let us give the poor head a drink."

So saying, he reached towards my parched lips a pannikin fixed on the end of a long handle. I quaffed eagerly the liquor which it contained. Ah! how grateful was that draught of brandy-and-water! I drained the cup to the bottom. But the bliss was short-lived. The flames hissed and crackled. My hair caught fire, and my poor head blazed like a Frenchman's "ponch-bol." The sparkles from the burning brands flew against my forehead and into my eyes, scorching and blinding me. My anguish was insufferable, and as a last desperate resource I cried out to the Count: "Take me from the fire—take me from the fire—I am overdone!"

The Count answered to this: "Patience, patience, head of a heathen! You are roasting beautifully. A few minutes more, and I will pour some Worcestershire sauce over you."

Worcestershire sauce! That essence of every peppery condiment known to civilized man! Worcestershire sauce, the delight of East Indian officers on half-pay, and the horror of Frenchmen who encounter it in London restaurants, and return to "La Belle" with excoriated palates; this biting, inflammatory stuff to be poured over a wretched head, whose scalp was cracking like the skin of a roasted apple—it was too much to endure, so I gave vent to my feelings in one unearthly shriek of agony and—awoke.

My head was hot, but, thank Heaven, it was not roasting. It was lying on a tumbled pillow across which a stream of the morning sunlight was pouring in a golden tide. There was no Count Goloptious—no circle of firebrands—no Worcestershire sauce—I was in bed, and alone in the Hotel de Coup d'OEil.

So soon as I had sufficiently recovered from the effects of my horrible dream, I sat up in bed, and inspected my apartment. It was large and lofty and sumptuously furnished. A touching attention to my necessities was visible as I glanced round the room. By my bedside, on a small buhl table, stood a large tumbler containing a creaming champagne cocktail. I drained it as a libation to the God of Morning. It was an appropriate sacrifice. The early sunlight itself seemed to flash through its amber globules. The white foam of dawn creamed in its effervescence. The tonic flavor of the fresh air that blows over the awaking earth was represented by the few drops of Boker's bitters with which it was tinctured. The immediate glow which it sent through every limb typified the healthy circulation produced by morning exercise.

I lay back on my pillow and began to speculate on the strange series of incidents which had befallen me. Who was

Count Goloptious? What weird hotel was this, of which I had beome an inmate? Were the days of enchantment indeed revived? Or did I merely dream of those myriads of beseeching hands and whispering mouths and ever-wakeful eyes?

I glanced involuntarily to the door at this juncture, and lo! there I beheld the eye which seemed set in the panel of my door. A full flood of the sunlight that poured across my bed struck across that side of my room, and I saw the eye winking drowsily in the blaze—drowsily, but yet wakefully, like one who is accustomed to watch between sleeping and waking; a sentinel which was never entirely somnolent.

The eye was watching me, despite the sleepy film with which it was overspread. Did I make any abrupt movement in the bed, its half-closed lid suddenly opened, and stared at me with appalling vigilance. There was no avoiding it. It commanded every corner of the room.

How was I to rise and attire myself, with so unpleasant a supervision? I had no longer the resource of extinguishing the light. The sun was beyond the reach of such a process. I meditated for a while, and at length hit upon the idea of constructing a species of wigwam out of the bedclothes, and dressing myself under its shelter. This I accomplished all the more easily, as I had laid my clothes, on retiring to rest, within easy reach of the bed; and as I constructed my impromptu tent, I thought I could discern an expression of drowsy disappointment shooting from underneath the half-closed lid of the Sentinel Eye.


## V     HOW I MAGNETIZED MY EYE.

Having finished my toilet sufficiently to justify my stepping from my bed, I was proceeding with my ablutions, when I heard a few chords struck upon a piano, in what seemed to be the next apartment. The moment after, a rich, luxurious contralto voice commenced to sing Schubert's beautiful serenade. I listened entranced. It seemed as if Alboni herself were singing. Those showers of rich, round notes falling in rhythmical sequence; that *sostenuto,* that, when first uttered, seemed a sound too weak to live, but growing and swelling every moment until it filled all the air with delicious sound, and then lessening and lessening till it almost died away, like distant music heard across the sea at night; those firm accentuations; the precision of those vocal descents, when the voice seemed to leap from the pinnacles of the gamut with the surety and fearlessness of a chamois-hunter leaping from Alpine peaks—all told me that I was listening to a queen of song.

I ran to the window of my room, and, opening it, thrust my head forth. There was a window next to mine, but I could see nothing. The blinds were down, but I could feel the glass panes vibrating with that wondrous tide of song.

A woman—a great singer—the greatest I had ever heard, lived next to me. What was she like? That heavenly voice could never come from a lean and withered chest, from a skeleton throat. She must be young, must be lovely. I determined on the instant to form her acquaintance.

But there was the Sentinel Eye! How to evade the vigilance of that abominable optic? Its horrible magnetic gaze followed me in every motion that I made. Magnetic gaze! There was an idea. It was doubtless an enchanted eye; but was there any enchantment that could stand against the human will? I was strong, body and soul. My magnetic power I had frequently proved to be of the highest force; why not exercise it on my sentinel? I resolved to attempt to magnetize The Eye!

I shut the window, and, taking a chair, seated myself opposite the demoniac optic. I fixed my eyes upon it, and, concentrating all the will of which I was master, sent a powerful magnetic current straight to the center of the glaring pupil. It would be a desperate struggle, I knew, but I was determined not to succumb. The Eye became uneasy. It glanced hither and thither, and seemed to wish to avoid my gaze. The painted eyelids drooped; the devilish pupil contracted and dilated, but still the orb always had to return and meet mine.

Presently the glaze of a magnetic sleep began to over-spread it. The scintillating lights that played within grew dim. The lid drooped, and, after lifting once or twice, I beheld the long, dark lashes fall, and slumber veiled my sentinel.

## VI   FAIR ROSAMOND.

No sooner was the Sentinel Eye fairly magnetized than I hastened to the window and flung it open. I possess a tolerable tenor voice, and as I thought vocalism was the simplest way of attracting the attention of the fair unknown, I sang the first verse of the charming serenade in the *Knight of Arva;* a melody full of grace and passion, for which Mr. Glover never obtained sufficient commendation. I had hardly concluded the first verse when I heard the neighboring window unclose. Unable to restrain my curiosity, I thrust my head out of my casement. Almost at the same instant a lovely face emerged from the window on the right. I had just time to get a flash of a glorious blond head, when the apparition disappeared. My head went in also. I waited a few moments, then cautiously, and after the manner of a turtle, protruded my caput once more. The Blond Head was out, but went in again like a flash. I remained with outstretched neck. After a brief pause I saw a gleam of fair curls. Then a white forehead, then a nose *retroussé,* then an entire face. I instantly withdrew into my shell. The Blond Head was timid, and I wished to encourage it.

Have you ever seen those philosophical toys which are constructed for the purpose of telling whether the day will be rainy or shiny? No. Then I will describe one to you.

There is a rustic house with two portals, one on either side. In the portal on the right a little man is concealed; in the portal on the left, a woman. They are both connected with a vertical coil of catgut, which runs from the base to the roof of the house, between the two. In dry weather the catgut relaxes, and the little man, by the action of such relaxation, is swung out of his portal into the open air. In wet weather the catgut contracts, and the woman enjoys the atmosphere. This toy has two advantages. One is, that it is infallible in its predictions, as it never announces fine weather until the weather is already fine; the other, that it affords an admirable illustration of the present social state of woman. When the day of storm arrives, in goes the man to his comfortable shelter, and out comes the woman to brave the elements. How many households does this typify! In sunshine and summer weather the husband is a charming fellow, and flaunts abroad in all his splendor; but when the clouds gather, when the fires goes out on the hearth for want of fuel, and duns are at the door, then poor woman is sent out to meet them, while the lord of creation hides in the cellar. I commend the toy to the consideration of Miss Lucy Stone.

Well, the Blond Head and myself played at weather-telling for five minutes. No sooner was one in than the other was out. It was a game of "tee to—tottering" performed after a new fashion. I resolved to put an end to it.

I gave three distinct hems.

There is a good deal of expression in a "hem." There is the hem of alarm, such as Alexis gives to Corydon, who is flirting in the garden with Phillis, when that young lady's mother is approaching. There is the hem of importance, such as that with which old Beeswax, the merchant, who is "worth his million, sir," prefaces a remark: the hem of confusion— the hem of derision or unbelief—the hem of satisfaction—the hem of disappointment—in short, a whole circle or hemmysphere of hems, each expressive in its way of a peculiar emotion. My hem was the hem of interrogation.

It was answered, and the next moment the Blond Head hovered, as it were, on the window-sill. It looked like a bird whose cage door has been opened after years of captivity, and who flutters on the threshold, not daring to advance into the free air.

I advanced my head boldly, and caught the Blond Head on the wing. It was retreating after the usual fashion, and with the usual rapidity, when I shot it with the word—

"Stay!"

It fluttered for an instant, and then remained still.

"We are neighbors," I remarked to the Blond Head. It was a truism, I know, but still it was a remark. After all, what does it matter what you say to most women, so that what you say is a remark?

"So I perceive," answered the Head, still fluttering a little.

"May I have the honor of knowing—" I commenced.

"Certainly," interrupted the Blond Head, "I am Rosamond."

"The fair Rosamond, I see," I interposed, in my gallantest manner.

"Yes," replied Rosamond, with wonderful *naïveté,* "fair perhaps, but very unhappy."

"Unhappy! How? Can I relieve you—be of any service?"

A glance of suspicion was shot at me from a pair of large, lustrous blue eyes.

"Are you not one of his satellites?" asked the Blond Head.

"I a satellite?" I answered indignantly—"I am no one's satellite—unless indeed it be yours," I added; "for I would gladly revolve round so fair a planet."

"Then you are not a friend of Count Goloptious?"

"No. I never saw him until last night. He brought me to this hotel, where I have been bewildered by enchantments."

"All my doing! all my doing!" cried Rosamond, wringing her hands.

"How your doing?" I inquired, with some astonishment.

"I am the artist—the fatal, the accursed artist. It was I who painted, I who modelled."

"Painted, modelled what?"

"Hush! you can save me, perhaps. I will see you again today. Is not the Eye watching you?"

"I have magnetized it."

"Good! you are a clever fellow," and Rosamond's eyes sparkled. "You must help me to escape."

"From what?"

"I will tell you—but quick shut your window. Count Goloptious is coming."

The Blond Head gave me a sweet smile, and retreated. I

did likewise, and closed my window. The next moment my door opened, and Count Goloptious entered.

## VII       THREE COLUMNS A DAY.

Count Goloptious entered. He seemed somewhat agitated and banged the door loudly. The shock dispelled the magnetic slumber of the Sentinel Eye, which suddenly opened its heavy lid and glared around with an expression which seemed to say, "I'd like to catch anybody saying that I have been asleep!"

"Sir," said the Count, "you have been misconducting yourself."

"I? Misconducting myself! What do you mean, Count Goloptious?"

"You have been singing love-songs, sir. In a tenor voice, too. If you were a bass I would not so much care, but to sing tenor—it's infamous!"

The blue goggles of the Count seemed to scintillate with anger as he glared at me.

"What the devil is the meaning of all this mystery?" I demanded angrily, for I really was getting savage at the incomprehensibility of everything that surrounded me. "What do your infernal eyes and hands and ears and mouths mean? If you are a nightmare, why don't you say so, and let me wake up? Why can't I sing love-songs if I like—and in a tenor voice, if I like? I'll sing alto if I choose, Count Goloptious."

"It is not for you to penetrate the mysteries of the Hotel de Coup d'OEil, sir," answered the Count. "You have enjoyed its hospitalities, and you can go. You have sung tenor songs, sir. You know, as well as I, the influence of the tenor voice upon the female heart. You are familiar with the history of the opera, sir. You have beheld penniless Italians, with curled mustaches, and with no earthly attraction except a peculiar formation of the windpipe, wreck the peace of the loveliest of our females. There is a female in this vicinity, sir. A poor, weak-minded girl, who has been placed under my guardian ship, and who is crazy on the subject of music. You have been singing to her, sir. Yes, with that accursed mellifluous voice of yours—that vocal honey in which you tenors administer the poison of your love—with that voice, sir, you are endeavoring to destroy the peace of mind of my ward. You have slept here, sir. You can go now.''

"I have not the slightest intention of going now, Count Goloptious. This hotel suits me admirably well. It has certain little drawbacks to be sure. It is not pleasant to be always overlooked and overhead in one's privacy.'' Here I pointed to the Ear and the Eye. "But still one can grow accustomed to that, I suppose. By the way, I should like some breakfast.''

My coolness took the Count completely by surprise. He stared at me without being able to utter a word. The fact was, that the Blond Head had bewitched me. Those clouds of golden hair that enfolded the wondrous oval of her face like a continual sunset had set my heart on fire. Never, never would I quit that hotel, unless I bore her with me. She had hinted at misfortune in our brief interview. She was a captive—a captive of the false Count, who now pretended that he was her guardian. Meshed in the countless spells and enchantments that surrounded her, she was helpless as those fair creatures we read of in the *Arabian Nights.* I would be her rescuer. I would discover the charm before which the bonds should melt. It was Andromache and Perseus and the sea-monster over again, in the year 1858. The Count, it is needless to say, was the monster. I had no Medusan shield, it is true, but I felt powerful as Perseus, for all that. My blond Andromache should be saved.

"So you won't go, eh?'' said Goloptious, after a long silence.

"No.''

"You had better.''

"This is a hotel. I have a right to accommodation here as long as I pay for it. Hotels belong to the public, when the puclic has money.''

"I know I can't force you to go, but I don't think, young

sir, that you will be able to pay for your board."

"How much do you charge here, by the day?"

"Three columns a day."

"Three what?"

"Three columns a day."

"I have heard of pillar dollars, but hang me if I ever heard of money that was called columns."

"We don't take money in pay at the Hotel de Coup d'OEil. Brain is the only currency that passes here. You must write me three columns of the best literary matter every day; those are our terms for this room. We have rooms higher up which rent for less. Some go as low as a paragraph. This is a four-column room usually, but you can have it for three."

Was the fellow laughing at me? His countenance was perfectly serious the whole time he was speaking. He talked as deliberately as if he had been a simple hotel clerk talking to a traveller, who was about pricing rooms. The whole thing struck me so comically that I could not refrain from a smile. I determined to carry the thing out in the Count's own vein.

"Meals are of course included?" I said inquiringly.

"Certainly, and served in your own room."

"I don't think the apartment dear," I continued, inspecting my chamber with a critical eye. "I'll take it."

"Very good"; and I saw a gleam of gratified malice shoot through the Count's great blue goggles.

"Now," said I, "perhaps you will inform me, Count Goloptious, why a few moments since you were so anxious to get rid of me, and why now you so tranquilly consent to my remaining an inmate of the Hotel de Coup d'OEil?"

"I have my reasons," said the Count, mysteriously. "You have now taken a room in the Hotel de Coup d'OEil; you will never quit it unless with my consent. The Eye shall watch you, the Ear shall hear you, the Hands shall detain you, the Mouths shall betray you; work is henceforth your portion. Your brain is my property; you shall spin it out as the spider his web, until you spin out your life with it. I have a lien on your intellect. There is one of my professions which I omitted in the catalogue which I gave you on our first meeting—I am a Publisher!"

## VIII   THE BLOND HEAD.

This last speech of the Count's I confess, stunned me. He was then a publisher. I, who for years had been anxiously keeping my individuality as an author intact, who had been strenuously avoiding the vortex of the literary whirlpool of which the publisher is the center, who had resisted, successfully, the absorbing process by which that profession succeeds in sucking the vitals out of the literary man, now suddenly found myself on the outer edge of the maelstrom, slowly but surely revolving towards the center funnel which was to swallow me.

An anticipation of unknown misfortunes seemed to overwhelm me. There was something sternly prophetic in the last tones of Goloptious's voice. He seemed to have had no turtle in his throat for several days. He was harsh and strident.

I determined to consult with the Blond Head in my extremity. It would, at least, be a consolation to me to gaze into those wondrous blue eyes, to bask in the sunshine of that luminous hair.

I raised my window, and hummed a bar of *Com'e Gentil.* In a moment the adjoining window was raised, and out came the Blond Head. The likeness of the weather-toy existed no longer: both our heads were out together.

"You have seen Goloptious," said the Blond Head. "What did he say?"

"Excuse me from continuing the conversation just at this moment," I replied. "I have forgotten something."

I had. The Ear and the Eye were in full play—one watching, the other listening. Such witnesses must be disposed of, if I was to hold any secret conversation with Rosamond. I retired therefore into my chamber again, and set to work to deliberately magnetize the eye. That organ did not seem to relish the operation at all, but it had no resource. In a few moments the film overspread it, and it closed. But what was to be done with the ear? I could not magnetize that. If, like the kind in Hamlet, I had only a little poison to pour into it, I might deafen it forever. Or, like the sailors of Ulysses, when passing the island of the Sirens—ah! Ulysses!—that was the

idea. Stop up the ear with wax! My bedroom candle was no
all burned out. To appropriate a portion of that luminary
soften it in my hands, and plaster it over the auricular orga
on my door was the work of a few moments. It was a triumph
of strategy. Both my enchanted guardians completely en
trapped, and by what simple means!

I now resumed my out-of-window conversation with
Rosamond with a feeling of perfect security.

"I have seen Goloptious," I said, in reply to her previou
question, "and am now a boarder in the Hotel de Coup
d'OEil."

"Great heavens, then you are lost!" exclaimed Rosa
mond, shaking her cloudy curls at me.

"Lost! How so?"

"Simply that you are the slave of Goloptious. He will live
on your brains, until every fiber is dried up. You will become
a mental atrophy—and, alas! worse."

"What do you mean? Explain, for Heaven's sake. You
mystify me."

"I cannot explain. But we must endeavor to escape. You
are ingenious and bold. I saw that by the manner in which you
overcame the Sentinel Eye by magnetism. This hotel is a den
of enchantments. I have been confined here for over a year
My profession is that of a sculptor, and I have been forced to
model all those demon hands and mouths and ears with which
the building is so thickly sown. Those weird glances that
strike through the countless corridors from the myriad eyes
are of my painting. Those ten thousand lips that fill this place
with unearthly murmurs are born of my fingers. It is I, who,
under the relentless sway of Goloptious, have erected those
enchanted symbols of which you are the victim. I knew no
what I did, when I made those things. But you can evade them
all. We can escape, if you will only set your ingenuity to
work."

"But, really, I see nothing to prevent our walking down
stairs."

"There is everything. You cannot move in this house
without each motion being telegraphed. The Hands that line

the staircase would clutch your skirts and hold you firm prisoner, were you to attempt to leave."

"The Hands be—dished!" I exclaimed.

At this moment there came a knock. I hastily drew my head in, and opened my door. I beheld the Hand of the night before, pleadingly extended; and at the same moment a running fire of murmurs from the Mouths informed me that he wanted the gold ring I had promised him. It was evident that this infernal hand would dun me to all eternity, unless he was paid.

I rushed to the window in my despair.

"Rosamond! fair Rosamond!" I shouted. "Have you got a gold ring?"

"Certainly," answered the Blond Head, appearing.

"Stretch as far as you can out of your window and hand it to me."

"Alas, I cannot stretch out of the window."

"Why not?"

"Do not ask me—oh! do not ask me," answered the Blond Head, with so much anguish in her tones that I inwardly cursed myself for putting so beautiful a creature to pain.

"But," I continued, "if I reach over to you with a pair of tongs, will you give it to me?"

"O, with pleasure!" and the Blond Head smiled a seraphic smile.

A pair of tongs being adjacent, a plain gold ring was quickly transferred from Rosamond's slender finger to my hand. With much ceremony I proceeded to place it on the smallest finger of the Hand, not being able, however, to get it farther than the first joint. Even this partial decoration seemed however to meet with approval, for the ten thousand hands commenced applauding vigorously, so much so that for a moment I fancied myself at the opera.

"Good heavens!" I thought, "what a *claque* these hands would make!"

There was one thing, however, that puzzled me much as I reentered my room.

Why was it that Fair Rosamond could not lean out of the

window? There was some mystery about it, I felt certain. I little thought in what manner or how soon that mystery was to be solved.

IX    ROSAMOND MAKES A GREEN BIRD.

No sooner was my debt to the Hand thus satisfactorily acquitted, than, in the elation of the moment at having for the first time in my life paid a debt on the appointed day, I immediately applied my lips to the Ear on the inside, and communicated my desire for some pens, ink, and paper. In an incredibly short space of time, the Hands, doubtless stimulated by the magnificence of my reward, passed a quantity of writing materials up the stairs, and in a few moments I was at work on my three columns, being determined from that time not to fall into arrears for my board.

"It is of the utmost importance," I thought, "that I should be unfretted by pecuniary liabilities, if I would rescue Rosamond from the clutches of this vile Count. I feel convinced of being able to baffle all his enchantments. Yes, Hands, ye may close, Ears, ye may listen, Eyes, ye may watch, Mouths, ye may scream the alarm, but I will deceive ye all! There is no magician who can outconjure the imagination of man."

Having mentally got rid of this fine sentence, I set myself regularly to work, and in a short space of time dashed off a stunning article on the hotel system of England as contrasted with that of America. If that paper was ever printed, it must have astonished the reader; for written as it was, under the influence of the enchantments of the Hotel de Coup d'OEil, it mixed up the real and the ideal in so inextricable a manner, that it read somewhat like a fusion of alternate passages from Murray's guide-book and the *Arabian Nights'* Entertainments. Such as it was, however, it being finished, I folded it up and sent it by the Hand, with my compliments to Count Goloptious, begging that he should at the same time be informed that I was hungry, and wanted my breakfast. My message whirred along the ten thousand Mouths, and faded away down into the hall below.

I had scarcely reentered my apartment when I heard the Blond Head open the window, and commence singing a strange wild sort of recitative, evidently with the view of attracting my attention. I listened, and found that it ran thus:—

*Rosamond sings:* "I have a bird, a bird, who was born today.

"Today the sunshine entered him through his eyes; his glittering wings rustled in the breath of the warm noon, and he began to live.

"He is merry and bold and wise, and is versed in the mysteries that are sung by the Unseen Spirits.

"Yet he knows not the mystical joys of the silently growing forests.

"No egg ever contained him.

"No down, white and silken, ever sheltered him from the cold.

"No anxious, bright-eyed mother ever brought him the oily grain of the millet to eat, or sat on the neighboring tree-tops, singing the holy hymns of maternal love.

"He never heard the sonorous melodies of the trees, when the wind with rushing fingers strikes the various notes of the forest, and Ash and Oak, Alder and Pine, are blent in the symphonic chords of the storm.

"Ten white fingers made him.

"The great sun—too far away to know what it was doing —hatched him into life, and in the supreme moment when his little heart just commenced to beat, and his magical blood to ebb and flow through the mystic cells of his frame, his maker cast from her lips, through his gaping golden bill, a stream of song, and gifted him with voice.

"This is the bird, bold and merry and wise, who will shake my salvation from his wings.

"Ah! until the hour of my delivery arrives, he shall be fed daintily on preserved butterflies, and shall scrape his bill on a shell of pearl!"

I opened my window as the last words of this strange song died away, and I had scarcely done so when a bright green bird, with an orange bill and cinnamon-colored legs, flew from Rosamond's window into my room, and perched on the table. It was a charming bird. Its shape was somewhat like that of the mockingbird—long, slender body, piquant head, and sweeping tail. Its color was of the most dazzling green, and its feathers shone like satin.

"Good morning, pretty bird," said I, holding out my finger to my visitor, who immediately flew to my hand and established himself there.

"Good morning," answered the Green Bird, in a voice so like Rosamond's that I was startled; "I am come to breakfast with you."

As the Green Bird spoke, a small bright feather dropped from its wing and fell slowly to the ground.

"I am delighted to have your society," I replied, with the utmost courtesy, "but I fear that I shall not be able to offer you any preserved butterflies. Nay, I have not as much as a beetle in pickle."

"Don't mention it," said the bird, with an off-hand flirt of his tail; "I can put up with anything. Besides, you know, one can always fall back on eggs."

To my surprise another bright green feather disengaged itself from the bird's plumage, and floated softly towards the carpet.

"Why, you'll lose all your feathers," said I. "Are you moulting?"

"No," answered the bird, "but I am gifted with speech on the condition that I shall lose a feather every time I use the faculty. When I lose all my feathers, which I calculate will not take place for about a year, I shall invent some artificial ornithological covering."

"Gracious!" I exclaimed, "what a figure—of speech you will be!"

At this moment the usual knock was heard at my door, on opening which I discovered a large tray covered with a snowy cloth, on which were placed a number of small porcelain covers, some bottles of red and white wine, a silver coffee-service, in short, everything necessary for a good breakfast.

## X    BREAKFAST,
## ORNITHOLOGICALLY CONSIDERED.

In a few moments my repast was arranged on the table, at which I seated myself, the Green Bird perching on the edge of a pretty dish of scarlet fruits at which he pecked, occasionally moistening his golden bill in the slender glass of Barsac which I placed near him.

"Breakfast," said the bird, looking at me with a glance of undisguised contempt while I was devouring a plate of *rognons au vin de champagne*—"breakfast is a meal utterly misinterpreted by human beings. What can be more unhealthy or more savage than the English or American breakfast? The latter is a miracle of indigestibility. The elastic, hot cakes. The tough, over-cooked meats. The half-boiled, muddy coffee. The half-baked, alum-tempered bread. Breakfast should be a light meal, invigorating, yet not overloading—fruits to purify the palate and the physical system, and a little red wine to afford nourishment to the frame, and enable it to go through the work of the day. In the morning man arises refreshed, not exhausted; his frame needs but little support; it is only when the animal vitality has been used up by a hard day's labor, that the meal of succulent and carbonized food is required. The French make their breakfast too elaborate; the English too heavy; the Americans too indigestible."

"Am I to understand, then," I asked, "that birds breakfast more sensibly than men?"

"Certainly," replied the Green Bird. "What is more delicate, and at the same time more easy of digestion, than the mucilaginous Caterpillar? The Dragon-fly, when carefully stripped of its corselet, is the lobster of the Insectivora. The green *acarus* is a dainty morsel, and the yellow roses sigh with relief when we gobble up their indolent enemy. The *coccinella,* or Lady-bird, is our turtle: with what dexterity is he stript of his upper shell and eaten palpitating!

"But the chief hygienic feature about the breakfast of us birds is, that we exercise in order that we may eat. Supposing the Blackbird, on withdrawing his head from under his crimson epaulet in the early morning, were merely to yawn, and stretch his wings, and, hopping lazily down branch by branch to the pool at the bottom of the tree on which he roosts, take his bath. That finished, we will suppose him retreating to his covert, when he rings a bell made of the blue campanula, and, being answered by an attendant Tom Tit, commands breakfast to be served. Tom Tit disappears, and after the usual absence returns with a meal of beetles, caterpillars, ripe cherries, and wild honey, neatly served on a satiny leaf of the Maple. Blackbird falls to and gorges himself. What an unhealthy bird he would be, compared with the Blackbird as he really is, stretching his wings at the first light of dawn, and setting off on a foraging expedition through the woods and fields! What glorious exercise and excitement there are in this chase after a breakfast! How all the physical powers are cultivated! The sight is sharpened. There is not a cranny in the bark of a tree, or a crevice in the earth, that the eye of the hungry bird does not penetrate. The extremist tip of the tail of a burrowing worm cannot remain undiscovered; he is whipped out and eaten in a moment. Then the long flight through the fresh air; the delicious draught of cool dew taken from time to time; the—"

"But," said I, interrupting the Green Bird, who I began to perceive was an interminable talker, "how is it possible for men to have the opportunity of pursuing their meals in the manner you describe? It would indeed present rather a ridiculous appearance, if at six o'clock in the morning I were to sally out, and run all over the fields turning up stones in order to find fried smelts, and diving into a rabbit burrow in the hope of discovering mutton chops *en papillotes.*"

"If I were a man," said the Green Bird, sententiously, "I would have my meals carefully concealed by the servants in various places, and then set to work to hunt them out. It would be twice as healthy as the present indolent method."

Here he took another sip at the Barsac, and looked at me so

queerly that I began to have a shrewd suspicion that he was drunk.

A brilliant idea here flashed across my mind. I would intoxicate the Green Bird, and worm out of him the reason why it was that the Blond Head was never able to stretch farther out of her window than the shoulders. The comicality of a drunken bird also made me favorable to the idea.

"As far as eating goes," said I, "I think that you are perhaps right; but as to drinking, you surely will not compare your insipid dew to a drink like this!" and, as I spoke, I poured out a glass of Richebourg, and handed it to the bird.

He dipped his bill gravely in it, and took one or two swallows.

"It is a fine wine," he said sententiously, "but it has a strong body. I prefer the Barsac. The red wine seems to glow with the fires of earth, but the white wine seems illumined by the sunlight of heaven."

And the Green Bird returned to his Barsac.


XI      LEG-BAIL.

"So the fair Rosamond made you," I said carelessly.

"Yes, from terra-cotta," answered the Green Bird; "and having been baked and colored, I came to life in the sun. I love this white wine, because the sun, who is my father, is in it"; and he took another deep draught.

"What induced her to construct you?" I asked.

"Why, with a view of escaping from this place, of course."

"O, then you are to assist her to escape?"

"Not at all—you are to assist her. I will furnish her with the means."

"What means?"

"With the wings."

"The what?" I asked, somewhat astonished.

"The wings!"

"What the deuce does she want of wings? She is not going

to escape by the window, is she?".

"Ha, ha, ha! Ho, ho, ho! He asks what Rosamond wants of wings!" And the bird, overcome with laughter at the ludicrousness of some esoteric jest, tumbled into his glass of Barsac, from which I rescued him draggled and dripping, all the more draggled as during our conversation he had been continually shedding his feathers.

"Well, what does she want of wings?" I asked, rather angrily, because a man does not like to see people laughing at a joke into the secret of which he is not admitted.

"To fly with," replied the Green Bird, nearly choking with the involuntary draught of white wine he had swallowed during his immersion.

"But why does she want to fly?"

"Because she has no legs—that's the reason she wants to fly," said the bird, a little crossly.

"No legs!" I repeated, appalled at this awful intelligence—"no legs! O, nonsense! you must be joking."

"No, I'm choking," answered the Green Bird.

"Why, she is like Miss Biffin, then, born without legs. Heavens! what a pity that so lovely a head shouldn't have a leg to stand on!"

"She wasn't born without legs," replied the Bird. "Her legs are down stairs."

"You don't mean to say that they have been amputated?"

"No. Count Goloptious was afraid she would escape; and as he wanted only her bust, that is, her brain, hands, and arms, he just took her legs away and put them in the storeroom. He'll take your legs away some day, too, you'll find. He wants nothing but heads in this hotel."

"Never!" I exclaimed, horror-stricken at the idea. "Sooner than part with my legs, I'd—"

"Take arms against him I suppose. Well, *nous verrons*. Gracious! what a lot of feathers I have shed!" suddenly continued the Bird, looking down at a whole pile of green feathers that lay on the floor. "I'm talking too much. I shan't have a feather left soon if I go on at this rate. By the way, where is your mirror? I must reproduce myself."

## XII    HOLDING THE MIRROR UP TO NATURE.

I handed the Green Bird a small dressing-glass which lay on the bureau—I mean, I placed it before him, for the impossibility of *handing* a bird anything will strike even the most uncultivated mind—and seated myself to watch his proceedings with a considerable amount of curiosity.

I wish, before proceeding any further, to make a few random remarks on the looking-glass in America.

I take a certain natural pride in my personal appearance. It is of no consequence if my nose is a trifle too long, my chin too retreating, or my head too angular. I flatter myself that the elegance of a man's appearance does not depend on his individual traits, but upon his *tout ensemble*. I feel, when regarding myself in a well-constituted mirror, that, in spite of any trifling defects in detail, my figure on the whole is rather *distingue*.

In the matter of mirrors, I have suffered. The hotel and boarding-house keepers of this country—actuated doubtless by a wholesome desire to crush that pet fly called "vanity," with which the Devil angles for human souls—have, I am convinced, entered into a combination against the admiration of the human face divine by its owner.

Like Proteus, I find myself changing my shape wherever I go. At the Bunkum House, I am a fat boy. At the St. Bobolink, a living skeleton. Once I was seriously alarmed on inspecting myself for the first time in the glass—on an occasion when I had just taken possession of a new boarding-house—at discovering that one of my eyebrows was in the middle of my forehead. I had been informed by a medical student—since plucked—from whom I derived most of my chirugical information, that paralysis not unfrequently produced such effects. I descended in some trepidation to the parlor, where I had an interesting interview with my landlady, who succeeded in removing the unpleasant impression from my mind that I was a victim to that unbecoming disease.

The glass was not, however, changed, and I never looked in it and beheld that eyebrow in the middle of my forehead, without the disagreeable sensation that in the end I should die a Cyclops.

The glass which I placed before the Green Bird possessed, I regret to say, certain defects in the plane of its surface which rendered self-contemplation by its aid anything but an agreeable occupation. I know no man egotist enough to—as the novels say—"spend hours before" such a mirror.

The Green Bird, as soon as he beheld himself in this abominable mirror, uttered a scream of disgust. I must say that, on looking over his shoulder, the image formed by him in the glass was not a graceful one. He was humped, one leg was shorter than the other, and his neck looked as if it had just been wrung by a schoolboy.

What attracted my attention most, however, were certain peculiarities in the reflected image itself. It scarcely seemed a reflection. It was semi-substantial, and stood out from the surface of the glass in a sort of half-relief, that grew more and more positive every moment. In a few seconds more, the so-called image detached itself from the mirror, and hopped out on the table, a perfect counterpart of the Green Bird, only humped, with one leg shorter than the other, and a wry neck. It was an ornithological caricature.

The Green Bird itself now sidled away from its position before the mirror, and the Caricature Bird took his place. If the image cast by the former was distorted, no words can convey the deformity of the image cast by the latter. It was a feathered cripple. It was all hump. It stood on one long attenuated leg. Its neck was tortuous as the wall of Troy.

This rickety, ornithological image produced itself in the mirror, in precisely the same fashion as did its predecessor, and, after gradually growing into substance, detached itself from the polished surface, and came out upon the table, taking its position before the mirror, *vice* the first humpback resigned.

What the image cast by the third bird was like I cannot at all attempt to portray. It was a chaos of neck and humps and feathers. The reproduction, nevertheless, went on, and the prolific mirror kept sending forth a stream of green abortions, that after a little while were no longer recognizable as belonging to any species of animal in the earth below, or the heavens above, or the caverns that lie under the earth. They filled my room. Swarms of limping, wall-eyed, one-legged, green-feathered things hustled each other on the floor. My bed was alive with a plumed mass of deformity. They filled the air, making lame efforts at flight, and blindly falling to the floor, where they tumbled about in inextricable confusion. The whole atmosphere seemed thick with green feathers. Myriads of squinting eyes glittered before me. Quintillions of paralytic yellow bills crookedly gaped at me.

I felt myself treading on a thick carpet of soft, formless life. The fluttering of embryonic wings, the twittering of sickly voices, the ruffling of lusterless plumages, produced a continuous and vague sound that filled me with horror. I was knee-deep in the creatures. From out the distorting mirror they poured in a constant stream, like a procession of nightmares, and the tide-mark of this sea of plumage rose higher and higher every instant. I felt as if I was about to be suffocated—as if I was drowning in an ocean of Green Birds. They were on my shoulders. Nestling in my hair. Crooning their loathsome notes into my ear. Filling my pockets, and brushing with their warm fuzzy breasts against my cheek. I grew wild with terror, and, making one desperate effort, struggled through the thick mass of life that pressed like a wall around me to the window, and, flinging it open, cried in a despairing voice: "Rosamond! Rosamond! Save me, Rosamond!"

XIII    A STUPID CHAPTER, AND I KNOW IT.

"What's the matter?" cried the Blond Head, appearing at her window, with all her curls in a flurry.

"Your Green Bird," I answered, "has been misconducting himself in the most abominable manner. He—"

"You surely have not let him get at a mirror?" screamed Rosamond.

"Unfortunately I have; and pretty things he has been doing with it. My room is full of Green Birds. If you don't call them away, or tell me how to get rid of them, I shall be killed, as the persons suspected of hydrophobia were formerly killed in Ireland, that is, I shall be smothered by a featherbed.''

"What a wretch of a bird to waste himself in such a foolish way, when he was so particularly wanted! But rest a moment. I will rid you of your unpleasant company.''

So saying, Rosamond withdrew her head from the window, and in a second or two afterwards a long shrill whistle came from her room, wild and penetrating as the highest notes of the oboe. The instant the Green Birds heard it, they all commenced jostling and crushing towards the open window, out of which they tumbled in a continual stream. As scarcely any of them could fly, only a few succeeded in reaching the sill of Rosamond's casement—the goal towards which they all struggled. The rest fell like a green cataract on the hard flags with which the yard underneath my window was paved. In this narrow enclosure they hustled, and crawled, and limped, and writhed, till the place, filled with such a mass of feathered decrepitude, resembled an ornithological *Cour des Miracles*.

So soon as my room was cleared of the bird multitude, I commenced sweeping up the mass of green feathers which lay on the floor, and which had been shed by the original Green Bird, during his conversation with me at breakfast. While engaged in this task, I heard a laugh which seemed to come from my immediate neighborhood. I turned, and there sat the Green Bird on the mantelpiece, arranging what feathers he had left with his bill.

"What," I said, "are *you* there? Why, I thought you had gone with the rest of them!"

"Go with such *canaille* as that set!" answered the Green Bird, indignantly. "Catch me at it! I don't associate with such creatures.''

"Then, may I ask, why the deuce did you produce all this *canaille* in my room, Green Bird?"

"It was your own fault. I intended to produce a few respectable and well-informed Green Birds, who would have been most entertaining society for you in your solitude, and materially aided you in your projects against Count Goloptious. But you presented me with a crooked mirror, and, instead of shapely and well-behaved Green Birds, I gave birth to a crowd of deformed and ill-mannered things, of no earthly use to themselves or anyone else. The worst of it is, they will build nests in the yard underneath, and bring forth myriads of callow deformities, so that unless they are instantly destroyed you will have no peace from them.''

"I'll shoot them.''

"Where's your gun?''

"Well, then, I'll fish for them with a rod, line, and hook, as the Chinese fish for swallows, and then wring their necks.''

"Poosh! that won't do. They'll breed faster than you can catch them. However, you need not trouble yourself about them; when the time comes I'll rid you of them. I owe you something for having caused this trouble; beside, your Barsac was very good.''

"Will you take another glass?'' I said.

"No, thank you,'' politely replied the Green Bird. "I have drunk enough already. About those feathers'' (I had just swept the green feathers up into a little heap)—''what are you going to do with them?''

"To burn them, of course. I can't have them littering my room.''

"My dear sir,'' said the Green Bird, "those feathers are immensely valuable. They will be needed to make Rosamond's wings. Put them into one of the drawers of the bureau, until they are wanted.''

I obeyed.


## XIV    ON THE ADVANTAGES OF MARRYING A WITCH.

"Now,'' continued the bird, "what are your plans for escape?''

"I haven't any, except a general idea of throttling Goloptious the next time he comes in here, gagging the Mouths, handcuffing the Hands, and bunging up all the Eyes, and then bolting somewhere or other with the Blond Head—that is, if we can recover her legs—say to Grace Church, where, with the blessing of Brown, we can become man and wife."

"Are you not afraid to marry a sorceress?"

"Why should I be? Haven't I been continually calling every woman with whom I have been in love an enchantress; and writing lots of verses about the 'spells' with which she encompassed me; and the magic of her glance, and the witchery of her smile? I'm not at all sorry, if the truth must be confessed, to meet an enchantress at last. She will afford me continual amusement. I need never go to see Professor Wyman, or Herr Dobler, or Robert Houdin. I can get up a little Parlor Magic whenever I choose. Fancy the pleasure of having Genii for servants, just like Aladdin! No Irish Biddies, to overroast your beef, and underboil your potatoes; to 'fix' her mop of capillary brushwood with your private, particular hairbrush; to drink your brandy and then malign the cat; to go out on Sunday evenings, 'to see his Reverence Father McCarthy,' touching some matter connected with the confessional, and come home towards midnight drunk as an owl; to introduce at two in the morning, through the convenient postern of the basement, huge 'cousins,' whose size prevents you from ejecting them with the speed they merit, and who impudently finish their toddies before they obey your orders to quit. Genii have no cousins, I believe. Happy were the people in the days of Haroun Al Raschid.

"On these grounds I esteem it a privilege to marry a witch. If you want dinner, all you have got to do is to notify your wife. She does something or other, kills a black hen, or draws a circle in chalk, and lo! an attendant Genius, who lived four years in his last place, appears, and immediately produces an exquisite repast, obtained by some inscrutable means, known only to the Genii, and you dine, without having the slightest care as to marketing, or butcher's or baker's bills.

"Then again, if your wife knits you a purse, what more easy for her than to construct it after the pattern of Fortunatus's? If she embroiders you a pair of slippers, they can just as well as not be made on the last of the seven-league boots. Your smoking-cap can possess the power of conferring invisibility like that of Fortunio.

"You can have money when you want. You can dress better at church than any of her acquaintances, because all the treasures of Solomon are at her disposal, to say nothing of those belonging to Jamshid. You can travel faster than any locomotive. You can amuse yourself with inspecting the private lives of your friends. You can win at cards when you desire it. You can at any moment take up your drawing-room carpet, and make it sail away with you and all your earthly possession to Minnesota, if you please. You can buy a block on Fifth Avenue, and build a palace in a night, and, in short, be always young, handsome, wealthy, happy, and respected. Marry an enchantress! why, it's even more profitable than marrying a Spirit Medium!"

"So you intend to marry Rosamond," remarked the Green Bird, with the slightest sneer in the world.

"Certainly. Why not?"

"I don't see how you're to do it. She has not got any legs, and may not be able to get away from here. You won't have any legs in a day or two. You are both in the power of Count Goloptious; and, even if you were to escape from your rooms, you would not be able to find the way out of the Hotel de Coup d'OEil."

"If I were forced to walk on my hands, I would bear Rosamond away from this cursed den of enchantment."

"An excellent speech for Ravel to make," replied the Green Bird, "but I fancy that your education as an Acrobat has been neglected."

"I think I see at what you are aiming," I answered. "You want to make terms. How much do you want to assist Rosamond and myself to escape? I learn from her song that you know the ropes."

"I know the stairs and the doors," said the Green Bird, indignantly, "and that is more to the purpose."

"Well, if you show us the way to get free, I will give you a golden cage."

"Good."

"You shall have as much hemp-seed as you can eat."

"Excellent."

"And as much Barsac as you can drink."

"No," here the Green Bird shook his head; "I won't drink any more of your wine, but I want every morning a saffron cocktail."

"A what?"

"A saffron cocktail. Saffron is our delight, not only of a shiny night, but also of a shiny morning, in all seasons of the year. It is the Congress Water of birds."

"Well, you shall have a saffron cocktail."

"And fresh groundsel every day."

"Agreed."

"Then I am yours. I will give my plot."

## THE GREEN BIRD MAKES A PLOT WHICH DIFFERS FROM ALL OTHER CONTEMPORARY PLOTS IN BEING SHORT AND SWEET.

"Sir," said the Green Bird, "you wish to escape."

"Undoubtedly."

"The chief enemies which you have at present to fear are the Hands that clutch, and the Mouths that betray."

"I am aware of that fact."

"It is necessary that you should visit Rosamond's room."

"I would give my life to accomplish such a call."

"All you want to enable you to accomplish it is a couple of lead-pencils and a paper of pins."

"Well?"

"Well, that's my plot. Order them at the Ear, and when you get them I will show you how to use them"; and the Green Bird ruffled out his feathers and gave himself airs of mystery.

I immediately went to the Ear, and, removing the wax with which I had deafened it, ordered the articles as prescribed. I confess, however, that I was rather puzzled to know how with the aid of two lead-pencils and a paper of pins I was to baffle the spells of Goloptious.

## XV    PREPARATIONS FOR FLIGHT.

While awaiting the arrival of the desired articles, I heard
Rosamond calling me through the window. I immediately
obeyed the summons.

"An idea has just struck me," said the Blond Head. "I am
exceedingly anxious, as you know, to get away from here,
and I have no doubt with your aid might succeed in doing so,
but how am I to take my trunks?"

"Your what?"

"Trunks. You did not suppose, surely, that I was staying
here without a change of dress."

"I always thought that imprisoned heroines contrived in
some miraculous manner to get along without fresh linen. I
have known, in the early days of my novel-reading, a young
lady run through six volumes, in the course of which she was
lost in forests, immersed in lakes, and imprisoned in dun-
geons, in a single white skirt and nothing on her head. I often
thought what a color that white skirt must have been at the end
of the novel."

"O," said Rosamond, "I have quite a wardrobe here."

"Well, I'm afraid you'll have to leave it behind."

"What! leave all those ducks of dresses behind! Why, I'd
rather stay here forever than part with them. It's so like a man
to say, in the coolest manner in the world, 'Leave them
behind.' " And the Blond Head here agitated her curls with
a certain tremulous motion, indicative of some indignation.

"My dear, you need not be angry," I said soothingly.
"Perhaps, after all, we can manage to get your trunks away
also. How much luggage have you got?"

"I will read you the list I made of it," answered
Rosamond.

This is her list—I jotted it down at the time in pencil. The
remarks are my own:—

One large trunk, banded with iron, and containing my
evening dresses.

One large square trunk containing my bonnets, two dozen.

(The excusable vanity of an individual having nothing but a head.)

One cedar chest containing my furs. (At this point I ventured a joke about a cedar chest being a great deal too good for such minkses. I was promptly suppressed by the dignified statement that they were sables.)

One circular box for carrying the incompressible skirt. (Doubtless an expansive package.)

A bird-cage.

A case for artificial flowers.

A feather case. (Containing the last feather which is supposed to be fatal to the Camel.)

A willow basket for bonnets. (More bonnets!)

Three large trunks. (Contents not stated—suspicious circumstance.)

Four small trunks. (What male who has ever travelled with a lady does not remember with terror her *small* parcels? The big ones gravitate naturally to the baggage-car; but you are requested to see after the little ones yourself. You carry them in your arms, tenderly, as if they were so many babies. What lamentations if they slip—and they are always doing it—and fall in the street! Something very precious must be inside. In the cars, you have to stow them away under the seat so that you have no room for your legs. Woe to you if one is lost or mislaid. It always contains *the* very thing of all others which the owner would not have lost for worlds.)

A bandbox. (The bandbox is the most terrible apparatus connected with the locomotion of females. It refuses utterly to accommodate itself to travel. Its lid comes off. It will fit into no shaped vehicle. Of its own accord it seems to place itself in positions favorable to its being sat upon. When crushed or in any way injured, it is capable of greater shabbiness of appearance than any other article of luggage.)

A dressing-case.

A portable bath.

An easel. (Easily carried.)

Three boxes of books. (A porter who was once removing my luggage called my attention to the weight of the box in which I had packed my books. They were certainly very heavy, and yet I had selected them with the greatest care.)

Here Rosamond stopped, and then proposed going over the list again, as she was sure she had forgotten something.

I respectfully declined the repetition, but asked her by what possible means she expected to transport such a quantity of luggage out of the Hotel de Coup d'OEil.

"You and the Green Bird can manage it, I suppose," she answered; "and I wish you would make haste, for I am getting very weary of not being able to walk. I shall enjoy so having my legs back again."

"Have you any idea where Count Goloptious put them?"

"O yes. They are in some cellar or other in a bin, with a number of other legs."

"Are the bins numbered?"

"Certainly."

"Do you know the number of your bin?"

"No. How should I?"

"It strikes me as rather awkward that you do not. For supposing that the Green Bird and myself succeed in getting down stairs in search of your legs, if we don't know the number of the bin we shall have some difficulty in finding the right ones, and it would be very disagreeable if you had to walk off with another person's legs."

"I never thought of that," said Rosamond, gravely. "A misfit would be horribly uncomfortable."

## XVI    A THRILLING CHAPTER.

We were certainly in a very unpleasant fix. To go down stairs on a wild-goose chase among the bins in search of the legs of the Blond Head would be anything but agreeable.

"Can you not make any pair do for the present?" I asked.

"Any pair? Certainly not. Could you get along with any other head but your own?"

The question rather took me aback. I confessed that such a change was not at all to be desire.

"Then go," said the Blond Head, "and search for them."

"Faint heart," etc.; a musty adage came into my head, and I answered, "I will do so." Turning to the Green Bird, I asked, "Will you come to the cellars?"

"Yes, at once," was the answer.

"Lead the way, then; you must be better acquainted here than I am."

The Green Bird led the way down the stairs, with all the hands before us; but not one moved now. Down! down! at least an hundred flights, then through a hall, and into a vast chamber black as midnight.

"How are we to find the legs in this plutonian darkness?" I asked.

"Silence!" said the Green Bird, and a falling feather aroused an echo that sounded like the beating of an hundred drums; "speak not if you would succeed!"

In silence I followed on through the cavernous chamber with its pitchy walls—on, still on. At last a small blue light appeared burning in the distance like the eye of a tiger. As we approached, it gradually increased in size, until, at last, as we neared it, it became magnified into an opening some sixty feet wide. Beyond, burned a lake of deadly blue sulphur, shedding a pale unearthly light. As we passed through the opening, a figure suddenly appeared before us. It was that of an old man. He carried a stick in his right hand, and walked with a feeble gait, but, what struck me as rather peculiar, his head, instead of being on his shoulders, he carried under his left arm.

"Who are you?" he asked, speaking from the head under his arm.

"I am an author," I replied.

"Look there?" he said, as he pointed to the burning lake.

I looked, and beheld what I had not before noticed. It was inhabited. Hundreds of poor wretches were there, burning and writhing in the seething flame.

"Who are those wretched beings?" I queried, in terror.

"Ha! ha! ha!" laughed the old man. "Those are authors!"

"Why doomed to a residence here?"

"Because, when on the earth beyond, they failed to fulfil their mission. They lost sight of their goal. They digressed from the path of honor. They—''

"I see. They went it blind."

"Exactly."

"There," and he pointed to a floating head near the edge of the lake—"there is a plagiarist. His is the A No. 1 degree. There," and he pointed to another, "is one who published and edited a newspaper."

"His offense?" I asked.

"Blackmailing. There is one who wrote flash novels."

"Jack Sheppard. *The Bhoys,*" I muttered.

"Ay; you be wise; avoid the broad path; keep faith; be true. And now what seek you here?"

I told him my errand.

"And you hope to find the legs?"

"I do."

"Come, then, with me. Here, carry my head."

I took the head, and, with the Green Bird by my side, followed the singular old man. He led us round by the lake, so close that, at times, the heat seemed to scorch my clothing. Presently he stopped opposite a great door of blue veined marble. Pushing that open, we entered a large and brilliantly lighted apartment. Here, upon every side, countless legs protruded from the wall. As we entered, the legs all at once commenced kicking as though they would eject us from their abode.

The old man took his head from us, and, putting it under his arm, commanded the legs to desist from their threatening attitudes. In an instant they all fell dormant.

"Here," he said, "are the legs of all who have ever slept in the Hotel de Coup d'OEil, and here you will find those of the Blond Head."

"But how am I to know them?" I said.

"That I cannot tell you."

"I can tell them," said the Green Bird, now speaking for the first time since we left the darkness; and it flew around the room, stopping to look at now one pair of legs, now another. At last it stopped opposite a remarkably crooked pair of limbs. "Here they are," he said.

"Nonsense! it cannot be. Such a beauty as the Blond Head

never propelled on such pedals as those."

"It is true," answered the bird. "Take them down, and see." I seized the legs, and with a sudden jerk pulled them from their place. What was my surprise on finding Count Goloptious before me. The legs were his.

"Ha!" he exclaimed, "you would trick me, but I have watched you. The Blond Head is safe."

"Safe!" I echoed.

"Ay, safe, safe in my stronghold, the Hotel de Coup d'OEil."

" 'Tis false!" cried the Green Bird. "She is here!" As it spoke, it flew to a small door in the wall which I had not before noticed. Tapping with its beak against it, it opened instantly, and, looking in, I beheld the Blond Head complete. Never did I behold a being so beautiful as she seemed to me at that glance. Grace, beauty, voluptuousness—well, imagine all the extensive descriptions of female loveliness you have ever read in two-shilling novels, put them all altogether, and pile on as much more, and then you have her description.

"Fair Rosamond," I exclaimed, as I started forward to gain her—"Fair Rosamond, you shall be saved."

"Never!" cried Count Goloptious—"never! Beware, rash youth! You have dared to criticize Italian opera, you have dared write political leaders, you have dared theatrical managers, you have dared a fickle public—all this you have done, but brave not me. If you would be safe, if you value your life, go, depart in peace!"

As he spoke, I felt the chivalric blood fast coursing through my veins. Go, and leave the fair being I loved in the power of a monster? No, I resolved upon the instant that I would die with her, or I would have her free.

"Count," I exclaimed in passionate tones, "I defy thee. I will never forsake yon wretched lady."

"Then your doom is sealed." He stamped three times upon the floor, and instantly the Green Bird disappeared. The place was wrapped in darkness. I felt myself borne through the murky, foul air of the cavern through which we had first passed, with the rapidity of a cannon-ball. Emerging from it,

I found myself in the arms of the Count; by his side stood the old man with his head under his arm.

"Here," cried the Count, "is the nine hundred and twentieth. Eighty more, and we are free."

A demoniacal laugh burst from the old man as he took me, unable to resist him, from Goloptious. "Go, go to your brother authors, to the blue lake of oblivion. Go," he exclaimed with a sardonic bitterness, as he pitched me from him into the burning lake.

A wild shriek. The burning sulphur entered my ears, my eyes, my mouth. My senses were going, when suddenly a great body, moving near, struck me. The liquid opened, and closed over me. I found myself going down, down. At last, I struck the bottom. One long scream of agony, and—

## XVII    HOW IT ALL HAPPENED.

"Good gracious! is that you? Why, how came you there?"
    "Dunno."
    "Bless me, you've almost frozen. Come, up with you."
    "What! Bunkler, that you? Where's the Blond Head?"
    "Blond what? You've been drinking."
    "Where's Count Goloptious?"
    "Count the deuce; you're crazy."
    "Where's the Green Bird?"
    "You're a Green Bird, or you wouldn't lie there in the snow. Come, get up."

In an instant I was awake. I saw it all. "What's the time?" I asked.

    "Just two!"

Could all that have happened in an hour! Yes. The Hotel de Coup d'OEil. The Blond Head. The Green Bird. The Count. The Blue Lake. The Hands. The Legs. The Eyes, the everything singular, were the creations of Pilgarlik's Burgundy. I had slipped in the snow at the door, and was dreaming.

The cold had revived me, and I was now shivering. I arose. My friend and fellow-boarder, Dick Bunkler, who had been tripping it on the light fantastic toe at a ball in the Apollo, was before me; and lucky it was for me that he had gone to that ball, for had I lain there all night, the probability is Coroner Connery would have made a V off my body, next day.

"How came you to lie there *outside* the door?" asked Dick.

"The door is fast; my night-key wouldn't work."

"Night-key! ha! ha! night-key!"

I looked at my hand, and beheld what? My silver pencil-case,—the only piece of jewelry I ever possessed.

Dick opened the door, and in a very short time was engaged in manufacturing the "Nightcap" which I had promised myself an hour before. Over it I told my dream in the snow, and we enjoyed a hearty laugh at the effect of the bottle of Burgundy which passed from HAND TO MOUTH.

# BODY AND SOUL
## *by* SEABURY QUINN

Probably the most popular and most effective occult detective to have appeared in American fiction is the character of Jules de Grandin, the post-middle-aged mercurial Frenchman born in *Weird Tales* magazine, October, 1925 in "The Horror on the Links." Contrary to general belief, the story did not cause an immediate sensation; it scarcely was mentioned in the readers' columns and was not listed in the monthly ratings of the most popular stories. However, as the series continued, it seemed to grow upon the readers and, more important, upon the editor Farnsworth Wright, who regarded it as a circulation sustainer. Though the peak of their popularity was in the late twenties and the thirties, new Jules de Grandin stories continued to appear in *Weird Tales* right up until 1951, a period of twenty-six years.

Actually, Jules de Grandin was but a slight variation on French characters which Seabury Quinn ran in quite a few of his stories, including "The Phantom Farmhouse," his first for *Weird Tales* which appeared in October, 1923, but in de Grandin all the character elements coalesced.

Despite the longevity of the series and perpetual popularity, neither Jules de Grandin nor Seabury Quinn have had anything close to the reprinting and critical appreciation of other weird tale authors such as H.P. Lovecraft, Robert E. Howard, Henry S. Whitehead, C.L. Moore, Henry Kuttner, Robert Bloch, Ray Bradbury, and numerous other frontliners.

The major reason is that there has been no Quinn champion to publicize his works nor any coterie to help keep his name alive. The first hardcover collection of Jules de Grandin stories appeared as recently as 1966 from the Mycroft &

Moran adjunct of Arkham House, Sauk City, Wisconsin, and it was published in a limited edition of only 2,000 copies as *The Phantom-Fighter*.

Though Jules de Grandin stories, from the first, were picked frequently for inclusion in the annual *Not at Night* series, published by Selwyn & Blount, London, and edited by Christine Campbell Thomson, these books had to be imported if Americans desired them. The first Jules de Grandin story to appear in an American anthology was "The House Where Time Stood Still," selected by Phil Strong for *The Other Worlds* (Wilfred Funk, 1941). There have been only a few other inclusions.

"Body and Soul" originally appeared in the September, 1928 *Weird Tales* and has never been reprinted. At the time of its publication Seabury Quinn resided at 34 Jefferson Ave., Brooklyn, N.Y., and received $115 for its 12,000 words. The rate of payment is an indication of his growing popularity, for his first story for *Weird Tales*, "The Phantom Farmhouse," was 8,400 words long and brought him but $40, indicating a rate increase of more than double in three years.

"Body and Soul" is a typical Jules de Grandin story of good quality. All of the idiosyncracies of the occult detective and his unofficial aide Dr. Trowbridge are brought into focus. The menace is actually supernatural (not all of Jules de Grandin's cases were), and the solution is a bit off-beat.

Seabury Quinn was actually a writer of above-average literary quality, but he wrote so much and at such odd hours that his work is uneven, sometimes within the story itself. This is true of "Body and Soul," but all is forgotten in the movement of the plot.

Quinn himself could easily have masqueraded for either de Grandin or Trowbridge. Small, slim, dapper, sharp-featured, at one period in his life he had the ideal profession for a writer of the supernatural—the editorship of a trade journal for morticians, entitled *Sunnyside and Casket!*

# BODY AND SOUL

by

**Seabury Quinn**

I had a strenuous day, for the mild epidemic of summer grippe had lasted over into September, and my round of calls had been double the usual number. "Thank heaven, I can relax for seven or eight hours," I murmured piously as I pulled the single blanket up around my chin and settled myself for the night. The hall clock had just struck twelve, and I had no appointments earlier than nine the following morning. "If only nobody is so inconsiderate as to break a leg or get the bellyache," I mumbled drowsily, "I'll not stir from this bed until—"

As if to demonstrate the futility of self-congratulation, there came a sudden thunderous clamor at the front door. Someone was beating the panels with both his fists, raining frenzied blows on the wood with his feet and shrieking at the top of his voice, "Let me in! Doctor—Dr. Trowbridge, let me in! For God's sake, let me in!"

"The devil!" I ejaculated, rising resentfully and feeling for my slippers and dressing-gown. "Couldn't he have had the decency to ring the bell?"

"Let me in, let me in, Dr. Trowbridge!" the frantic hail came again as I rounded the bed of the stairs. "Let me in—quick!"

"All right, all right!" I counseled testily, undoing the lock and chain-fastener. "Just a min—"

The caller ceased his battering-ram assault on the door as I swung it back and catapulted past me into the hall, almost carrying me off my feet as he did so. "Quick, shut it—shut the door!" he gasped, wheeling in his tracks to snatch the knob from my hand and force the door to. "It's out there—it's outside there, I tell you!"

"What the mischief—" I began, half puzzled, half angry, as I took quick stock of the intruder.

He was a young man, twenty-five or -six, I judged, dressed somewhat foppishly in a suit of mohair dinner clothes, his jacket and waistcoat badly rumpled, his once stiff evening shirt and collar reduced to a pulpy mass of sweat-soaked linen, and the foamy froth of drool disfiguring the corners of his flaccid mouth. As he turned on me to repeat his hysterical warning, I noticed that he caught his breath with considerable difficulty and that there was a strong hint of liquor in his speech.

"See here, young man, what do you mean?" I demanded sternly. "Haven't you any better sense than to knock a man out of bed at this ungodly hour to tell him that—"

"Ssssh!" he interrupted with the exaggerated caution of the half-tipsy. "Sssssh, Dr. Trowbridge, I think I hear it coming up the steps. Is the door locked? Quick, in here!" Snatching me by the arm he dragged me unceremoniously into the surgery.

"Now see here, confound you!" I remonstrated. "This is going a bit too far. If you expect to get away with this sort of thing, I'll mighty soon show you—"

"Trowbridge, *mon vieux*, what is it? What does the alarm portend?" Jules de Grandin, a delicate mauve-silk dressing-gown drawn over his lilac pajamas, slippers of violet snakeskin on his womanishly small feet, tiptoed into the room, his little blue eyes round with wonder and curiosity. "I thought I heard someone in extremity calling," he continued, looking from the visitor to me, then back again with his quick, stock-taking glance. "Is it that someone dies and requires our assistance through the door to the better world, or—"

"It looks as if some drunken young fool is trying to play a practical joke on us," I returned grimly, bending a stern look on the boy who cowered in the chair beside my desk. "I've half a mind to prescribe four ounces of castor oil and stand by while he takes it!"

De Grandin regarded the young man with his steady, unwinking stare a moment, then: "What frightens you, *mon brave?*" he demanded, far too gently, I thought. "*Parbleu*, but you look as though you had been playing tag with Satan himself!"

"I have—I have!" the youth replied quaveringly. "I tell you, it jumped at me just as I came past the park entrance, and I wasn't a hundred yards ahead when Dr. Trowbridge let me in!"

"U'm?" the Frenchman twisted the ends of his little blond mustache meditatively. "And this 'It' which pursued you, it is what?"

"I don't know," the other responded. "I was walking home from a dance at the Sigma Delta Tau house—been stagging it, you know—and stopped by the Victory Monument to light a cigarette when something—dam' if I know what—jumped out o' the bushes at me and made a grab at my throat. It missed my neck by a couple o' inches, but snatched my hat, and I didn't take any time to see what it would do next. I'd 'a' been going yet if my wind hadn't given out, and I happened to think that Dr. Trowbridge lives in this block and that he'd most likely be up, or within call, anyhow, so I rushed up the steps and hammered on the door till he let me in.

"Will you let me stay here overnight?" he concluded, turning to me appealingly. "I'm Dick Ratliff—Henry Ratliff's nephew, you know—and honest, Doctor, I'm scared stiff to go out in that street again till daylight."

"H'm," I murmured judicially, surveying the young fool reflectively. He was not a bad-looking boy—quite otherwise—and I could well imagine he presented a personable enough appearance when his clothing was in better array and his head less fuddled with bad liquor. "How much have you had to drink tonight, young man?"

"Two drinks, sir," he returned promptly, looking me squarely in the eye, and, though my better judgment told me he was lying like a witness at a Senate investigation, I believed him.

"I think you're a damn fool," I told him with more candor than courtesy. "You were probably so full of rotgut that your own shadow gave you a start back there by the park gate, and you've been trying to outrace it for the last four blocks. You'll be heartily ashamed of yourself in the morning, but I've a spare bed, and you may as well sleep off your debauch here as in some police station, I suppose."

"Thank you, sir," he answered humbly. "I don't blame you for thinking I've got the jimjams—I know my story sounds crazy—but I'm telling you the truth. Something did jump out at me, and almost succeeded in grabbing me by the throat. It wasn't just imagination, and it wasn't booze, either, but—my God, *look!*"

The exclamation ended in a shrill crescendo, and the lad half leaped from his chair, pointing with a shaking forefinger at the little window over the examination table, then slumped back as though black-jacked, his hands falling limply to the floor, his head lolling drunkenly forward on his breast.

Both de Grandin and I wheeled about, facing the window. "Good lord!" I exclaimed as my gaze penetrated the shining, night-backed panes.

"*Grand Dieu—c'est le diable en personne!*" the little Frenchman cried.

Staring into the dimly lighted room was such a visage as might bring shudders of horripilation to a bronze statue. It was a long, cadaverous face, black with the dusky hue of old and poorly cured rawhide, bony as a death's-head, yet covered with a multitude of tiny horizontal wrinkles. The fleshless, leathery lips were drawn back from a set of broken and discolored teeth which reminded me somehow of the cruel dentition of a shark, and the corded, rugous neck supporting the withered face was scarcely thicker than a man's wrist. From the bare, black scalp there hung a single lock of coarse, straggling hair. But terrible as the features were, terrifying as were the unfleshed lips and cheeks and brow, the tiny, deep-set eyes almost fallen backward from their sockets were even more horrible. Small as the eyes of a rodent, set, unwavering in their stare, they reminded me, as they gleamed with hellish malevolence in their settings of shrunken, wrinkled skin, of twin poisonous spiders awaiting the chance to pounce upon their prey. It might have been a trick of the lamplight, but to me it seemed that the organs shone with a diabolical luminance of their own as they regarded us with a sort of mirthless smile.

"Good heavens, what is it?" I choked, half turning to my companion, yet keeping most of my glance fixed on the baneful, hypnotic orbs glaring at me through the window-pane.

"God knows," returned de Grandin, "but by the belly of Jonah's whale, we shall see if he be proof against shot and powder!" Whipping a tiny Ortgies automatic from his dressing-gown pocket he brought its blunt muzzle in line with the window and pressed the trigger. Seven, eight shots rang out so quickly that the last seemed no more than the echo of the first; the plate glass pane was perforated like a sieve within an area of three square inches; and the sharp, acrid smell of smokeless powder bit the mucous membrane of my nostrils.

"After him, Friend Trowbridge!" de Grandin cried, flinging aside the empty pistol and bolting through the door, down the hallway and across the porch. *"Barbe d'une oie,* but we shall see how he liked the pills I dealt him!"

The September moon rode serenely in the dark-blue sky; a little vagrant breeze, coming from the bay, rustled the boughs of the curbside maple trees; and from the downtown section there came to us, faintly, the muted clangor of the all-night trolley cars and the occasional hoot of a cruising taxicab's horn. After the bedlam of the Frenchman's shots the early autumn night seemed possessed of a stillness which bore in on our eardrums like a tangible sound, and, like visitors in an empty church, we pursued our quest in silence, communicating only in low, breathless whispers. From house to hedge, over lawn and rosebed and tennis court we pushed our search, scanning every square inch of land. peering under rosebushes and rhododendron plants, even turning over the galvanized iron trash-can which stood by my kitchen stoop. No covert large enough to have shielded a rat did we leave unexplored, yet of the awful thing which had gazed through the surgery window we found no sign or trace, though we hunted till the eastern sky began to pale with streaks of rose and pearl and amethyst and the rattling milk carts broke the nighttime quiet with their early-morning clatter.

"Good mornin', Dr. de Grandin."

Detective Sergeant Costello rose from his seat in the consulting room as de Grandin and I entered. " 'Tis sorry I am to be disturbin' ye so early in th' mornin', more especially as I know what store ye set by yer breakfast"—he grinned broadly at his sally—"but th' fact is, sor, there's been a tidy little murder committed up th' street, an' I'm wondering if ye'd be discommodin' yerself to th' extent o' comin' up to Professor Kolisko's house and takin' a look around before th' coroner's physician messes everything up an' carts th' remains off to the morgue for an autopsy."

"A murder?" de Grandin's little eyes snapped with sudden excitement. "Do you say a murder? My friend, you delight me!"

"Yes, sor, I knew y'd be pleased to hear about it," the Irishman answered soberly. "Will we be goin' up to th' house at once, sor?"

"But of course, by all means," de Grandin assented. "Trowbridge, my friend, you will have the charity to convey us thither, will you not? Come, let us hasten to this Monsieur Kolisko's house and observe what we can see. And"—his little eyes twinkled as he spoke—"I beseech you, implore the so excellent Nora to reserve sufficient breakfast against the time of our return. *Mordieu*, already I feel my appetite assuming giant proportions!"

Two minutes later the detective, de Grandin and I were speeding uptown toward the isolated cottage where Urban Kolisko, one-time professor of psychology at the University at Warsaw, had passed the declining years of his life as a political refugee.

"Tell me, Friend Costello," the Frenchman demanded; "this Monsieur Kolisko, how did he die?"

"H'm, that's just what's puzzlin' all of us," the detective admitted. "All we know about th' case is that Murphy, who has th' beat where th' old felly lived, wuz passin' by there a little after midnight an' heard th' devil's own row goin' on inside. Th' lights wuz all goin' in th' lower part o' th' house, which warn't natural, an' when Murphy stopped to hear what it wuz all about, he thought he heard someone shoutin' an swearin', an' once or twice th' crack o' a whip, then nothin' at all.

"Murphy's a good lad, sor; I've knowed him, man an' boy, these last eighteen years, an' he did just what I'd expected o' him. Went up an' knocked on th' door, an' when he couldn't get no response, broke it in. There was hell broke loose for certain, sor."

"Ah?" returned de Grandin. "What did the excellent Murphy observe?"

"Plenty," Costello replied laconically. "Ye'll be seein' it for yerself in a minute."

Inside the Kolisko house was that peculiar hush which does reverence to the Grim Reaper's visits. Acting on telephoned instructions, Officer Murphy mounted guard before the door, permitting no one to enter the place, and the scene in the small, poorly lighted livingroom was exactly as he had come upon it several hours earlier.

Like most dyed-in-the-wool students, Kolisko had regarded his home merely as a place to sleep, eat and store books. The room was lined from floor to ceiling on all sides with rough deal shelving which groaned and sagged under the weight of ponderous volumes in every language known to print. Piles of other books, unable to find accommodation on the shelves, were littered about the floor. The rough, benchlike table and the littered, untidy desk which stood between the two small windows were also piled high with books.

Between the desk and table, flat on its back, staring end

lessly at the rough whitewashed ceiling with bulging, sightless eyes, lay the relic of Professor Kolisko. Clothed in a tattered bathrobe and soiled pajamas the body lay, and it was not a pretty sight even to a medical man to whom death in its unloveliest phases is no stranger. Kolisko had been thin to the point of emaciation, and his scrawniness was accentuated in death. His white-thatched head was thrown back and bent grotesquely to one side, his straggling white beard thrust upward truculently, and his lower jaw had fallen downward with the flaccidity of death, half an inch or so of tongue protruding beyond the line of his lower teeth. Any doctor, soldier or undertaker—any man whose business has to do habitually with death—could not fail to recognize the signs. The man was dead, and had been so for upward of seven hours.

"Howly-Mither!" Costello's brogue came strongly to the surface as he blessed himself involuntarily. "Will ye be lookin' at th' awfulness o' him, sors?"

"U'm," murmured Jules de Grandin, sinking to one knee beside the corpse, raising the lolling head and fingering the back of the neck with quick, practiced hands, then brushing back the bristling beard to examine the scrawny throat attentively, "he had cause to be dead, this one. See, Friend Trowbridge"—taking my hand he guided my fingers slowly down the dead man's neck, then pointed to the throat—"there is a clean fracture of the spine between the third and fourth dorsal vertebrae, probably involving a rupture of the cord, as well. The autopsy will disclose that. And here"—he tapped the throat with a well-manicured forefinger—"are the marks of strangulation. *Mordieu,* whatever gripped this poor one's neck possessed a hold like Death himself, for he not only choked him, but broke his spine as well! If it were not for one thing, I should say such strength—such ferocity of grip— could only have been exerted by one of the great apes, but—"

He broke off, staring with preoccupied, unseeing eyes at the farther wall.

"But what, sor?" Costello prompted as the little man's silence continued.

"*Parbleu,* it could not be an ape and leave such a thumb-mark, my friends,'' de Grandin returned. ''The gorilla, the orangutan, the chimpanzee, all have such strength of hand as to accomplish what we see here, but they are not human, no matter how much they parody mankind. Their thumbs are undeveloped; the thumb which closed on this one's neck was long and thin, more like a finger than a thumb. See for yourselves, it closed about the throat, meeting the fingers which clasped it on the other side. *Mordieu,* if we are to find this murderer we must look for one with twice the length and five times the strength of hand of the average man. Bethink you—this one's grip was great enough to snap Kolisko's spine like a clay-pipe stem by merely squeezing his neck! *Dieu de Dieu,* but he will be an uncomfortable one to meet in the dark!''

''Sergeant Costello,'' Murphy's hail came sharply from the cottage door, ''they're comin'; Coroner Martin an' Dr. Schuester just drove up!''

''All right, Murphy, good lad!'' Costello returned, then glanced sharply at de Grandin. ''Leave him be, Doc,'' he ordered. ''If th' coroner an' Dr. Schuester catch us monkeyin' with their property there'll be hell poppin' at headquarters.''

''Very good, my friend,'' de Grandin rejoined, rising and brushing the dust from his trousers knees, ''we have seen as much of the body as we desire. Let them have it and perform their gruesome rites; we shall look elsewhere for what we seek.''

Coroner Martin and his physician came bustling in almost as the little Frenchman ceased speaking, glanced casually at Costello and suspiciously at de Grandin and me, then went at their official duties with only a mumbled word of greeting.

''What do you make of it?'' I inquired as we drove toward my house.

''*Eh bien,* as yet I make nothing,'' de Grandin returned. ''The man was killed by paralysis resulting from a broken neck, although the pressure on his windpipe would have been sufficient to have slain him, had it but continued long enough. We know his murderer possessed hands of extraordinary strength and size, and is, therefore, in all probability, a man of more than usual height. Thus far we step with assurance. When the coroner has finished with the deceased gentleman's premises, we shall afford ourselves the pleasure of a protracted search; before that we shall request our good friend Costello to inquire into Monsieur Kolisko's antecedents and discover if he possess any enemies, especially any enemies capable of doing him to death in this manner. Meantime I famish for my breakfast. I am hungry as a cormorant.''

The boasted appetite was no mere figure of speech. Three bowls of steaming cereal, two generous helpings of bacon and eggs, half a dozen cups of well-creamed coffee disappeared into his interior before he pushed back his chair and lighted a rank-smelling French cigarette with a sigh of utter content. *''Eh bien,* but it is difficult to think on an empty stomach,'' he assured me as he blew a column of smoke toward the ceiling. ''Me, I am far from my best when there is nothing but flatulence beneath my belt. I require stimu— *Mon Dieu,* what a fool I am!''

Striking his forehead with the heel of his hand, he rose so abruptly that his chair almost capsized behind him.

''What's the matter?'' I asked, but he waved my question and me aside with an impatient hand.

*''Non, non,* do not stop me, do not hinder me, my friend!'' he ordered. ''Me, I have important duties to perform, if it be not too late to do them. Go upon your errands of mercy, Friend Trowbridge, and should you chance to return before I quit the surgery, I pray you leave me undisturbed. I have to do that which is needful, and I must do it uninterrupted, if you please.''

Having thus served notice on me that I would be unwelcome in my own workshop, he turned and fled toward the front door like a luckless debtor pursued by collectors.

It was nearly four o'clock that afternoon when I returned from my round of calls and tiptoed past the surgery door, only to find my caution unnecessary, for de Grandin sat in the cool, darkened library, smoking a cigar and chuckling over some inane story in *L'Illustration.*

"Finish the important duties?" I asked regarding him ironically.

"But certainly," he returned. "First, dear friend, I must apologize most humbly for my so abominable rudeness of this morning. It is ever my misfortune, I fear, to show only incivility to those who most deserve my courtesy, but I was all afire with the necessity of haste when I spoke. Great emptyhead that I was, I had completely forgotten for the moment that one of the best places to seek clues of a murder is the person of the victim himself, and when I did remember I was almost beside myself until I ascertained to which *entrepreneur des pompes funèbres*—how do you say it? under-taker?—my God, what a language!—Monsieur Kolisko's body had been entrusted by the coroner. Friend Costello informed me that Monsieur Mitchell was in charge, and to the excellent Mitchell I hurried post-haste, begging that he would permit me one little minute alone with the deceased before he commenced his ministrations."

"H'm, and did you find anything?" I asked.

"*Parbleu,* yes; I found almost too much. From the nails of Monsieur Kolisko's hands I rescued some fragments, and in your surgery I subjected them to microscopic examination. They proved to be—what do you say?"

"Tobacco?" I hazarded.

"Tobacco!" he scoffed. "Friend Trowbridge, sometimes I think you foolish; at others I fear you are merely stupid. Beneath the dead man's fingernails I found some bits of human skin—and a fragment of human hair."

"Well," I returned unenthusiastically, "what of it? Kolisko was an exceedingly untidy sort of person—the kind who cared so little for social amenities that he was apt to scratch himself vigorously when he chose and probably he was also addicted to the habit of scrabbling through his beard with his fingers. Most of those European scientists with birds' nests sprouting from their chins are that sort, you know. He was shockingly uncouth, and—"

"And you annoy me most thoroughly, Friend Trow-bridge," the little Frenchman broke in. "Listen, attend me, regard that which I am about to tell you: The skin and hair which I did find were black, my friend, black as bitumen, and subjected to chemical reagents, showed themselves to be strongly impregnated with natron, oil of cedar and myrrh. What have you to say now?''

"Why—"

"And if these things suggest an Egyptian mummy to you, as they may if you think steadily for the next ten or more years, I make so bold as to ask what would a professor of psychology be doing in contact with a mummy. *Hein?* Answer me that, if you please. Had he been an Egyptologist, or even a student of comparative anatomy, there would be reason for it, but a psychologist—it does not make sense!''

"Well, then, why bother about it?'' I retorted.

"Ah, but I think maybe, perhaps there is an answer to the riddle, after all,'' he insisted. "Recall the events of last night, if you please. Remember how that young Monsieur Ratliff came bawling like a frightened calf to our door, begging to be taken in and protected from something which assaulted him in the public thoroughfares. Recollect how we suspected him of an overindulgence in alcohol, and how, as we were about to turn him out, there appeared at our window a most unpleasant-looking thing which made mock of Jules de Grandin's marksmanship. *Parbleu,* yes, you will recall all that, as well as that the ungrateful Ratliff child did sneak away from the house without so much as saying 'thank you' for our hospitality while we were out with Sergeant Costello viewing Monsieur Kolisko's remains.''

"Then you'd suggest—'' I began incredulously, but he rose with an impatient shrug.

"Ah, bah, I think nothing, my friend,'' he assured me. "He who thinks without knowing is a fool. A connection there may be between that which we saw last night and that which we viewed this morning. We shall see, perhaps. I have an engagement to search Kolisko's house with Sergeant Costello this evening, and I suggest you accompany us. There may be that there which shall cause your eyes to pop from out your face with wonder. Meantime, I hear visitors in the reception room. Go to your duties, my friend. Some neurotic old lady undoubtlessly desires you to sympathize with her latest symptoms.''

"Well, sor,'' confided Sergeant Costello as he, de Grandin and I set out for the Kolisko cottage that evening, "this case beats th' Jews, an' the' Jews beat the devil.''

"Indeed?'' responded de Grandin politely.

"It sure does. We've been over Kolisko's antecedents, as ye might call 'em, an' th' devil a thing can we find that might lead us to a clue as to who killed him. 'Twas little enough they knew about him, at best, for he was a standoffish old felly, wid never a word for annybody, except when he wanted sumpin, which warn't often. He had a few Polack cronies, but they wuz few an' far between. Five months ago a felly broke into his house an' stole some stuff o' triflin' value, an' shot up a state trooper while tryin' to escape to th' next town. Kolisko appeared agin 'im at th' trial, as wuz his dooty, for he wuz subpenaed, an' later visited 'im in jail, I understand, but this felly—name o' Heschler, he wuz—didn't take anny too kindly to th' professor's visits, an' he cut 'em out.''

"Ah,'' de Grandin nursed his narrow chin in the cradle of his hand, "perhaps it is that this Heschler harbored malice and wreaked vengeance on Monsieur Kolisko for the part he had in his conviction?''

"P'raps,'' agreed Costello shortly, "but 'tain't likely.''

"And why not?'' the Frenchman demanded shortly. Like most men who keep their own counsel, he was easily annoyed by others' reticence.

"Because they burned him at Camden last night, sor.''

"Burned? How do you mean—''

"Sure, burned him. Bumped 'im off, rubbed 'im out, gave 'im th' chair—electrocuted 'im. He was a murderer, warn't he?'' Costello elucidated.

"U'm,'' the Frenchman gulped over the information like one trying to clear his mouth of an unpalatable morsel, "you are doubtless right, Sergeant; we may regard this Heschler as eliminated—perhaps.''

"P'raps?'' echoed the amazed Irishman⸻ ⸻ the car to a halt before the cottage door. ''P you'll listen to me, I'll say he's been eliminated altogether entirely be th' state executioner!''

Our search was startlingly unproductive. A few letters in envelopes with foreign postmarks, receipts for small bills for groceries and kindred household items, one or two invitations to meetings of learned societies—this was the sum total produced by an hour's rummaging among the dead man's papers.

*"Tiens,* it would seem we have come on the chase of the wild goose," de Grandin admitted disconsolately, wiping the sweat from his forehead with a pale blue silk handkerchief. *"Zut,* it seems impossible that any man should have so much paper of so little importance. Me, I think that—"

"Here's sumpin that might help us, if it's papers ye're after," Costello interrupted, appearing at the kitchen door with a rough wooden box in his hand. "I found it behint th' stove, sor. Most of it seems of little enough account, but you might find sumpin that'd—"

"Aside, stand aside, my friend!" the Frenchman ordered, leaping on the box like a famished cat on a mouse and scattering its contents over the living-room table. "What have we here? *Mordieu,* another receipt from that twenty-times-damned Public Service Company! Name of a rooster, did the man do nothing but contract and pay bills for electric light? Another one—and another! *Grand Dieu,* if I find but one more of these receipts I shall require a strait-waistcoat to restrain myself. What, another—ah, *triomphe!* At last we find something else!" From the pile of scrambled papers he unearthed a small, black-leather book and began riffling through its pages.

Pausing to read an inscription at random, he regarded the page with upraised brows and pursed lips, seated himself beside the table and brought his eyes to within a few inches of the small, crabbed writing with which the book seemed filled.

Five minutes he sat thus studying the memoranda, his brows rising till I feared they would impinge upon the line of his smoothly combed blond hair. Finally: "My friends, this is of the importance," he assured us, looking quickly from one to the other with his queer, direct glance. "Monsieur Kolisko made these entries in his diary in mingled Polish and French. I shall endeavor to render them into English tonight, and tomorrow morning we shall go over them together. Thus far I have read little, but that little may explain much, or I am much mistaken."

"Trowbridge, my friend," de Grandin requested the following morning when my round of calls was finished, "will you please read what I have written? All night I labored over this translation, and this morning my eyes are not sufficient to the task of reading my own script."

He thrust a sheaf of neatly written foolscap into my hands, then lighted a cigarette and leaned back in his chair, his small hands locked behind his head, his eyes half closed, as he surveyed Costello and me lazily.

Glancing from de Grandin to the waiting detective, I set my pince-nez firmly on my nose and began:

*April 5*—Michel was here again last night, nagging me with his silly talk of the soul and its immortality. To think that one so well educated should entertain such childish ideas! I would have ordered him from the house in anger, as I did once before, had he not been more than usually insulting. After taunting me with the old story about a body's being weighed a few minutes after death and found lighter than before, thereby proving that something of material weight had passed from it, he challenged me to prove the nonexistence of any entity separate from the physical being. Fool! It is he who asserts the proposition, not I. Yet I must think of some way to confound him, or he will be everlastingly reminding me that I failed to meet his test.

*April 10*—Michel is a greater fool than I thought. I hold him and his faith in the hollow of my hand, and by his own act. Last night he proposed the wildest scheme ever broached

by man. The burglar who broke into my house last month has
been sentenced to death for killing a policeman. Michel
would have me see the fellow in prison, arrange for a trans-
migration of his soul to a body which he will secure, and
await results of the experiment. It is a childish folly; I insult
my own intelligence by agreeing to it, but I must silence
Michel and his everlasting patter of the soul's immortality. I
shall undertake the task, if only to prove my cousin a fool.

*May 16*—Yesterday I saw Heschler in prison. The poor
fellow was almost beside himself with joy when I told him of
Michel's wild plan. Not dying, but fear of punishment in the
world to come seems to terrify the man. If I can provide a
tenement for his soul which will enable it to remain away
from the seat of judgment a little longer, he will be content,
even though he has to live in the body of a child, a cripple or
one already bowed with age. Living out the span of life in the
second body we provide, he will so conduct himself as to win
pardon for misdeeds committed in the frame he now wears,
he vows. Poor, hoodwinked fool! Like all Christians, he is
bound hand and foot by the old superstitions which have
come down to us through the ages. That Heschler, the burglar, should adhere to the *Christus* myth, the God fairly-tale,
is not surprising, for he is but an ignorant clod; but that my
cousin Michel Kolisko, a learned man, should give credit to
beliefs which were outworn and disproved in the nineteenth
century is beyond my understanding.

*May 30*—Today I had another talk with Heschler. He is
pitiably anxious to begin the experiment. It was childishly
simple. Ordering him to gaze steadfastly into my eyes
through the bars of his cell, I soon had him completely
hypnotized. "You will hereafter cease to dread your coming
execution," I told him. "From this time forth you will think
of nothing but the opportunity of living on in another body
which is to be afforded you. At the moment of execution you
will concentrate all your will upon entering the body which
will be waiting at my home to receive your soul." He nodded
as I gave each command, and I left him. It will not be
necessary to repeat my orders. He was already half insane

with the obsession of prolonging his life. My work was more than half done before I gave him the directions. I shall not see him again.

The next page bore a clipping from the *Newark Call:*

Adolph Heschler, confined in the penitentiary at Camden awaiting execution for the murder of State Trooper James Donovan on the night of March 20th last, seems resigned to his fate. When first taken to the state prison he seemed in deadly fear of death and spent most of his time in prayer. Prison officials say that he began to show signs of resignation following the memorial services on May 20th, and it is said he declares his conscience is cleared by the thought that he shall be allowed the opportunity of atoning for his misdeeds. Curiously enough, Heschler, who has heretofore shown the most devout appreciation of the ministrations of the prison's Catholic chaplain, will have nothing further to do with the spiritual advisor, declaring "atonement for his sins has been arranged." There is talk of having him examined by a lunacy commission before the date set for his execution.

Another translation of the diary followed:

*August 30*—Michel has come with the body. It is a mummy! When I expressed my astonishment, he told me it was the best possible corpse for the purpose. After hearing him, I realized he has the pseudo-logic of the mildly insane. The body of one who has died from natural causes or by violence would be unfitted for our purposes, he says, since some of its organs must inevitably be unable to function properly. This mummy is not a true mummy, but the body of an Egyptian guilty of sacrilege, who was sealed up alive in a tomb during the Hyksos dynasty. He died of asphyxia, in all probability, and his body is in perfect condition, except for the dehydration due to lying so many thousands of years in a perfectly dry atmosphere. Michel rescued the mummy during his last expedition to Egypt, and tells me there was evidence of the man's having made a terrific struggle before death put an end to his sufferings. Other bodies, properly mummified, were found in the same tomb, and the dying man had overturned many of the cases and spilled their contents about the place. His body was so thoroughly impregnated with the odor of the spices and preservatives, absorbed from the mummies lying in the tomb, that it was not for some time his discoverers realized he had not been eviscerated and embalmed. Michel assures me the dead man will be perfectly able to act as an envelope for Heschler's soul when the electrocution has been performed. Cousin Michel, if this body does but so much as wiggle its fingers or toes after the authorities have killed Heschler, I will believe—I will believe.

I laid down the final page of de Grandin's translation and looked wonderingly at him. "Where's the rest of it?" I demanded. "Couldn't you do any more last night?"

"The rest," he answered ironically, "is for us to find out, my friends. The journal stops with the entry you have just read. There was no more."

"Humph," Sergeant Costello commented, "crazy as a pair o' fish out o' water, weren't they? Be gorry, gentlemen, I'm thinkin' it's a crazy man we'd best be lookin' for. I can see it all plain, now. This here Cousin Michael o' Professor Kolisko's was a religious fy-nat-ic, as th' felly says, an' th' pair o' 'em got to fightin' among themselves an' the' professor came out second best. That's th' answer, or my name ain't—"

The sudden shrilling of the office telephone interrupted him. "Sergeant Costello, please," a sharp voice demanded as I picked up the receiver.

"Yeah, this is Costello speakin'," the detective announced, taking the instrument from me. "Yep. All right, go ahead, *What?* Just like th' other one? My Gawd!"

"What is it?" de Grandin and I asked in chorus as he put down the receiver and turned a serious face to us.

"Miss Adkinson, an old lady livin' by herself out by th' cemetery, has been found murdered," he replied slowly, *"an' th' marks on her throat tally exactly wid those on Professor Kolisko's!"*

*"Cordieu!"* de Grandin shouted, leaping from his chair as if it had suddenly become white-hot. "We must hasten, we must rush, we must fly to that house, my friends! We must examine the body, we must assure ourselves before some bungling coroner's physician spoils everything!"

Two minutes later we were smashing the speed ordinances in an effort to reach the Adkinson house before Coroner Martin arrived.

Stark tragedy repeated itself in the Adkinson cottage. The old lady, gaunt with the leanness of age to which time has not been over-kind, lay in a crumpled heap on her kitchen floor, and a moment's examination disclosed the same livid marks on her throat and the same horrifying limberness of neck which we had observed when viewing Professor Kolisko's body.

"By Gawd, gentlemen, this is terrible!" Costello swore as he turned from the grisly relic. "Here's an old man kilt at night an' a harmless old woman murdered in broad daylight, an' no one to tell us anything certain about th' murderer!"

*"Ha,* do you say so?" de Grandin responded sharply, his little eyes flashing with excitement. *"Parbleu,* my friend, but you are greatly wrong, as wrong as can be. There is one who can tell us, and tell us he shall, if I must wring the truth from him with my bare hands!"

"What d'ye mean—?" Sergeant Costello began, but the little Frenchman had already turned toward the door, dragging frantically at my elbow.

"Clutch everything, *mes amis,"* he commanded. "Retain all; me, I go to find him who can tell us what we need to know. *Mordieu,* I shall find him though he takes refuge in the nethermost subcellar of hell! Come, Trowbridge, my friend; I would that you drive me to the station where I can entrain for New York."

Shortly after seven o'clock that evening I answered the

furious ringing of my telephone to hear de Grandin's excited
voice come tumbling out of the receiver. "Come at once, my
friend," he ordered, fairly stuttering in his elation. "Rush
with all speed to the Carmelite Fathers' retreat in East Thirty-
second Street. Bring the excellent Costello with you, too, for
there is one here who can shed the light of intelligence on our
ignorance."

"Who is it—?" I began, but the sharp click of a receiver
smashed into its hook cut short my query, and I turned in
disgust from the unresponsive instrument to transmit the
Frenchman's message to Sergeant Costello.

Within sight of Bellevue's grim mortuary, enshrouded by
the folds of drab East River fog as a body is wrapped in its
winding-sheet, the little religious community seemed as
incongruously out of place in the heart of New York's pover-
ty-ridden East Side as a nun in a sweatshop. Striding up and
down the polished floor of the bare, immaculately clean
reception room was Jules de Grandin, a glowing cigarette
between his fingers, his tiny, waxed mustache standing
straight out from the corners of his mouth like the whiskers of
an excited tomcat. "At last!" he breathed as Costello and I
followed the porter from the front door to the public room.
"*Morbleu*, I thought you had perished on the way!

"*Monsieur*," he paused in his restless pacing and stopped
before the figure sitting motionless in the hard, straight-
backed chair at the farther side of the room, "you will please
tell these gentlemen what you have told me and be of haste in
doing so. We have small time to waste."

I glanced curiously at the seated man. His strong resem-
blance to the dead Kolisko was remarkable. He possessed a
mop of untidy, iron-gray hair and a rather straggling gray
beard; his forehead was high, narrow and startlingly white,
almost transparent, and the skin of his face was puckered into
hundreds of little wrinkles as though his skull had shrunk,
leaving the epidermis without support. His eyes, however,
differed radically from Kolisko's, for even in death the professor's orbs had shown a hard, implacable nature, whereas

this man's eyes, though shaded by beetling, overhanging brows, were soft and brown. Somehow, they reminded me of the eyes of an old and very gentle dog begging not to be beaten.

"I am Michel Kolisko," he began, clearing his throat with a soft, deprecating cough. "Urban Kolisko was my cousin, son of my father's brother. We grew up together in Poland, attended the same schools and colleges, and dreamed the same dreams of Polish independence. I was twenty, Urban was twenty-three when the Tsar's officers swooped down on our fathers, carried them off to rot in Siberia, and confiscated most of our family's fortune. Both of us were suspected of complicity in the revolutionary movement, and fled for our lives, Urban to Paris, I to Vienna. He matriculated at the Sorbonne and devoted himself to the study of psychology; I studied medicine in Vienna, then went to Rome, and finally took up Egyptology as my life's work.

"Twenty years passed before I saw my cousin again. The Russian proscription had been raised, and he had gone to Warsaw, where he taught in the university. When I went there to visit him, I was shocked to learn he had abandoned God and taken to the worship of the material world. Kant, Spencer, Richet, Wundt—these were his prophets and his priests; the God of our fathers he disowned and denied. I argued with him, pleaded with him to return to his childhood's belief, and he turned me out of his house.

"Once again he earned the displeasure of the Tsar and escaped arrest only by a matter of moments. Fleeing to this country, he took up residence in your city, and devoted himself to penning revolutionary propaganda and atheistic theses. Broken in health, but with sufficient money to insure me of a quiet old age, I followed him to America and made it the work of my declining years to convert him from his apostasy.

"This spring it seemed I was beginning to succeed, for he showed more patience with me than ever before; but he was a hardened sinner, his heart was steeled against the call of consciousness, even as was Pharaoh's of old. He challenged me to offer evidence of God's truth, and promised he would turn again to religion if I could.''

For a moment the speaker paused in his monotonous, almost mumbled recitation, wrung his bloodless hands together in a gesture of despair, pressed his fingers to his forehead, as though to crowd back departing reason, then took up his story, never raising his voice, never stressing one word more than another, keeping his eyes fixed on vacancy. He reminded me of a child reciting a distasteful lesson by rote.

"I see we were both mad, now," he confided drearily. "Mad, mad with the sense of our own importance, for Urban defied divine providence, and I forgot that it is not man's right to attempt to prove God's truth as revealed to us by his ordained ministers. It is ours to believe, and to question not. But I was carried away by the fervor of my mission. 'If I can shake Urban's doubts, I shall surely win a crown of glory,' I told myself, 'for surely there is great joy in heaven over one sinner who repents.' And so I went about the sacrilegious business of the test.

"Among the curios I had brought from Egypt was the body of a man sealed alive in a tomb during the Hyksos rule. It was not really a mummy, for no embalming had been performed, but the superheated atmosphere of the tomb in which he had been incarcerated had shriveled his tissues until it was difficult to tell him from a body mummified by artificial methods. Only three or four such bodies are known; one is the celebrated Flinders mummy, and the others are in French and British museums. I had intended leaving mine to the Metropolitan when I died.

"I brought this body to Urban's house the night before Heschler, the condemned murderer, was to be executed, and we laid it on the library table. Urban viewed it with disgust and skepticism, but I prayed over it, begging God to work a miracle, to permit the body to move, if only very slightly, and so convince my poor, misguided cousin. You know, gentlemen"—he turned his sorrowful lackluster eyes on us with a melancholy smile—"such things are not entirely unknown.

Sudden changes in temperature or in the moisture content of the atmosphere often lead to a movement as the dehydrated tissues take up water from the air. The mummy of Rameses the Great, for instance, moved its arm when first exposed to the outdoor air.

"A few minutes after midnight was the time set for Heschler's electrocution, and as the town clocks began sounding the hour I felt as though the heavens must fall if no sign were manifested to us.

"Urban sat beside the mummy, smoking his pipe and sneering—part of the time reading an impious book by Freud. I bowed my head in silent prayer, asking for a miracle to save him despite his hardness of heart. The city hall clock struck the quarter-hour, then the half, and still there was no sound. Urban laid his pipe and book aside and looked at me with his familiar sneer, then turned as though to thrust the body of the Egyptian from the table—*then it sat up!*

"Like a sleeper waking from a dream, like a patient coming forth from the ether it was—the corpse that had been dead four thousand years rose from the table and looked at us. For a moment it seemed to smile with its fleshless lips, then it looked down at itself, and gave a scream of surprise and fury.

" 'So!' it shrieked; 'so *this* is the body you've given me to work out my salvation! This is the form in which I must walk the earth until my sins be wiped away, is it? You've tricked me, cheated me, but I'll have vengeance. No one living can harm me, and I'll take my toll of human kind before I finally go forth to stew and burn in Satan's fires!'

"It was stiff and brittle, but somehow it managed to crawl from the table and make at Urban. He seized a heavy whip which hung on the wall and struck the thing on the head with its loaded butt. The blow would have killed an ordinary man—indeed, I saw the mummy's dried-up skull cave in beneath the force of Urban's flailings, but it never faltered in its attack, never missed a step in its pursuit of vengeance.

"Then I went mad. I fled from that accursed house and buried myself in this retreat, where I have spent every moment since, denying myself both food and sleep, deeming every second left me all too short to beg divine forgiveness for the terrible sacrilege I have committed.''

"So, my friends, you see?" de Grandin turned to Costello and me as the half-hysterical Pole concluded his preposterous narrative.

"Sure, I do," the detective returned. "Didn't th' felly say he's mad? Be dad, they say crazy folks tell th' truth, an' he ain't stretchin' it none when he says his steeple's full o' bats.''

"Ah bah!" de Grandin shot back. "You weary me, my friend.''

To Kolisko he said: "Your story supplies the information which we so sorely needed, sir. Whatever the result of your experiment, your motives were good, nor do I think the good God will be too hard upon you. If you do truly wish forgiveness, pray that we shall be successful in destroying the monster before more harm is done. *Cordieu,* but we shall need all your prayers, and a vast deal of luck as well, I think; for killing that which is already dead is no small task.''

"Now what?" demanded Costello with a sidelong glance at de Grandin as we emerged from the religious house. "Got some more loonies for us to listen to?"

"*Parbleu,* if you will but give ear to your own prattle, you shall have all that sort of conversation you wish, I think, *cher Sergent,*" the little Frenchman jerked back with a smile which took half the acid from his words. Then:

"Friend Trowbridge, convoy our good, unbelieving friend to Harrisonville and await my return. I have one or two things to attend to before I join you; but when I come I think I can promise you a show the like of which you have not before seen. *Au revoir, mes enfants.*"

Ten o'clock sounded on the city's clocks; eleven; half-past. Costello and I consumed innumerable cigars and more than one potion of some excellent cognac I had stored in my cellar since the days before prohibition; still no sign of my little friend. The sergeant was on the point of taking his departure when a light step sounded on the porch and de Grandin came bounding into the consulting room, his face wreathed in smiles, a heavy-looking parcel gripped under his right arm.

"*Bien,* my friends, I find you in good time," he greeted, poured himself a monstrous stoup of amber liquor, then helped himself to one of my cigars. "I think it high time we were on our way. There is that to do which may take considerable doing this night, but I would not that we delay our expedition because of difficulties in the road."

"Be gorry, he's caught it from th' other nut!" Costello confided to the surrounding atmosphere with a serio-comic grimace. "Which crazy house are we goin' to now, sor?"

"Where but to the house of Monsieur Kolisko?" returned the Frenchman with a grin. "I think there will be another there before long, and it is highly expedient that we be there first."

"Humph, if it's Coroner Martin or his physician, you needn't be worryin' yourself anny," Costello assured him. "They'll be takin' no more interest in th' case till someone else gets kilt, I'm thinkin'."

"*Morbleu,* then their days of interest are ended, or Jules de Grandin is a colossal liar," was the response. "Come; *allons vite!*"

The lowest workings of a coal mine were not darker than the Kolisko house when we let ourselves in some fifteen minutes later. Switching on the electric light, de Grandin proceeded to unpack his parcel, taking from it a folded black object which resembled a deflated association football. Next he produced a shining nickel-plated apparatus consisting of a thick upright cylinder and a transverse flat piece which opened in two on hinges, disclosing an interior resembling a waffle-iron with small, close-set knobs. Into a screw-stopped opening in the hollow cylinder of the contrivance he poured several ounces of gray-black powder; then, taking the flat rubber bag, he hurried from the house to my car, attached the valve of the bag to my tire pump and proceeded to inflate the rubber bladder almost to the bursting point. This done, he attached the bag to a valve in the nickeled cylinder by a two-foot length of rubber hose, poured some liquid over the corrugated ''waffle-iron'' at the top of the cylinder, and, with the inflated bag hugged under his arm, as a Highland piper might hold the bag of his pipes, he strode across the room, snapped off the light, and took his station near the open window.

Several times Costello and I addressed him, but each time he cut us short with a sharp, irritable "Sssh!" continuing his crouching watch beside the window, staring intently into the shaded garden beyond.

It must have been some three-quarters of an hour later that we sensed, rather than heard, the scuffling of light footfalls on the grass outside, heard the door-knob cautiously tested, then the scuttering of more steps, scarcely louder than the sound of wind-blown leaves, as the visitant rounded the cottage wall and made for the window beside which de Grandin mounted guard.

A puff of autumn wind, scented with the last blooms of summer's rose beds, sent the light clouds drifting from before the moon's pale lantern, and, illuminated in the pallid light of the night's goddess, we saw framed at the window-square the terrifying vision which had followed young Ratliff's story of his escape two nights before.

"My Gawd!" Costello's bass voice was shrill and treble with sudden terror as the thing gazed malevolently in at us. Next instant his heavy service revolver was out, and shot after shot poured straight into the hideous, grinning face at the window.

He might as well have fired boiled beans from a pea-shooter for all the effect his bullets had. Distinctly I saw a portion of the mummy's ear clipped off by a flying slug of lead, saw an indentation sink in the thing's head half an inch above the right eye as a soft-nosed bullet tore through skin and withered flesh and frontal bone; but the emaciated body never paused in its progress. One withered leg was lifted across the window-sill; two long, unfleshed arms, terminating in hands of enormous length, were thrust out toward the

Irishman; a grin of such hellish hatred and triumph as I have never conceived possible disfigured the object's visage as it pressed onward, its long, bony fingers opening and closing convulsively, as though they already felt their victim's neck within their grasp.

"*Monsieur,* you do play truant from hell!" De Grandin's announcement was made in the most casual manner as he rose from his half-kneeling posture beside the window and placed himself directly in the mummy's path, but there was a quaver in his voice which betrayed the intensity of his emotion.

A noise—you could hardly call it a snarl nor yet a scream, but a sound midway between the two—emanated from the thing's desiccated throat as it turned on him, threw out one hand and snatched at his throat.

There was a tiny spark of light, as though a match had been struck, then a mighty, bursting blaze, as if time had turned backward in its flight for a second and the midday sun had thrown its beams through the midnight blackness of the room, a swishing whistling sound, as of air suddenly released from tremendous pressure, and a shriek of mad, unsupportable anguish. Then the fierce blazing of some inflammable substance suddenly set alight. My eyes started from my face as I seemed to see the mummy's scraggly limbs and emaciated torso writhe within a very inferno of fire. Then:

"*Cher Sergent,* it might be well to call the fire department; this place will surely burn about our ears unless *les pompiers* hurry with their hose, I fear," remarked Jules de Grandin as calmly as though advising us the night was fine.


"But—but—howly Mither o' Moses!" Sergeant Costello demanded as we turned from watching the firemen salvaging the remnants of Kolisko's cottage; "how did ye manage it, Doctor de Grandin, sor? May I never eat another mess o' corned beef an' cabbage if I didn't shoot th' thing clean through th' head wid me gun, an' it never so much as batted an eye, yet ye burned it up as clean as—"

"Precisely, *mon vieux,*" the Frenchman admitted with a chuckle. "Have you never heard the adage that one must

fight the Devil with fire? It was something like that which I
did.

"No later than night before last a young man came crying
and whimpering at Friend Trowbridge's door, begging for
shelter from some ghastly thing which pursued him through
the streets. Both Trowbridge and I thought he suffered from
an overdose of the execrable liquor with which Mosieur
Volstead has flooded this unhappy land, but before we could
boot him from the door, behold, the same thing which you so
unsuccessfully shot tonight did stick its unlovely countenance against our window and I who always go armed lest
some miscreant do me a mischief, did fire eight shots directly
into his face. Believe me, my friend, when Jules de Grandin
shoots, he does not miss, and that night I shot exceptionally
well. Yet when Friend Trowbridge and I searched the garden,
neither hide nor hair of the one who should have been eight
times dead did we find. 'There is something here which will
take much explaining,' I say to me after we could not find
him.

"Next morning you did come and tell us of Professor
Kolisko's murder and when we had viewed his remains, I
wondered much what sort of creature could have done the
thing. The pressure exerted on his neck was superhuman, but
the marks of the hand were not those of an ape, for no ape
possesses such a long, thin thumb.

"Then we did find the dead professor's diary and I have
the tiny shivers playing tag with each other up and down my
back as I read and translate it. It sounds like the dream of one
crazed with dope, I know, but there was the possibility of
truth in it. Do you know the vampire, my friends?"

"The vampire?" I echoed.

"*Précisément;* the vampire, you have said it. He is not
always one who can not die because of sin or misfortune in
life. No. Sometimes he is a dead body possessed by some
demon—perhaps by some unhappy, earthbound spirit. Yes.

"Now as I read the professor's journal, I see that everything which had transpired were most favorable for the
envampirement of that body which his cousin had brought
from Egypt so long ago. Yet the idea seemed—how do you

say?—ah, yes—to have the smell of the fish on it.

"But when you come and say Miss Adkinson have been erased in the same manner as Professor Kolisko, I begin to wonder if perhaps I have not less nuts in my belfry than I at first thought. In Professor Kolisko's journal there was reference to his cousin. 'How does it come that this cousin have not come forward and told us what, if anything, he knows?'' I ask me as we view the poor dead woman's body, and the answer was, 'He has most doubtless seen that which will not be believed, and hides because he fears arrest on a false charge of murder.'

"Right away I rush to New York and inquire at the *Musée Metropolitain* for the address of Monsieur Michel Kolisko the Egyptologist. I find his living-quarters in East Eighty-sixth Street. There they tell me he have gone to the Carmelite retreat. *Morbleu,* had he hidden in lost Atlantis, I should have hunted him out, for I desired speech with him!

"At first he would not talk, dreading I intended to drag him to the jail, but after I had spoken with him for a time, he opened his heart, and told me what he later told you.

"Now, what to do? By Monsieur Kolisko's story, it were useless to battle with this enlivened mummy, for the body of him was but the engine moved by an alien spirit—he had no need of brains, hearts and such things as we must use. Also, I knew from experience, bullets were as useless against him as puffs of wind against a fortress wall. 'Very well,' I tell me, 'he may be invulnerable to bullets and blows, but living or dead, he is still a mummy—a dry, desiccated mummy—and we have had no rain lately. It are entirely unlikely that he have gotten greatly moistened in his trips through the streets, and all mummies are as tinder to fire. *Mordieu,* did they not once use them as fuel for locomotives in Egypt when railways were first built there? Yes.'

"And so I prepare the warm reception for him. At one time and another I have taken photographs at night, and to do so I have used magnesium flares—what you call flashlight powder. At a place where they sell such things in New York I procure a flashlight burner—a hollow cylinder for the powder magazine with a benzine wick at its top and a tube through which air can be blown to force the powder through the burning petrol and so give a continuous blaze. I get me also a rubber bag which I can inflate and attach to the windpipe of the apparatus, thus leaving my lips free for swearing and other important things, and also giving a greater force of air.

"I reason: 'Where will this living mummy go most naturally? Why not to the house where he received his new life, for the town in which he goes about committing murder is still new to him?'' And so, when *Monsieur la Momie* returns to the place of his second nativity, I am all ready for him. Your shots, they are as ineffectual as were mine two nights ago, but I have my magnesium flare ready, and as he turns on me I blow the fierce flame from it all over him. He are dry like tinder, the fire seized on him like a hungry little boy on a jam-tart, and—*pouf*—he is burn up, incinerated; he is no more!''

"Do you actually mean Heschler's soul entered that dried-up body?" I demanded.

The Frenchman shook his head. "I do not know," he replied. "Perhaps it were Heschler; more likely not. The air is full of strange and terrible things, my friend. Not for nothing did the old divines call Satan the Prince of the Powers of the Air. How do we know some of those elementals who are ever on the watch to do mankind an injury did not hear the mad Koliskos' scheme and take advantage of the opportunity to enter the mummy's body? Such things have been before; why may they not be again?''

"But—" I commenced.

"But—" expostulated Sergeant Costello.

"But, my friends," the little man cut in, "did you behold how dry that so abominable mummy was before I applied the fire?''

"Yes," I answered wonderingly.

"*Cordieu,* he was wet as the broad Atlantic Ocean beside the dryness of Jules de Grandin at this moment! Friend Trowbridge, unless my memory plays me false, I beheld a bottle of cognac upon your office table. Come, I faint, I die, I perish; talk to me no more till I have consumed the remainder of that bottle, I do beseech you!''

# UNSEEN—UNFEARED
### *by* FRANCIS STEVENS

Francis Stevens was probably the greatest woman writer of science fantasy in the period between Mary Wollstonecraft Shelley and C.L. Moore. Twice she has achieved recognition and twice her name has faded from popularity. It may enjoy a contemporary revival with the publication in 1970 of her fine novel, *The Citadel of Fear* at this editor's behest, but it is questionable that she is around to enjoy it. Born in 1884 as Gertrude Barrows, she would be eighty-seven if still alive today, but the last word ever received from her was a letter to her daughter dated September 1, 1939 from the state of California. No further information concerning her presence has come to light since that date.

Brought up by a bookish family in Minneapolis, she never got further than a grammer school education, though both her mother and father were book lovers and had a house full of volumes. Her initial aspiration was to be an illustrator and though working, she studied art nights, but finally gave up her ambitions in that direction. It is possible that she further improved her education with evening classes, but apparently the talent for writing came naturally to her. In one of the very few letters of hers ever to have appeared in print, she said: "I wrote my first story when I was seventeen and working in the office of a department store. It had just one merit, as I remember it, and that was a rather grotesque originality. Of course, in the writer's estimation it was a very wonderful story, but nevertheless, I was more than surprised when *The Argosy,* the first magazine to which it was submitted, accepted it. Within a week or so of that the *Youth's Compan-*

*ion* accepted a couple of verses, also a first offering, and naturally, being seventeen and optimistic, I believed my literary career established. But they were both 'beginner's luck'—flukes—and though I persisted, for a while my success did not. So I dropped the 'literary career,' and several years intervened before I even attempted anything save desultory scribbling for my own amusement . . . Then I spent a year in newspaper work, which I detested; but it reawoke the ambition to write. Again I was fortunate with a first story, and since then have not deserted the field.''

It has commonly been supposed that the first story she had published was ''The Nightmare,'' a long, garish but thrilling science fiction novelette which appeared in *All-Story Weekly,* April 14, 1917. Reading the above letter, it was obvious that such an assumption would be an error, and a search conducted by this editor and bibliophile Lester Mayer, revealed that first story under her maiden name G.M. Barrows to be ''The Curious Experience of Thomas Dunbar,'' published in *The Argosy* for March, 1904. The story had never been listed in a bibliography of her works or ever directly or indirectly related to her before the writing of this preface. In keeping with her bent for the fantastic, it was science fiction, dealing with a man hit by an automobile, who is nursed back to health by a scientist who is half Japanese and half American. The room where he is kept adjoins a laboratory and factory. The contact of the patient with a newly discovered element, stellarite, converts him into an incredibly powerful physical superman. There is a good note of the mystery and the bizarre in the story, but it is not an important work.

''Unseen—Unfeared'' has in common with that first story by Gertrude Barrows, that it has been never listed by bibliographers, and except for a previous mention by this editor is almost unknown. Unlike ''The Curious Experience of Thomas Dunbar,'' it is a product of the author's mature writing talent and appeared in an important magazine of the period, *People's Favorite Magazine* for February 10, 1919. ''Unseen—Unfeared'' is a science fiction horror story, and though in no ways similar in plotting, in general background and subject it appears to show the influence of

Fitz-James O'Brien, particularly his two stories "The Diamond Lens" and "The Wondersmith." It is almost redundant to state that this is the first time the story has ever been reprinted.

# UNSEEN—UNFEARED

by

**Francis Stevens**

I had been dining with my ever-interesting friend, Mark Jenkins, at a little Italian restaurant near South Street. It was a chance meeting. Jenkins is too busy, usually, to make dinner engagements. Over our highly seasoned food and sour, thin, red wine, he spoke of little odd incidents and adventures of his profession. Nothing very vital or important, of course. Jenkins is not the sort of detective who first detects and then pours the egotistical and revealing details of achievement in the ears of every acquaintance, however appreciative.

But when I spoke of something I had seen in the morning papers, he laughed. "Poor old 'Doc' Holt! Fascinating old codger, to anyone who really knows him. I've had his friendship for years—since I was first on the city force and saved a young assistant of his from jail on a false charge. And they had to drag him into the poisoning of this young sport, Ralph Peeler!"

"Why are you so sure he couldn't have been implicated?" I asked.

But Jenkins only shook his head, with a quiet smile. "I have reasons for believing otherwise," was all I could get out of him on that score, "But," he added, "the only reason he was suspected at all is the superstitious dread of these ignorant people around him. Can't see why he lives in such a

168

place. I know for a fact he doesn't have to. Doc's got money of his own. He's an amateur chemist and dabbler in different sorts of research work, and I suspect he's been guilty of 'showing off.' Result, they all swear he has the evil eye and holds forbidden communion with invisible powers. Smoke?''

Jenkins offered me one of his invariably good cigars, which I accepted, saying thoughtfully: ''A man has no right to trifle with the superstitions of ignorant people. Sooner or later, it spells trouble.''

''Did in his case. They swore up and down that he sold love charms openly and poisons secretly, and that, together with his living so near to—somebody else—got him temporarily suspected. But my tongue's running away with me, as usual!''

''As usual,'' I retorted impatiently, ''you open up with all the frankness of a Chinese diplomat.''

He beamed upon me engagingly and rose from the table, with a glance at his watch. ''Sorry to leave you, Blaisdell, but I have to meet Jimmy Brennan in ten minutes.''

He so clearly did not invite my further company that I remained seated for a little while after his departure; then took my own way homeward. Those streets always held for me a certain fascination, particularly at night. They are so unlike the rest of the city, so foreign in appearance, with their little shabby stores, always open until late evening, their unbelievably cheap goods, displayed as much outside the shops as in them, hung on the fronts and laid out on tables by the curb and in the street itself. Tonight, however, neither people nor stores in any sense appealed to me. The mixture of Italians, Jews and a few Negroes, mostly bareheaded, unkempt and generally unhygienic in appearance, struck me as merely revolting. They were all humans, and I, too, was human. Some way I did not like the idea.

Puzzled a trifle, for I am more inclined to sympathize with poverty than accuse it, I watched the faces that I passed. Never before had I observed how bestial, how brutal were the countenances of the dwellers in this region. I actually shuddered when an old-clothes man, a gray-bearded Hebrew, brushed me as he toiled past with his barrow.

There was a sense of evil in the air, a warning of things which it is wise for a clean man to shun and keep clear of. The impression became so strong that before I had walked two squares I began to feel physically ill. Then it occurred to me that the one glass of cheap Chianti I had drunk might have something to do with the feeling. Who knew how that stuff had been manufactured, or whether the juice of the grape entered at all into its ill-flavored composition? Yet I doubted if that were the real cause of my discomfort.

By nature I am rather a sensitive, impressionable sort of chap. In some way tonight this neighborhood, with its sordid sights and smells, had struck me wrong.

My sense of impending evil was merging into actual fear. This would never do. There is only one way to deal with an imaginative temperament like mine—conquer its vagaries. If I left South Street with this nameless dread upon me, I could never pass down it again without a recurrence of the feeling. I should simply have to stay here until I got the better of it—that was all.

I paused on a corner before a shabby but brightly lighted little drug store. Its gleaming windows and the luminous green of its conventional glass show jars made the brightest spot on the block. I realized that I was tired, but hardly wanted to go in there and rest. I knew what the company would be like at its shabby, sticky soda fountain. As I stood there, my eyes fell on a long white canvas sign across from me, and its black-and-red lettering caught my attention.

## SEE THE GREAT UNSEEN!

### Come in! This Means You!

## FREE TO ALL!

A museum of fakes, I thought, but also reflected that if it were a show of some kind I could sit down for a while, rest, and fight off this increasing obsession of nonexistent evil. That side of the street was almost deserted, and the place itself might well be nearly empty.

## II

I walked over, but with every step my sense of dread increased. Dread of I knew not what. Bodiless, inexplicable horror had me as in a net, whose strands, being intangible, without reason for existence, I could by no means throw off. It was not the people now. None of them were about me. There, in the open, lighted street, with no sight nor sound of terror to assail me, I was the shivering victim of such fear as I had never known was possible. Yet still I would not yield.

Setting my teeth, and fighting with myself as with some pet animal gone mad, I forced my steps to slowness and walked along the sidewalk, seeking entrance. Just here there were no shops, but several doors reached in each case by means of a few iron-railed stone steps. I chose the one in the middle beneath the sign. In that neighborhood there are museums, shops and other commercial enterprises conducted in many shabby old residences, such as were these. Behind the glazing of the door I had chosen I could see a dim, pinkish light, but on either side the windows were quite dark.

Trying the door, I found it unlocked. As I opened it a party of Italians passed on the pavement below and I looked back at them over my shoulder. They were gayly dressed, men, women and children, laughing and chattering to one another; probably on their way to some wedding or other festivity.

In passing, one of the men glanced up at me and involuntarily I shuddered back against the door. He was a young man, handsome after the swarthy manner of his race, but never in my life had I see a face so expressive of pure, malicious cruelty, naked and unashamed. Our eyes met and his seemed to light up with a vile gleaming, as if all the wickedness of his nature had come to a focus in the look of concentrated hate he gave me.

They went by, but for some distance I could see him watching me, chin on shoulder, till he and his party were swallowed up in the crowd of marketers farther down the street.

Sick and trembling from that encounter, merely of eyes though it had been, I threw aside my partly smoked cigar and

entered. Within there was a small vestibule, whose ancient
tesselated floor was grimy with the passing of many feet. I
could feel the grit of dirt under my shoes, and it rasped on my
rawly quivering nerves. The inner door stood partly open,
and going on I found myself in a bare, dirty hallway, and was
greeted by the sour, musty, poverty-stricken smell common
to dwellings of the very ill-to-do. Beyond there was a stair-
way, carpeted with ragged grass matting. A gas jet, turned
low inside a very dusty pink globe, was the light I had seen
from without.

Listening, the house seemed entirely silent. Surely, this
was no place of public amusement of any kind whatever.
More likely it was a rooming house, and I had, after all,
mistaken the entrance.

To my intense relief, since coming inside, the worst agony
of my unreasonable terror had passed away. If I could only
get in some place where I could sit down and be quiet,
probably I should be rid of it for good. Determining to try
another entrance, I was about to leave the bare hallway when
one of several doors along the side of it suddenly opened and
a man stepped out into the hall.

"Well?" he said, looking at me keenly, but with not the
least show of surprise at my presence.

"I beg your pardon," I replied. "The door was unlocked
and I came in here, thinking it was the entrance to the
exhibit—what do they call it?——the 'Great Unseen.' The
one that is mentioned on that long white sign. Can you tell me
which door is the right one?"

"I can."

With that brief answer he stopped and stared at me again.
He was a tall, lean man, somewhat stooped, but possessing
considerable dignity of bearing. For that neighborhood, he
appeared uncommonly well dressed, and his long, smooth-
shaven face was noticeable because, while his complexion
was dark and his eyes coal-black, above them the heavy
brows and his hair were almost silvery-white. His age might
have been anything over the threescore mark.

I grew tired of being stared at. "If you can and—won't,

then never mind," I observed a trifle irritably, and turned to go. But his sharp exclamation halted me.

"No!" he said. "No—no! Forgive me for pausing—it was not hesitation, I assure you. To think that one—one, even, has come! All day they pass my sign up there—pass and fear to enter. But you are different. *You* are not of these timorous, ignorant foreign peasants. You ask me to tell you the right door? Here it is! Here!"

And he struck the panel of the door, which he had closed behind him, so that the sharp yet hollow sound of it echoed up through the silent house.

Now it may be thought that after all my senseless terror in the open street, so strange a welcome from so odd a showman would have brought the feeling back, full force. But there is an emotion stronger, to a certain point, than fear. This queer old fellow aroused my curiosity. What kind of museum could it be that he accused the passing public of fearing to enter? Nothing really terrible, surely, or it would have been closed by the police. And normally I am not an unduly timorous person. "So it's in there, is it?" I asked, coming toward him. "And I'm to be sole audience? Come, that will be an interesting experience." I was half laughing now.

"The most interesting in the world," said the old man, with a solemnity which rebuked my lightness.

With that he opened the door, passed inward and closed it again—in my very face. I stood staring at it blankly. The panels, I remember, had been originally painted white, but now the paint was flaked and blistered, gray with dirt and dirty finger marks. Suddenly it occurred to me that I had no wish to enter there. Whatever was behind it could be scarcely worth seeing, or he would not choose such a place for its exhibition. With the old man's vanishing my curiosity had cooled, but just as I again turned to leave, the door opened and this singular showman stuck his white-eyebrowed face through the aperture. He was frowning impatiently. "Come in—come in!" he snapped, and promptly withdrawing his head, once more closed the door.

"He has something there he doesn't want should get out,"

was the very natural conclusion which I drew. "Well, since it can hardly be anything dangerous, and he's so anxious I should see it—here goes!"

With that I turned the soiled white porcelain handle, and entered.

The room I came into was neither very large nor very brightly lighted. In no way did it resemble a museum or lecture room. On the contrary, it seemed to have been fitted up as a quite well-appointed laboratory. The floor was linoleum-covered, there were glass cases along the walls whose shelves were filled with bottles, specimen jars, graduates, and the like. A large table in one corner bore what looked like some odd sort of camera, and a larger one in the middle of the room was fitted with a long rack filled with bottles and test tubes, and was besides littered with papers, glass slides, and various paraphernalia which my ignorance failed to identify. There were several cases of books, a few plain wooden chairs, and in the corner a large iron sink with running water.

My host of the white hair and black eyes was awaiting me, standing near the larger table. He indicated one of the wooden chairs with a thin forefinger that shook a little, either from age or eagerness. "Sit down—sit down! Have no fear but that you will be interested, my friend. Have no fear at all—of anything!"

As he said it he fixed his dark eyes upon me and stared harder than ever. But the effect of his words was the opposite of their meaning. I did sit down, because my knees gave under me, but if in the outer hall I had lost my terror, it now returned twofold upon me. Out there the light had been faint, dingily roseate, indefinite. By it I had not perceived how this old man's face was a mask of living malice—of cruelty, hate and a certain masterful contempt. Now I knew the meaning of my fear, whose warning I would not heed. Now I knew that I had walked into the very trap from which my abnormal sensitiveness had striven in vain to save me.

### III

Again I struggled within me, bit at my lip till I tasted blood, and presently the blind paroxysm passed. It must have been longer in going than I thought, and the old man must have all that time been speaking, for when I could once more control my attention, hear and see him, he had taken up a position near the sink, about ten feet away, and was addressing me with a sort of "platform" manner, as if I had been the large audience whose absence he had deplored.

"And so," he was saying, "I was forced to make these plates very carefully, to truly represent the characteristic hues of each separate organism. Now, in color work of every kind the film is necessarily extremely sensitive. Doubtless you are familiar in a general way with the exquisite transparencies produced by color photography of the single-plate type."

He paused, and trying to act like a normal human being, I observed: "I saw some nice landscapes done in that way—last week at an illustrated lecture in Franklin Hall."

He scowled, and made an impatient gesture at me with his hand. "I can proceed better without interruptions," he said. "My pause was purely oratorical."

I meekly subsided, and he went on in his original loud, clear voice. He would have made an excellent lecturer before a much larger audience—if only his voice could have lost that eerie, ringing note. Thinking of that I must have missed some more, and when I caught it again he was saying:

"As I have indicated, the original plate is the final picture. Now, many of these organisms are extremely hard to photograph, and microphotography in color is particularly difficult. In consequence, to spoil a plate tries the patience of the photographer. They are so sensitive that the ordinary darkroom ruby lamp would instantly ruin them, and they must therefore be developed either in darkness or by a special light produced by interposing thin sheets of tissue of a particular shade of green and of yellow between lamp and plate, and even that will often cause ruinous fog. Now I, finding it hard to handle them so, made numerous experiments with a view of discovering some glass or fabric of a color which should add to the safety of the green, without robbing it of all efficiency. All proved equally useless, but intermittently I persevered—until last week.''

His voice dropped to an almost confidential tone, and he leaned slightly toward me. I was cold from my neck to my feet, though my head was burning, but I tried to force an appreciative smile.

"Last week," he continued impressively, "I had a prescription filled at the corner drug store. The bottle was sent home to me wrapped in a piece of what I first took to be whitish, slightly opalescent paper. Later I decided that it was some kind of membrane. When I questioned the druggist, seeking its source, he said it was a sheet of 'paper' that was around a bundle of herbs from South America. That he had no more, and doubted if I could trace it. He had wrapped my bottle so, because he was in haste and the sheet was handy.

"I can hardly tell you what first inspired me to try that membrane in my photographic work. It was merely dull white with a faint hint of opalescence, except when held against the light. Then it became quite translucent and quite brightly prismatic. For some reason it occurred to me that this refractive effect might help in breaking up the actinic rays— the rays which affect the sensitive emulsion. So that night I inserted it behind the sheets of green and yellow tissue, next the lamp, prepared my trays and chemicals, laid my plate holders to hand, turned off the white light and—turned on the green!''

There was nothing in his words to inspire fear. It was a wearisomely detailed account of his struggles with photography. Yet, as he again paused impressively, I wished that he might never speak again. I was desperately, contemptibly in dread of the thing he might say next.

Suddenly, he drew himself erect, the stoop went out of his shoulders, he threw back his head and laughed. It was a hollow sound, as if he laughed into a trumpet. "I won't tell you what I saw! Why should I? Your own eyes shall bear witness. But this much I'll say, so that you may better understand—later. When our poor, faultily sensitive vision can perceive a thing, we say that it is visible. When the nerves of touch can feel it, we say that it is tangible. Yet I tell you there are beings intangible to our physical sense, yet whose presence is felt by the spirit, and invisible to our eyes merely because those organs are not attuned to the light as reflected from their bodies. But light passed through the screen, which we are about to use has a wave length novel to the scientific world, and by it you shall see with the eyes of the flesh that which has been invisible since life began. Have no fear!''

He stopped to laugh again, and his mirth was yellow-toothed—menacing.

*''Have no fear!''* he reiterated, and with that stretched his hand toward the wall, there came a click and we were in black, impenetrable darkness. I wanted to spring up, to seek the door by which I had entered and rush out of it, but the paralysis of unreasoning terror held me fast.

I could hear him moving about in the darkness, and a moment later a faint green glimmer sprang up in the room. Its source was over the large sink, where I suppose he developed his precious ''color plates.''

Every instant, as my eyes became accustomed to the dimness, I could see more clearly. Green light is peculiar. It may be far fainter than red, and at the same time far more illuminating. The old man was standing beneath it, and his face by that ghastly radiance had the exact look of a dead man's. Besides this, however, I could observe nothing appalling.

''That,'' continued the man, ''is the simple developing light of which I have spoken—now watch, for what you are about to behold no mortal man but myself has ever seen before.''

For a moment he fussed with the green lamp over the sink. It was so constructed that all the direct rays struck downward. He opened a flap at the side, for a moment there was a streak of comforting white luminance from within, then he inserted something, slid it slowly in—and closed the flap.

The thing he put in—that South American ''membrane'' it must have been—instead of decreasing the light increased it—amazingly. The hue was changed from green to greenish-gray, and the whole room sprang into view, a livid, ghastly chamber, filled with—overcrawled by—what?

My eyes fixed themselves, fascinated, on something that moved by the old man's feet. It writhed there on the floor like a huge, repulsive starfish, an immense, armed, legged thing, that twisted convulsively. It was smooth, as if made of rubber, was whitish-green in color; and presently raised its great round blob of a body on tottering tentacles, crept toward my host and writhed upward—yes, climbed up his legs, his body. And he stood there, erect, arms folded, and stared sternly down at the thing which climbed.

But the room—the whole room was alive with other creatures than that. Everywhere I looked they were—centipedish things, with yard-long bodies, detestable, furry spiders that lurked in shadows, and sausage-shaped translucent horrors that moved—and floated through the air. They dived here and there between me and the light, and I could see its bright greenness through their greenish bodies.

Worse, though; far worse than these were the *things with human faces*. Mask-like, monstrous, huge gaping mouths and slitlike eyes—I find I cannot write of them. There was that about them which makes their memory even now intolerable.

The old man was speaking again, and every word echoed in my brain like the ringing of a gong. "Fear nothing! Among such as these do you move every hour of the day and night. Only you and I have seen, for God is merciful and has spared our race from sight. But I am not merciful! I loathe the race which gave these creatures birth—the race which might be so surrounded by invisible, unguessed but blessed beings—and chooses these for its companions! All the world shall see and know. One by one shall they come here, learn the truth, and perish. For who can survive the ultimate of terror? Then I, too, shall find peace, and leave the earth to its heritage of man-created horrors. Do you know what these are—whence they come?"

His voice boomed now like a cathedral bell. I could not answer him, but he waited for no reply. "Out of the ether—out of the omnipresent ether from whose intangible substance the mind of God made the planets, all living things, and

man—man has made these! By his evil thoughts, by his
selfish panics, by his lusts and his interminable, never-ending
hate he has made them, and they are everywhere! Fear
nothing—but see where there comes to you, its creator, the
shape and the body of your FEAR!''

And as he said it I perceived a great Thing coming toward
me—a Thing—but consciousness could endure no more. The
ringing, threatening voice merged in a roar within my ears,
there came a merciful dimming of the terrible, lurid vision,
and blank nothingness succeeded upon horror too great for
bearing.

## IV

There was a dull, heavy pain above my eyes. I knew that
they were closed, that I was dreaming, and that the rack full
of colored bottles which I seemed to see so clearly was no
more than a part of the dream. There was some vague but
imperative reason why I should rouse myself. I wanted to
awaken, and thought that by staring very hard indeed I could
dissolve this foolish vision of blue and yellow-brown bottles.
But instead of dissolving they grew clearer, more solid and
substantial of appearance, until suddenly the rest of my
senses rushed to the support of sight, and I became aware that
my eyes were open, the bottles were quite real, and that I was
sitting in a chair, fallen sideways so that my cheek rested
most uncomfortably on the table which held the rack.

I straightened up slowly and with difficulty, groping in my
dulled brain for some clue to my presence in this unfamiliar
place, this laboratory that was lighted only by the rays of an
arc light in the street outside its three large windows. Here I
sat, alone, and if the aching of cramped limbs meant anything, here I had sat for more than a little time.

Then, with the painful shock which accompanies awakening to the knowledge of some great catastrophe, came memory. It was this very room, shown by the street lamp's rays to
be empty of life, which I had seen thronged with creatures too
loathsome for description. I staggered to my feet, staring
fearfully about. There were the glass-doored cases, the book-

shelves, the two tables with their burdens, and the long iron sink above which, now only a dark blotch of shadow, hung the lamp from which had emanated that livid, terrifically revealing illumination. Then the experience had been no dream, but a frightful reality. I was alone here now. With callous indifference my strange host had allowed me to remain for hours unconscious, with not the least effort to aid or revive me. Perhaps, hating me so, he had hoped that I would die there.

At first I made no effort to leave the place. Its appearance filled me with reminiscent loathing. I longed to go, but as yet felt too weak and ill for the effort. Both mentally and physically my condition was deplorable, and for the first time I realized that a shock to the mind may react upon the body as vilely as any debauch of self-indulgence.

Quivering in every nerve and muscle, dizzy with headache and nausea, I dropped back into the chair, hoping that before the old man returned I might recover sufficient self-control to escape him. I knew that he hated me, and why. As I waited, sick, miserable, I understood the man. Shuddering, I recalled the loathsome horrors he had shown me. If the mere desires and emotions of mankind were daily carnified in such forms as those, no wonder that he viewed his fellow beings with detestation and longed only to destroy them.

I thought, too, of the cruel, sensuous faces I had seen in the streets outside—seen for the first time, as if a veil had been withdrawn from eyes hitherto blinded by self-delusion. Fatuously trustful as a month-old puppy, I had lived in a grim, evil world, where goodness is a word and crude selfishness the only actuality. Drearily my thoughts drifted back through my own life, its futile purposes, mistakes and activities. All of evil that I knew returned to overwhelm me. Our gropings toward divinity were a sham, a writhing sunward of slime-covered beasts who claimed sunlight as their heritage, but in their hearts preferred the foul and easy depths.

Even now, though I could neither see nor feel them, this room, the entire world, was acrawl with the beings created by our real natures. I recalled the cringing, contemptible fear to which my spirit had so readily yielded, and the faceless Thing to which the emotion had given birth.

Then abruptly, shockingly, I remembered that every moment I was adding to the horde. Since my mind could conceive only repulsive incubi, and since while I lived I must think, feel, and so continue to shape them, was there no way to check so abominable a succession? My eyes fell on the long shelves with their many-colored bottles. In the chemistry of photography there are deadly poisons—I knew that. Now was the time to end it—now! Let him return and find his desire accomplished. One good thing I could do, if one only. I could abolish my monster-creating self.

## V

My friend Mark Jenkins is an intelligent and usually a very careful man. When he took from "Smiler" Callahan a cigar which had every appearance of being excellent, innocent Havana, the act denoted both intelligence and caution. By very clever work he had traced the poisoning of young Ralph Peeler to Mr. Callahan's door, and he believed this particular cigar to be the mate of one smoked by Peeler just previous to his demise. And if, upon arresting Callahan, he had not confiscated this bit of evidence, it would have doubtless been destroyed by its regrettably unconscientious owner.

But when Jenkins shortly afterward gave me that cigar, as one of his own, he committed one of those almost inconceivable blunders which, I think, are occasionally forced upon clever men to keep them from overweening vanity. Discovering his slight mistake, my detective friend spent the night searching for his unintended victim, myself, and that his search was successful was due to Pietro Marini, a young Italian of Jenkins' acquaintance, whom he met about the hour of 2:00 A.M. returning from a dance.

Now, Marini had seen me standing on the steps of the house where Doctor Frederick Holt had his laboratory and living rooms, and he had stared at me, not with any ill intent, but because he thought I was the sickest-looking, most ghastly specimen of humanity that he had ever beheld. And, sharing the superstition of his South Street neighbors, he wondered if the worthy doctor had poisoned me as well as Peeler. This suspicion he imparted to Jenkins, who, however, had the best of reasons for believing otherwise. Moreover, as he informed Marini, Holt was dead, having drowned himself late the previous afternoon. An hour or so after our talk in the restaurant, news of his suicide reached Jenkins.

It seemed wise to search any place where a very sick-looking young man had been seen to enter, so Jenkins came straight to the laboratory. Across the fronts of those houses was the long sign with its mysterious inscription, "See the Great Unseen," not at all mysterious to the detective. He knew that next door to Doctor Holt's the second floor had been thrown together into a lecture room, where at certain hours a young man employed by settlement workers displayed upon a screen stereopticon views of various deadly bacilli, the germs of diseases appropriate to dirt and indifference. He knew, too, that Doctor Holt himself had helped the educational effort along by providing some really wonderful lantern slides, done by micro-color photography.

On the pavement outside, Jenkins found the two-thirds remnant of a cigar, which he gathered in and came up the steps, a very miserable and self-reproachful detective. Neither outer nor inner door was locked, and in the laboratory he found me, alive, but on the verge of death by another means that he had feared.

In the extreme physical depression following my awakening from drugged sleep, and knowing nothing of its cause, I believed my adventure fact in its entirety. My mentality was at too low an ebb to resist its dreadful suggestion. I was searching among Holt's various bottles when Jenkins burst in. At first I was merely annoyed at the interruption of my purpose, but before the anticlimax of his explanation the mists of obsession drifted away and left me still sick in body, but in spirit happy as any man may well be who has suffered a delusion that the world is wholly bad—and learned that its badness springs from his own poisoned brain.

The malice which I had observed in every face, including young Marini's, existed only in my drug-affected vision.

Last week's "popular-science" lecture had been recalled to my subconscious mind—the mind that rules dreams and delirium—by the photographic apparatus in Holt's workroom. "See the Great Unseen" assisted materially, and even the corner drug store before which I had paused, with its green-lit show vases, had doubtless played a part. But presently, following something Jenkins told me, I was driven to one protest. "If Holt was not here," I demanded, "if Holt is dead, as you say, how do you account for the fact that I, who have never seen the man, was able to give you an accurate description which you admit to be that of Doctor Frederick Holt?"

He pointed across the room. "See that?" It was a life-size bust portrait, in crayons, the picture of a white-haired man with bushy eyebrows and the most piercing black eyes I had ever seen—until the previous evening. It hung facing the door and near the windows, and the features stood out with a strangely lifelike appearance in the white rays of the arc lamp just outside. "Upon entering," continued Jenkins, "the first thing you saw was that portrait, and from it your delirium built a living, speaking man. So, there are your white-haired showman, your unnatural fear, your color photography and your pretty green golliwogs all nicely explained for you, Blaisdell, and thank God you're alive to hear the explanation. If you had smoked the whole of that cigar—well, never mind. You didn't. And now, my very dear friend, I think it's high time that you interviewed a real, flesh-and-blood doctor. I'll phone for a taxi."

"Don't," I said. "A walk in the fresh air will do me more good than fifty doctors."

"Fresh air! There's no fresh air on South Street in July," complained Jenkins, but reluctantly yielded.

I had a reason for my preference. I wished to see people, to meet face to face even such stray prowlers as might be about at this hour, nearer sunrise than midnight, and rejoice in the goodness and kindliness of the human countenance—particularly as found in the lower classes.

But even as we were leaving there occurred to me a curious inconsistency.

"Jenkins," I said, "you claim that the reason Holt, when I first met him in the hall, appeared to twice close the door in my face, was because the door never opened until I myself unlatched it."

"Yes," confirmed Jenkins, but he frowned, foreseeing my next question.

"Then why, if it was from that picture that I built so solid, so convincing a vision of the man, did I see Holt in the hall before the door was open?"

"You confuse your memories," retorted Jenkins rather shortly.

"Do I? Holt was dead at that hour, but—*I tell you I saw Holt outside the door!* And what was his reason for committing suicide?"

Before my friend could reply I was across the room, fumbling in the dusk there at the electric lamp above the sink. I got the tin flap open and pulled out the sliding screen, which consisted of two sheets of glass with fabric between, dark on one side, yellow on the other. With it came the very thing I dreaded—a sheet of whitish, parchmentlike, slightly opalescent stuff.

Jenkins was beside me as I held it at arm's length toward the windows. Through it the light of the arc lamp fell—divided into the most astonishingly brilliant rainbow hues. And instead of diminishing the light, it was perceptibly increased in the oddest way. Almost one thought that the sheet itself was luminous, and yet when held in shadow it gave off no light at all.

"Shall we—put it in the lamp again—and try it?" asked Jenkins slowly, and in his voice there was no hint of mockery.

I looked him straight in the eyes. "No," I said, "we won't. I was drugged. Perhaps in that condition I received a merciless revelation of the discovery that caused Holt's suicide, but I don't believe it. Ghost or no ghost, I refuse to ever again believe in the depravity of the human race. If the air and the earth are teeming with invisible horrors, they are *not* of our making, and—the study of demonology is better let alone. Shall we burn this thing, or tear it up?"

"We have no right to do either," returned Jenkins thoughtfully, "but you know, Blaisdell, there's a little too darn much realism about some parts of your 'dream.' I haven't been smoking any doped cigars, but when you held that up to the light, I'll swear I saw—well, never mind. Burn it—send it back to the place it came from."

"South America?" said I.

"A hotter place than that. Burn it."

So he struck a match and we did. It was gone in one great white flash.

A large place was given by morning papers to the suicide of Doctor Frederick Holt, caused, it was surmised, by mental derangement brought about by his unjust implication in the Peeler murder. It seemed an inadequate reason, since he had never been arrested, but no other was ever discovered.

Of course, our action in destroying that "membrane" was illegal and rather precipitate, but, though he won't talk about it, I know that Jenkins agrees with me—doubt is sometimes better than certainty, and there are marvels better left unproved. Those, for instance, which concern the Powers of Evil.

# THE PENDULUM
## *by* RAY BRADBURY

The literary world is understandably fascinated by the details of how any given famous or popular author created, sold, and published a first story or first book. Magazines of seventy-five years past frequently ran monthly series of articles giving full details of an author's first sale. The more important an author is, the more fascinating the subject.

Ray Bradbury is today acknowledged to be one of the great names among masters of the horror tale, not to mention science fiction. His first hardcover collection of tales of horror and the supernatural, *Dark Carnival* (Arkham House, 1947), took many years to go out of print but now commands extremely high prices. *The October Country*, another fine collection of the macabre (Ballantine Books, 1955), stays perpetually in print. Yet, Bradbury's first professional sale, "Pendulum" in collaboration with Henry Hasse, has never seen hard covers, until now.

There were actually two versions of "Pendulum." The first, written by Ray Bradbury alone, was finished when he was nineteen years old. He couldn't sell it so he published it in the Fall, 1939 issue of his fan magazine *Futuria Fantasia*. The original story was about 1,800 words long, was published anonymously, mimeographed in green ink with a small illustration by Hannes Bok, then a professionally unpublished artist.

Another contributor to *Futuria Fantasia* was Henry Hasse, a young author who had made a number of sales to the science fiction magazines and had been particularly acclaimed for his long novelette "He Who Shrank" (*Amazing Stories*, August, 1936), which would eventually be anthologized in *Adventures in Time and Space,* edited by Raymond J. Healy and J. Francis McComas (Random House, 1946), which anthology has never been out of print since its original publication.

Bradbury prevailed upon Hasse to help him rewrite his story in line with the style preferred by the science fiction magazines of that day. The length of the story was extended to over 5,000 words and with a certain amount of pressure, Julius Schwartz, a New York literary agent who specialized in science fiction, agreed to try to sell the story. Rejected by all, it gradually trickled down to the lower paying markets until it arrived at Popular Publications, a pulp house which published *Astonishing Stories* and *Super Science Stories*, edited by Fred Pohl.

Pohl remembers reading the manuscript, but was leaving his job after a disagreement on salary and the magazines were taken over by Alden H. Norton, a veteran Popular Publications editor. This leaves a bit murky the credit for the discovery of Bradbury, but the story was published in the November, 1941 *Super Science Stories,* and was actually accepted July 18, 1941, with a grand total of $27.50 paid for it. That meant that after the 10% agent's commission and splitting down the middle with Henry Hasse, Bradbury had a maximum of $12.38 to spend anyway he saw fit!

The question of just how much Hasse actually contributed to the collaboration has often been raised. The question can be answered to a great degree by comparing the original story as Bradbury wrote and published it, with the final version as it appeared in collaboration with Henry Hasse. For this purpose both versions are printed here and both in book form for the first time.

Bradbury would sell several more collaborations with Henry Hasse, "Gabriel's Horn" *(Captain Future,* Spring, 1943) and "Final Victim" (*Amazing Stories,* February, 1946) and he would on several occasions enlist the assistance of Henry Kuttner and Leigh Brackett before he would venture out completely on his own.

# THE PENDULUM

by

## Ray Bradbury

Up and down, back and forth, up and down. First the quick flight skyward, gradually slowing, reaching the pinnacle of the curve, poising a moment, then flashing earthward again, faster and faster at a nauseating speed, reaching the bottom and hurtling aloft on the opposite side. Up and down. Back and forth. Up and down.

How long it had continued this way Layeville didn't know. It might have been millions of years he'd spent sitting here in the massive glass pendulum watching the world tip one way and another, up and down, dizzily before his eyes until they ached. Since first they had locked him in the pendulum's round glass head and set it swinging it had never stopped or changed. Continuous, monotonous movements over and above the ground. So huge was this pendulum it shadowed one hundred feet or more with every majestic sweep of its gleaming shape, dangling from the metal intestines of the shining machine overhead. It took three or four seconds for it to traverse the one hundred feet one way, three or four seconds to come back.

*The Prisoner of Time!* That's what they called him now! Fettered to the very machine he had planned and constructed. A pris-on-er—of——time! A—pris-on-er—of——time! With every swing of the pendulum it echoed in his thoughts.

Forever like this until he went insane. He tried to focus his eyes on the arching hotness of the earth as it swept past beneath him.

They had laughed at him a few days before. Or was it a week? A month? A year? He didn't know. This ceaseless pitching had filled him with an aching confusion. They had laughed at him when he said, some time before all this, he could bridge time gaps and travel into futurity. He had designed a huge machine to warp spaces, invited thirty of the world's most gifted scientists to help him finish his colossal attempt to scratch the future wall of time.

The hour of the accident spun back to him now through misted memory. The display of the time machine to the public. The exact moment when he stood on the platform with the thirty scientists and pulled the main switch! The scientists, all of them, blasted into ashes from wild electrical flames! Before the eyes of two million witnesses who had come to the laboratory or were tuned in by television at home! He had slain the world's greatest scientists!

He recalled the moment of shocked horror that followed. Something radically wrong had happened to the machine. He, Layeville, the inventor of the machine, had staggered backward, his clothes flaming and eating up about him. No time for explanations. Then he had collapsed in the blackness of pain and numbing defeat.

Swept to a hasty trial, Layeville faced jeering throngs calling out for his death. "Destroy the Time Machine!" they cried. "And destroy this murderer with it!"

Murderer! And he had tried to help humanity. This was his reward.

One man had leaped onto the tribunal platform of the trial, crying, "No! Don't destroy the machine! I have a better plan! A revenge for this—this man!" His finger pointed at Layeville where the inventor sat unshaven and haggard, his eyes failure-glazed. "We shall rebuild his machine, take his precious metals, and put up a monument to his slaughtering! We'll put him on exhibition for life within his executioning device!" The crowd roared approval like thunder shaking the tribunal hall.

Then, pushing hands, days in prison, months. Finally, led forth into the hot sunshine, he was carried in a small rocket car to the center of the city. The shock of what he saw brought him back to reality. THEY had rebuilt his machine into a towering timepiece with a pendulum. He stumbled forward, urged on by thrusting hands, listening to the roar of thousands of voices damning him. Into the transparent pendulum head they pushed him and clamped it tight with weldings.

Then they set the pendulum swinging and stood back. Slowly, very slowly, it rocked back and forth, increasing in speed. Layeville pounded futilely at the glass, screaming. The faces became blurred, were only tearing pink blobs before him.

On and on like this—for how long?

He hadn't minded it so much at first, that first night. He couldn't sleep, but it was not uncomfortable. The lights of the city were comets with tails that pelted from right to left like foaming fireworks. But as the night wore on, he felt a gnawing in his stomach, that grew worse. He got very sick and vomited. The next day he couldn't eat anything.

They never stopped the pendulum, not once. Instead of letting him eat quietly, they slid the food down the stem of the pendulum in a special tube, in little round parcels that plunked at his feet. The first time he attempted eating he was unsuccessful, it wouldn't stay down. In desperation, he hammered against the cold glass with his fists until they bled, crying hoarsely, but he heard nothing but his own weak, fear-wracked words muffled in his ears.

After some time had elapsed he got so that he could eat, even sleep while traveling back and forth this way. They allowed him small glass loops on the floor and leather thongs with which he tied himself down at night and slept a soundless slumber without sliding.

People came to look at him. He accustomed his eyes to the swift flight and followed their curiosity-etched faces, first close by in the middle, then far away to the right, middle again, and to the left.

He saw the faces gaping, speaking soundless words, laughing and pointing at the prisoner of time traveling forever nowhere. But after awhile the town people vanished and it was only tourists who came and read the sign that said: THIS IS THE PRISONER OF TIME—JOHN LAYEVILLE—WHO KILLED THIRTY OF THE WORLD'S FINEST SCIENTISTS! The school children, on the electrical moving sidewalk, stopped to stare in childish awe. THE PRISONER OF TIME!

Often he thought of that title. God, but it was ironic, that he should invent a time machine and have it converted into a clock, and that he, in its pendulum, would mete out the years—traveling *with* time.

He couldn't remember how long it had been. The days and nights ran together in his memory. His unshaven cheeks had developed a short beard and then ceased growing. How long a time? How long?

Once a day they sent down a tube after he ate and vacuumed up the cell, disposing of any wastes. Once in a great while they sent him a book, but that was all.

The robots took care of him now. Evidently the humans thought it a waste of time to bother over their prisoner. The robots brought the food, cleaned the pendulum cell, oiled the machinery, worked tirelessly from dawn until the sun crimsoned westward. At this rate it it could keep on for centuries.

But one day as Layeville stared at the city and its people in the blur of ascent and descent, he perceived a swarming darkness that expanded in the heavens. The city rocket ships that crossed the sky on pillars of scarlet flame darted helplessly, frightenedly for shelter. The people ran like water splashed on tiles, screaming soundlessly. Alien creatures fluttered down, great gelatinous masses of black that sucked out the life of all. They clustered thickly over everything, glistening momentarily upon the pendulum and its body above, over the whirling wheels and roaring bowels of the metal creature once a Time Machine. An hour later they dwindled away over the horizon and never came back. The city was dead.

Up and down, Layeville went on his journey to nowhere, in his prison, a strange smile etched his lips. In a week or more, he knew, he would be the only man alive on earth. Elation flamed within him. This was *his* victory! Where the other men had planned the pendulum as a prison it had been an asylum against annihilation now!

Day after day the robots still came, worked, unabated by the visitation of the black horde. They came every week, brought food, tinkered, checked, oiled, cleaned. Up and down, back and forth—THE PENDULUM! . . . a thousand years must have passed before the sky again showed life over the dead earth. A silvery bullet of space dropped from the clouds, steaming, and hovered over the dead city where now only a few solitary robots performed their tasks. In the gathering dusk the lights of the metropolis glimmered on. Other automations appeared on the rampways like spiders on twisting webs, scurrying about, checking, piling, working in their crisp mechanical manner.

And the creatures in the alien projectile found the time mechanism, the pendulum swinging up and down, back and forth, up and down. The robots still cared for it, oiled it, tinkering.

A thousand years this pendulum had swung. Made of glass the round disc at the bottom was, but now when food was lowered by the robots through the tube it lay untouched. Later, when the vacuum tube came down and cleaned out the cell it took that very food with it.

Back and forth—up and down.

The visitors saw something inside the pendulum. Pressed closely to the glass side of the cell was the face of a whitened skull—a skeleton visage that stared out over the city with empty sockets and an enigmatic smile wreathing its lipless teeth.

Back and forth—up and down.

The strangers from the void stopped the pendulum in its course, ceased its swinging and cracked open the glass cell, exposing the skeleton to view. And in the gleaming light of the stars, the skull face continued its weird grinning as if it knew that it had conquered something. Had conquered time.

The Prisoner of Time, Layeville, had indeed traveled along the centuries.

And the journey was at an end.

# PENDULUM

by

**Ray Bradbury
and Henry Hasse**

"I think," shrilled Erjas, "that this is our most intriguing discovery on any of the worlds we have yet visited! It's almost frightening."

His wide, green-shimmering wings fluttered, his beady bird eyes flashed excitement. His several companions bobbed their heads in agreement, the greenish-gold down on their slender necks ruffling softly. They were perched on what had once been a moving sidewalk but was now only a twisted ribbon of wreckage overlooking the vast expanse of a ruined city.

"Yes," Erjas continued, "it's baffling, fantastic! It—it has no reason for being." He pointed unnecessarily to the object of their attention, resting on the high stone plaza a short distance away. "Look at it! Just a huge tubular pendulum hanging from that towering framework! And the machinery, the coggery which must have once sent it swinging . . . I flew up there a while ago to examine it, but it's hopelessly corroded."

"But the head of the pendulum!" another of the bird creatures said awedly. "A hollow chamber—transparent, glassite—and that awful thing staring out of it . . ."

Pressed close to the inner side of the pendulum head was a

single human skeleton. The whitened skull seemed to stare out over the desolate, crumbling city as though regarding with amusement the heaps of powdery masonry and the bare steel girders that drooped to the ground, giving the effect of huge spiders poised to spring.

"It's enough to make one shudder—the way that thing grins! Almost as though—"

"The grin means nothing!" Erjas interrupted annoyedly. "That is only the skeletal remains of one of the mammal creatures who once, undoubtedly, inhabited this world." He shifted nervously from one spindly leg to the other, as he glanced again at the grinning skull. "And yet, it does seem to be almost triumphant! And why are there no more of them around? Why is he the only one . . . and why is he encased in that fantastic pendulum head?"

"We shall soon know," another of the bird creatures trilled softly, glancing at their spaceship which rested amidst the ruins, a short distance away. "Orfleew is even now deciphering the strange writing in the book he salvaged from the pendulum head. We must not disturb him."

"How did he get the book? I see no opening in that transparent chamber."

"The long pendulum arm is hollow, apparently in order to vacuum out the cell. The book was crumbling with age when Orfleew got it out, but he saved most of it."

"I wish he would hurry! Why must he—"

"Shh! Give him time. Orfleew will decipher the writing; he has an amazing genius for alien languages."

"Yes, I remember the metal tablets on that tiny planet in the constellation—"

"Here he comes now!"

"We shall soon know the story . . ."

The bird creatures fairly quivered as Orfleew appeared in the open doorway of their spaceship, carefully carrying a sheaf of yellowed pages. He waved to them, spread his wings and soared outward. A moment later he alighted beside his companions on their narrow perch.

"The language is simple," Orfleew told them, "and the story is a sad one. I will read it to you and then we must depart, for there is nothing we can do on this world.''

They edged closer to him there on the metal strand, eagerly awaiting the first words. The pendulum hung very straight and very still on a windless world, the transparent head only a few feet above the plaza floor. The grinning skull still peered out as though hugely amused or hugely satisfied. Orfleew took one more fleeting look at it . . . then he opened the crumbling notebook and began to read . . .

My name is John Layeville. I am known as "The Prisoner of Time." People, tourists, from all over the world come to look at me in my swinging pendulum. School children, on the electrically moving sidewalks surrounding the plaza, stare at me in childish awe. Scientists, studying me, stand out there and train their instruments on the swinging pendulum head. Oh, they could stop the swinging, they could release me—but now I know that will never happen. This all began as a punishment for me, but now I am an enigma to science. I seem to be immortal. It is ironic.

A punishment for me! Now, as through a mist, my memory spins back to the day when all this started. I remember I had found a way to bridge time gaps and travel into futurity. I remember the time device I built. No, it did not in any way resemble this pendulum—my device was merely a huge box-like affair of specially treated metal and glassite, with a series of electric rotors of my own design which set up conflicting, but orderly, field of stress. I had tested it to perfection no less than three times, but none of the others in the Council of Scientists would believe me. They all laughed. And Leske laughed. Especially Leske, for he has always hated me.

I offered to demonstrate to prove. I invited the Council to bring others—all the greatest minds in the scientific world. At last, anticipating an amusing evening at my expense, they agreed.

I shall never forget that evening when a hundred of the world's greatest scientists gathered in the main Council laboratory. But they had come to jeer, not to cheer. I did not care, as I stood on the platform beside my ponderous machine and listened to the amused murmur of voices. Nor did I care that millions of other unbelieving eyes were watching by television, Leske having indulged in a campaign of mockery against the possibility of time travel. I did not care, because I knew that in a few minutes Leske's campaign would be turned into victory for me. I would set my rotors humming. I would pull the control switch—and my machine would flash away into a time dimension and back again, as I had already seen it do three times. Later we would send a man out in the machine.

The moment arrived. But fate had decreed it was to be my moment of doom. Something went wrong, even now I do not know what or why. Perhaps the television concentration in the room affected the stress of the time-fields my rotors set up. The last thing I remember seeing, as I reached out and touched the main control switch, were the neat rows of smiling white faces of the important men seated in the laboratory. My hand came down on the switch . . .

Even now I shudder, remembering the vast mind-numbing horror of that moment. A terrific sheet of electrical flame, greenish and writhing and alien, leaped across the laboratory from wall to wall, blasting into ashes everything in its path!

Before millions of television witnesses I had slain the world's greatest scientists!

No, not all. Leske and myself and a few others who were behind the machine escaped with severe burns. I was least injured of all, which seemed to increase the fury of the populace against me. I was swept to a hasty trial, faced jeering throngs who called out for my death.

"Destroy the time machine," was the watchword, and "destroy this murderer with it!"

Murderer! I had only sought to help humanity. In vain I tried to explain the accident, but popular resentment is a thing not to be reasoned with.

One day, weeks later, I was taken from my secret prison and hurried, under heavy guard, to the hospital room where Leske lay. He raised himself on one arm and his smouldering eyes looked at me. That's all I could see of him, just his eyes; the rest of him was swathed in bandages. For a moment he just looked; and if ever I saw insanity, but a cunning insanity, in a man's eyes, it was then.

For about ten seconds he looked, then with a great effort he pointed a bulging, bandaged arm at me.

"No, do not destroy him," he mumbled to the authorities gathered around. "Destroy his machine, yes, but save the parts. I have a better plan, a fitting one, for this man who murdered the world's greatest scientists."

I remembered Leske's old hatred of me, and I shuddered.

In the weeks that followed, one of my guards told me with a sort of malicious pleasure of my time device being dismantled, and secret things being done with it. Leske was directing the operations from his bed.

At last came the day when I was led forth and saw the huge pendulum for the first time. As I looked at it there, fantastic and formidable, I realized as never before the extent of Leske's insane revenge. And the populace seemed equally vengeful, equally cruel, like the ancient Romans on a gladiatorial holiday. In a sudden panic of terror, I shrieked and tried to leap away.

That only amused the people who crowded the electrical sidewalks around the plaza. They laughed and shrieked derisively.

My guards thrust me into the glass pendulum head and I lay there quivering, realizing the irony of my fate. This pendulum had been built from the precious metal and glassite of my own time device! It was intended as a monument to my slaughtering! I was being put on exhibition for life within my own executioning device! The crowd roared thunderous approval, damning me.

Then a little click and a whirring above me, and my glass prison began to move. It increased in speed. The arc of the pendulum's swing lengthened. I remember how I pounded at the glass futilely screaming, and how my hands bled. I remember the rows of faces becoming blurred white blobs before me . . .

I did not become insane, as I had thought at first I would. I did not mind it so much that first night. I couldn't sleep but it wasn't uncomfortable. The lights of the city were comets with tails that pelted from right to left like foaming fireworks. But as the night wore on I felt a gnawing in my stomach that grew worse until I became very sick. The next day was the same and I couldn't eat anything.

In the days that followed they never stopped the pendulum, not once. They slid my food down the hollow pendulum stem in little round parcels that plunked at my feet. The first time I attempted eating I was unsuccessful; it wouldn't stay down. In desperation I hammered against the cold glass with my fists until they bled again, and I cried hoarsely, but heard nothing but my own weak words muffled in my ears.

After an infinitude of misery, I began to eat and even sleep while traveling back and forth this way . . . they had allowed me small glass loops on the floor with which I fastened myself down at night and slept a sound slumber, without sliding. I even began to take an interest in the world outside, watching it tip one way and another, back and forth and up and down, dizzily before my eyes until they ached. The monotonous movements never changed. So huge was the pendulum that it shadowed one hundred feet or more with every majestic sweep of its gleaming shape, hanging from the metal intestines of the machine overhead. I estimated that it took four or five seconds for it to traverse the arc.

On and on like this—for how long would it be? I dared not think of it . . .

Day by day I began to concentrate on the gaping, curiosity-etched faces outside—faces that spoke soundless words, laughing and pointing at me, the prisoner of time, traveling forever nowhere. Then after a time—was it weeks or months or years?—the town people ceased to come and it was only tourists who came to stare . . .

Once a day the attendants sent down my food, once a day they sent down a tube to vacuum out the cell. The days and nights ran together in my memory until time came to mean very little to me . . .

It was not until I knew, inevitably, that I was doomed forever to this swinging chamber, that the thought occurred to me to leave a written record. Then the idea obsessed me and I could think of nothing else.

I had noticed that once a day an attendant climbed into the whirring coggery overhead in order to drop my food down the tube. I began to tap code signals along the tube, a request for writing materials. For days, weeks, months, my signals remained unanswered. I became infuriated—and more persistent.

Then, at long last, the day when not only my packet of food came down the tube, but with it a heavy notebook and writing materials! I suppose the attendant above became weary at last of my tappings! I was in a perfect ecstasy of joy at this slight luxury.

I had spent the last few days in recounting my story, without any undue elaboration. I am weary now of writing, but I shall continue from time to time—in the present tense instead of the past.

My pendulum still swings in its unvarying arc. I am sure it has been not months, but years! I am accustomed to it now. I think if the pendulum were to stop suddenly I should go mad at the motionless existence!

(*Later*): There is unusual activity on the electrically moving sidewalks surrounding me. Men are coming, scientists, and setting up peculiar-looking instruments with which to study me at a distance. I think I know the reason. I guessed it some time ago. I have not recorded the years, but I suspect that I *have already outlived Leske and all the others*. I know my cheeks have developed a short beard which suddenly ceased growing, and I feel a curious, tingling vitality. I feel that I shall outlive them all! I cannot account for it, nor can they out there, those scientists who now examine me so scrupulously. And they dare not stop my pendulum, my little world, for fear of the effect it may have on me!

(*Still later*): These men, these puny scientists, have dropped a microphone down the tube to me. They have actually remembered that I was once a great scientist, encased here cruelly. In vain they have sought the reason for my longevity; now they want me to converse with them, giving my symptoms and reactions and suggestions! They are perplexed, but hopeful, desiring the secret of eternal life to which they feel I can give them a clue. I have already been here two hundred years, they tell me: they are the fifth generation.

At first I said not a word, paying no attention to the microphone. I merely listened to their babblings and pleadings until I wearied of it. Then I grasped the microphone and looked up and saw their tense, eager faces, awaiting my words.

"One does not easily forgive such an injustice as this," I shouted. "And I do not believe I shall be ready to until five more generations."

Then I laughed. Oh, how I laughed.

"He's insane!" I heard one of them say: "The secret of immortality may be somehow with him, but I feel we shall never learn it; and we dare not stop the pendulum—that might break the timefield, or whatever it is that's holding him in thrall . . ."

*(Much later)*: It has been a longer time than I care to think, since I wrote those last words. Years . . . I know not how many. I have almost forgotten how to hold a pencil in my fingers to write.

Many things have transpired, many changes have come in the crazy world out there.

Once I saw wave after wave of planes, so many that they darkened the sky, far out in the direction of the ocean moving toward the city; and a host of planes arising from here, going out to meet them; and a brief, but lurid and devastating battle in which planes fell like leaves in the wind; and *some* planes triumphantly returning, I know not which ones . . .

But all that was very long ago, and it matters not to me. My daily parcels of food continue to come down the pendulum stem; I suspect that it has become a sort of ritual, and the inhabitants of the city, whoever they are now, have long since forgotten the legend of why I was encased here. My little world continues to swing in its arc, and I continue to observe the puny little creatures out there who blunder through their brief span of life.

*Already I have outlived generations! Now I want to outlive the very last one of them! I shall!*

. . . another thing, too, I have noticed. The attendants who daily drop the parcels of food for me, and vacuum out the cell, are robots! Square, clumsy, ponderous and four-limbed things—unmistakably metal robots, only vaguely human in shape.

. . . I begin to see more and more of these clumsy robots about the city. Oh, yes, humans too—but *they* only come on sightseeing tours and pleasure jaunts now; *they* live, for the most part, in luxury high among the towering buildings. Only the robots occupy the lower level now, doing all the menial and mechanical tasks necessary to the operation of the city. This, I suppose, is progress as these self-centered beings have willed it.

. . . robots are becoming more complicated, last words. Years . . . I know not how many more human in shape and movements . . . and more numerous . . . uncanny . . . I have a premonition . . .

*(Later):* It has come! I knew it! Vast, surging activity out there . . . the humans, soft from an aeon of luxury and idleness could not even escape . . . those who tried in their rocket planes were brought down by the pale, rosy electronic beams of the robots . . . others of the humans, mcre daring or desperate, tried to sweep low over the central robot base and drop thermite bombs—but the robots had erected an electronic barrier which hurled the bombs back among the planes, causing inestimable havoc . . .

The revolt was brief, but inevitably successful. I suspect that all human life except mine has been swept from the earth. I begin to see, now, how cunningly the robots devised it.

The humans had gone forward recklessly and blindly to achieve their Utopia; they had designed their robots with more and more intricacy, more and more finesse, until the great day when they were able to leave the entire operation of the city to the robots—under the guidance perhaps of one or two humans. But somewhere, somehow, one of those robots was imbued with a spark of intelligence; it began to think, slowly but precisely; it began to add unto itself, perhaps secretly; until finally it had evolved itself into a terribly efficient unit of inspired intelligence, a central mechanical Brain which planned this revolt.

At least, so I pictured it. Only the robots are left now—but very intelligent robots. A group of them came yesterday and stood before my swinging pendulum and seemed to confer among themselves. They surely must recognize me as one of the humans, the last one left. Do they plan to destroy me too?

No. I must have become a legend, even among the robots. My pendulum still swings. They have now encased the operating mechanism beneath a protective glassite dome. They have erected a device whereby my daily parcel of food is dropped to me mechanically. They no longer come near me; they seem to have forgotten me.

This infuriates me! Well, I shall outlast them too! After all, they are but products of the human brain . . . I shall outlast everything even remotely human! I swear it! To that end, I shall exert all my knowledge!

*(Much later):* Is this really the end? *I have seen the end of the reign of the robots!* Yesterday, just as the sun was crimsoning in the west, I perceived the hordes of things that came swarming out of space, expanding in the heavens . . . alien creatures fluttering down, great gelatinous masses of black that clustered thickly over everything . . .

I saw the robot rocket planes crisscrossing the sky on pillars of scarlet flame, blasting into the black masses with their electronic beams—but the alien things were unperturbed and unaffected! Closer and closer they pressed to earth, until the robot rockets began to dart helplessly for shelter.

To no avail. The silvery robot ships began crashing to earth in ghastly devastation.

And the black gelatinous masses came ever closer, to spread over the earth, to crumble the city and corrode all exposed metal.

Except my pendulum. They came dripping darkly down over it, over the glassite dome which protects the whirring wheels and roaring bowels of the mechanism. The city has crumbled, the robots are destroyed, but my pendulum still moves, the only thing in this world now . . . and I know that fact puzzles these alien things and they will not be content until they have stopped it . . .

This all happened yesterday. I am lying very still now, watching them. Most of them are gathering out there over the ruins of the city, preparing to leave—except a few of the black quivering things that are still hanging to my pendulum, almost blotting out the sunlight; and a few more above, near the operating machinery, concentrating those same emanations by which they corroded the robots. They are determined to do a complete job here. I know that in a few minutes they will begin to take effect even through the glassite shield. I shall continue to write until my pendulum stops swinging . . . it is happening now. I can feel a peculiar grinding and grating in the coggery above. Soon my tiny glassite world will ease its relentless arc.

I feel now only a fierce elation flaming within me, for after all, this is *my* victory! I have conquered over the men who planned this punishment for me, and over countless other generations and over the final robots themselves! There is nothing more I desire except annihilation, and I am sure that will come automatically when my pendulum ceases, bringing me to a state of unendurable motionlessness . . .

It is coming now. Those black, gelatinous shapes above are drifting away to join their companions. The mechanism is grinding raucously. My arc is narrowing . . . smaller . . . I feel . . . so strange . . .

# THE POOL OF THE STONE GOD
*by* W. FENIMORE

It is one of the great losses to lovers of the fantastic that A. Merritt, one of the finest and most popular writers to emerge out of the pulp magazines should have written so little. His novels, *The Moon Pool, Seven Footprints to Satan, Dwellers in the Mirage, Ship of Ishtar,* and others, have been brought back into print repeatedly for the past half-century and there is no indication that his following will diminish in the future.

The unfortunate part for those who admire Merritt's works is that he never was a full-time writer. Most of his working life was spent as associate editor and then as full editor of *American Weekly* when it was at the height of its profitability and circulation. The job was too big and time-consuming to allow him much opportunity to write what he wished, so his stories were infrequent and relatively few.

After A. Merritt died of a heart attack August 21, 1943, a probe was begun to see if he had any unpublished works. Paul Dennis O'Connor, a New York City antiquarian bookman, made contact with the estate and secured the beginnings of two uncomplete novels. The first was *The Fox Woman,* which he had finished by Hannes Bok and published under his own imprint in a special edition in 1946 (New Collectors' Group); and the second was *The Black Wheel,* also completed by Hannes Bok and published by the New Collectors' Group in 1947.

Avon Books had begun reprinting A. Merritt's novels in paperback form in 1942 and they did so well that reprintings were frequent. In order to add another Merritt title to their line, Donald A. Wollheim, their editor, in 1949 collected all the short stories of A. Merritt into a paperback, leading off with the portion of *The Fox Woman* Merritt had completed, including a fragment titled "When Old Gods Wake," initially published in *Avon Fantasy Reader* Number 7, 1948, which were the first few thousand words of an intended sequel to *The Snake Mother*. Another fragment, a little over 1,000 words long, titled "The White Road," was also printed, and this was intended to be a possible follow-up for his first story, "Through the Dragon Glass." As an aside to collectors, 100 copies of the Avon paperback were bound in hardcovers with little coverjackets printed for them by Lloyd Arthur Eshback, publisher of Fantasy Press, and sold for $1.00.

The Avon *Fox Woman* seemed to wind up the excavation of unpublished Merritt until a Baltimore fan and bibliographer named George Wetzel got the idea of going through the old files of *American Weekly*, which sometimes published fiction, to see if there was anything in its pages which might have been written by Merritt in the thirty-one years he had been associated with it.

George Wetzel was fascinated by bibliography, particularly in the field of the fantastic, had done some good pieces for *Fantasy Commentator*, had edited six brochures in *The Lovecraft Collectors Library* (SSR Publications, 1952), and was then working on *HPL: Memoirs Critiques, & Bibliographies* (SSR Publications, 1955), which, with the help of Robert Briney, would contain the most complete Lovecraft bibliography to that date.

The results of George Wetzel's search of the pages of *American Weekly* were published in the Summer, 1954 issue of *Tellus,* issued by a San Jose enthusiast named Page Brownton. Through wading through all the interminable pages of axe murders, pseudo-science, celebrity interviews, exotic locales, and the idle rich, he was only able to pin down one story that appeared to have been written by A. Merritt. That story was "The Pool of the Stone God," credited to W. Fenimore. There was no further confirmation, other than subject matter and internal evidence. *American Weekly* never answered George Wetzel's inquiries about the story and now since that publication has long-since been discontinued, it is unlikely that anyone ever will.

The safest thing to do in these cases is to present the story and let the reader make up his or her own mind as to whether it is authentic Merritt. I am a bit more courageous than that, knowing something about Merritt and the publishing business.

First, Merritt's story appeared in the issue for September 23, 1923. He was still a working editor on the *American Weekly,* fourteen years away from rising to the top spot. The paper was large and with weekly deadlines there must have been a need to dive in and fill a last-minute hole many times. Merritt had been hired because of the "excellence," of his stories of executions, murders, suicides, hangings, and lynchings. It is safe to say that from the time he went to work for the *American Weekly* in 1912 until he died he wrote literally thousands of stories for them, most of them "fact" features and most of them anonymous.

"The Pool of the Stone God" is written almost with the terseness of a synopsis; it was the work of a skilled newspaper writer. The imaginative image conveyed in the story with droplets of blood on the black winged statue, in effect resembles the great golden tears flowing down the cheeks of a carven image in "The Face in the Abyss," which appeared in *Argosy-All-Story* later the same year. The island locale, with its evidence of a lost and ancient civilization, corresponds closely with *The Moon Pool.*

It is my opinion that Merritt dashed it off as a filler at deadline time and in the process produced a condensed horror tale of undeniable distinction. That Merritt was doing some writing for the publication right until the end of his career is confirmed by the appearance of a hardcover book written by him, titled *The Story Behind the Story,* published by *American Weekly* in 1942 to assist the sales staff in selling advertising to prospective customers by telling what went into the planning of eighteen major features.

# THE POOL OF
# THE STONE GOD

by

## W. Fenimore

This is Professor James Marston's story. A score of learned bodies have courteously heard him tell it, and then among themselves have lamented that so brilliant a man should have such an obsession. Professor Marston told it to me in San Francisco, just before he started to find the island that holds his pool of the stone god and the wings that guard it. He seemed to me very sane. It is true that the equipment of his expedition was unusual, and not the least curious part of it are the suits of fine chain mail and masks and gauntlets with which each man of the party is provided.

The five of us, said Professor Marston, sat side by side on the beach. There was Wilkinson the first officer, Bates and Cassidy the two seamen, Waters the pearler and myself. We had all been on our way to New Guinea, I to study the fossils for the Smithsonian. The *Moranus* had struck the hidden reef the night before and had sunk swiftly. We were then, roughly, about five hundred miles northeast of the Guinea coast. The five of us had managed to drop a lifeboat and get away. The boat was well stocked with water and provisions. Whether the rest of the crew had escaped we did not know. We had sighted the island at dawn and had made for her. The lifeboat was drawn safely up on the sands.

"We'd better explore a bit, anyway," said Waters. "This may be a perfect place for us to wait rescue. At least until the typhoon season is over. We've our pistols. Let's start by following this brook to its source, look over the place and then decide what we'll do."

The trees began to thin out. We saw ahead an open space. We reached it and stopped in sheer amazement. The clearing was perfectly square and about five hundred feet wide. The trees stopped abruptly at its edges as though held back by something unseen.

But it was not this singular impression that held us. At the far end of the square were a dozen stone huts clustered about one slightly larger. They reminded me powerfully of those prehistoric structures you see in parts of England and France. I approach now the most singular thing about this whole singular and sinister place. In the center of the space was a pool walled about with huge blocks of cut stone. At the side of the pool rose a great stone figure, carved in the semblance of a man with outstretched hands. It was at least twenty feet high and was extremely well executed. At the distance the statue seemed nude and yet it had a peculiar effect of drapery about it. As we drew nearer we saw that it was covered from ankles to neck with the most extraordinary carved wings. They looked exactly like bat wings when they were folded.

There was something extremely disquieting about this figure. The face was inexpressibly ugly and malignant. The eyes, Mongol-shaped, slanted evil. It was not from the face, though, that this feeling seemed to emanate. It was from the body covered with wings—and especially from the wings. They were part of the idol and yet they gave one the idea that they were clinging to it.

Cassidy, a big brute of a man, swaggered up to the idol and laid his hand on it. He drew it away quickly, his face white, his mouth twitching. I followed him and conquering my unscientific repugnance, examined the stone. It, like the huts and in fact the whole place, was clearly the work of that forgotten race whose monuments are scattered over the Southern Pacific. The carving of the wings was wonderful. They were batlike, as I have said, folded and each ended in a little ring of conventionalized feathers. They ranged in size from four to ten inches. I ran my fingers over one. Never have I felt the equal of the nausea that sent me to my knees before the idol. The wing had felt like smooth, cold stone, but I had the sensation of having touched back of the stone some monstrous obscene creature of a lower world. The sensation came of course, I reasoned, only from the temperature and texture of the stone—and yet this did not really satisfy me.

Dusk was soon due. We decided to return to the beach and examine the clearing further on the morrow. I desired greatly to explore the stone huts.

We started back through the forest. We walked some distance and then night fell. We lost the brook. After a half hour's wandering we heard it again. We started for it. The trees began to thin out and we thought we were approaching the beach. Then Waters clutched my arm. I stopped. Directly in front of us was the open space with the stone god leering under the moon and the green water shining at his feet!

We had made a circle. Bates and Wilkinson were exhausted. Cassidy swore that devils or no devils he was going to camp that night beside the pool!

The moon was very bright. And it was so very quiet. My scientific curiosity got the better of me and I thought I would examine the huts. I left Bates on guard and walked over to the largest. There was only one room and the moonlight shining through the chinks in the wall illuminated it clearly. At the back were two small basins set in the stone. I looked in one and saw a faint reddish gleam reflected from a number of globular objects. I drew a half dozen of them out. They were pearls, very wonderful pearls of a peculiarly rosy hue. I ran toward the door to call Bates—and stopped!

My eyes had been drawn to the stone idol. Was it an effect of the moonlight or did it move? No, it was the wings! They stood out from the stone and waved—they waved, I say, from the ankles to the neck of that monstrous statue.

Bates had seen them, too. He was standing with his pistol raised. Then there was a shot. And after that the air was filled with a rushing sound like that of a thousand fans. I saw the wings loose themselves from the stone god and sweep down in a cloud upon the four men. Another cloud raced up from the pool and joined them. I could not move. The wings circled swiftly around and about the four. All were now on their feet and I never saw such horror as was in their faces.

Then the wings closed in. They clung to my companions as they had clung to the stone.

I fell back into the hut. I lay there through the night insane with terror. Many times I heard the fan-like rushing about the enclosure, but nothing entered my hut. Dawn came, and silence, and I dragged myself to the door. There stood the stone god with the wings carved upon him as we had seen him ten hours before!

I ran over to the four lying on the grass. I thought that perhaps I had had a nightmare. But they were dead. That was not the worst of it. Each man was shrunken to his bones! They looked like collapsed white balloons. There was not a drop of blood in them. They were nothing but bones wrapped around in thin skin!

Mastering myself, I went close to the idol. There was something different about it. It seemed larger—as though, the thought went through my mind, as though it had eaten. Then I saw that it was covered with tiny drops of blood that had dropped from the ends of the wings that clothed it!

I do not remember what happened afterward. I awoke on the pearling schooner *Luana* which had picked me up, crazed with thirst as they supposed in the boat of the *Moranus*.

**NEVERMORE...must you ponder weak and
weary searching out forgotten lore...
BERKLEY OFFERS THE BEST IN
TALES OF HORROR**